Emuna Elon

IF YOU AWAKEN LOVE

TRANSLATED BY

David Hazony

The Toby Press

If You Awaken Love
First English Language Edition 2007
The Toby Press LLC
POB 8531, New Milford, CT 06776-8531, USA
& POB 2455, London W1A 5WY, England
www.tobypress.com

Originally published in Hebrew as *Simha Gdola Bashamayim*

ISBN-10 1 59264 145 8, ISBN-13 978 1 59264 145 1, *paperback*

A CIP catalogue record for this title is
available from the British Library.

Printed and bound in the United States
by Thomson-Shore Inc., Michigan.

Chapter one

You wouldn't have thought it possible, Yair, but lately I've grown a little taller. I, too, never imagined that a forty-year-old woman could suddenly grow like a girl, like someone whose life is spread out before her instead of trailing behind her like a puddle that's muddied her feet. But it is a fact: My pants have recently gotten shorter on me, the counters in my kitchen and the workspaces in my studio have gotten lower, and when I walked with Maya today after she surprised me at work and later came home with me, she suddenly stopped and declared, astonished, "Mom, did you notice we're the same height?"

"Impossible," I stated, adopting a mature, motherly tone, despite the fact that inside I was elated that she sees it too.

But it wasn't my new height that made me feel such glee. Surely the five feet and six inches that had come between me and the ground for most of my life had been enough. I was just pleased to learn that I really *had* grown taller, although probably not the way kids grow but more of a *lengthening*, perhaps because of all the exercise I've been doing, the yoga, the self-awareness, but maybe it's more than that; maybe it's a clear sign that I'm all right, that I'm surviving, that finally I've learned to live without you, even to grow. There have been other signs, too, like the relative satisfaction I've gotten out of a couple of post-modern apartments I've designed this year, and the new vegetarian diet I've maintained against all odds, and of course the sweet, laid-back relationship I've struck up with Yossi Sorek, a *moshavnik* widower whom I met on an organized tour of Scandinavia I went on last summer with my friend Eden.

The ability to go on an organized tour is just one of the changes that have come over me since I stopped being your partner in changing the world and became just an ordinary person. Sometimes I look at it as making do with little, sometimes I call it a "surrogate life," and sometimes I take a look at myself and find it hard to believe that this ordinary woman living out her gray, ordinary days, year upon year, is the same stormy, spiritual Shlomtzion whom you once loved—or so it seemed.

I was genuinely content today when Maya and I got out of the car with our shopping bags bursting with fruits and vegetables and soft cheeses and hard cheeses and whole-grain bread, climbing the stairs as in some everyday family scene, as though we were still a young mother with her little girl, though now Maya is almost twenty and wears clothes I didn't buy her, an ankle-length denim skirt and a baggy, long-sleeved cotton blouse; and I was filled with satisfaction when we entered the house and put away the groceries and got straight to work on dinner with an intensity and a gaiety that hadn't been seen here in a long time. Maya chopped onions and green peppers and ripe tomatoes and fried up the *shakshuka* that has been her trademark dish since she was nine, and I cooked some wholesome bulgur for my new vegetarian diet, and we set the table with colorful paper napkins and flowers in a vase, and we sat and ate and chatted and laughed as we used to before she started up with all this repentance of hers. And apparently Maya was also happy about this, for when she finished her meal she grew serious for a minute, looked into my eyes and said, "I'm really grateful, Mom, that you made the kitchen kosher for me and bought these new dishes. You have no idea how much I appreciate this," and I gently put my hand on her shoulder and replied, "Oh well, what wouldn't I have done just to taste your delicious *shakshuka* once again in this life?" and Maya laughed, relieved.

Only the TV news, which we had turned on while clearing the table and washing the dishes, threatened to spoil the moment. Naturally I got annoyed when they showed the latest of the ugly, raucous demonstrations your friends have been holding, this time in response to the murder of an Israeli cab driver whose body was found the night before on the road to Jenin. I wanted to tell Maya that people who support the Oslo accords also see the murder as a tragedy which should never have been allowed to happen, but that precisely *because* of tragedies like this we all have to give peace a chance. But instead I decided to keep quiet, and she too remained silent when Rabin appeared on the screen and, with the harshest of words and his face red with anger, answered the claims of the opposition. She just sighed a deep sigh, tossed a fork into the sink, and quickly began wiping down the table.

"You're unhappy about what Rabin said," I offered in the most empathetic voice I could find.

"Let him say whatever he wants," Maya muttered, gathering up the crumbs off the table with a rag. "It just hurts to know my prime minister couldn't care less about me. But I can live with it." She rinsed out the rag in the sink and then added, her voice trembling with anger and affront, "If I have to, I can also die with it."

❧

I was so pleased to have my only daughter come for such a nice visit, I felt so gratified at having things with her be so right, that I neglected to ask myself why, exactly, she had left her seminary in the middle of the week, missing classes in Torah and faith, and had made the trip from her settlement all the way to Tel Aviv.

Only later, when I had set up my drafting table in order to go over the plans I had brought home from the studio to find all the little things that the computer had missed, things that my hands alone know how to fix, and Maya came out of the shower with her wet fragrant curls, wearing her pajamas, and walked toward me hesitantly with an expression on her face that looked like she had something to announce—only then did I understand that this visit had a specific purpose.

"What are you working on?" She began questioning me, her penetrating look examining the rolls of paper spread out before me.

"What is it, darling? Is there something you want to tell me?"

"It's such a shame, Mom, that you became an interior decorator and not an artist. With talent like yours—"

"You came to Tel Aviv today to talk to me about my talent?"

"It's much more than talent, Mom. It's Vision. Originality. You could have been a great painter, you could have—"

"Mayaleh—"

"Okay Mom," she said, running the fingers of both hands through her hair as she has done since childhood whenever she experienced uncontainable emotion. "I'm getting married."

❧

I had heard about Ariel before, of course, but in all honesty I had preferred not to show too much interest in what Maya had told me about him. Her eyes would sparkle when she mentioned him every now and again, I knew that he lived in the same settlement where her seminary was and that things were starting to heat up between them, but I preferred to think that this entire religious phase of hers would soon pass. That she would repent of all this repentance of hers and fulfill the role of the unencumbered, complex-free daughter I had assigned her since birth. That is why I put off making the kitchen kosher until just two months ago, and when I finally scraped clean all the pots and the countertops like someone possessed, and climbed up into the attic to sadly stow away all my beautiful treif china, and when I brought my cousin Shlomo over with his students from the yeshiva to work through the night with boiling water and hot stones—all this I did just to draw Maya closer in the hope that this would bring her back to me, bring her back to sanity, bring her back to a good, peaceful life.

Now I heard her saying, "Okay Mom, I'm getting married," and I knew that what she was really saying was *Okay Mom, I'm cutting myself off from you once and for all, I'm going over to their side*, and I knew that if for the last twenty years there had still been some doubt, from this moment on it was overwhelmingly clear that your people have defeated me. That I have lost everything.

I put down my pens and my sketching rulers and walked over to my daughter around my old drafting table, around the remnants of my shattered dreams, around my life that ended before it began, and I reached her and hugged her desperately, with the kind of force that is reserved for someone very dear just before parting ways for a very long time, maybe forever. And she, who may or may not have understood what I was going through, hugged me back and said in a choked but amazed voice, "Look, Mom, we really are the same height."

❧

"Tell me all about him, Mayaleh," I somehow managed to say, and she spread out her arms and fluttered like a butterfly over to the window, putting her burning cheeks up against the cool glass and looking dreamily into the night outside.

"Oh Mom," she breathed, turning her glowing face toward me, "Ariel is so wonderful, so magical, so brilliant, so righteous, that I really don't know if I deserve to marry him, if I'm good enough for him—"

"Don't be silly," I snapped, but when I saw how she started to recoil I tried to take the edge off my voice. *I really shouldn't impose our cloudy past, yours and mine, on her crystal-clear present*, I reminded myself. *I mustn't weigh down her joy with the burden of my pain.* So I took a deep breath, and I smiled to her, and I caressed her cheek and said, "It's just not healthy to speak that way, sweetie. If you love him, and he loves you, then of course you are good enough for him."

"Tomorrow or the day after, Mom, we'll come to visit you," Maya promised, the light returning to her face. "I wanted to introduce you long before we got engaged, but Ariel is finishing his basic training in another three weeks, and it suddenly dawned on us that we ought to get married right after that."

"You're getting married in *three weeks*?" I exclaimed, as if I had already gotten used to the idea that my daughter was about to turn into a settler's wife wearing a headscarf and surrounded by babies, and all I asked was that all this not take place in *three weeks*' time but perhaps, if it was not too much to ask, in about four.

Maya laughed. "No, no," she assured me, as though this was all it would take to calm me down. "The wedding will be in about two months, hopefully around Hanukah."

With her damp curls swirling about her forehead and her light pajamas with pictures of teddy bears on them, she almost looked to me, just for a moment, like the secular girl whom I had so wanted her to be.

"You haven't even told me his full name, other than Ariel."

"Ariel Berman," Maya proclaimed. "You've probably heard of his father, Rabbi Yair Berman."

❧

You've probably heard of him, she tells me. How could she know that the name Yair Berman would fall on me like a boulder and hurl me all at once into the deep chasm that is always inside of me? How could she know that from the moment I heard that name, from the moment I understood that her fiancé is your son, I would need every ounce of strength just to keep breathing evenly and to hide behind a smile until, after midnight, after she talked and talked and talked and after she gave me a soft, comforting goodnight kiss like the kisses she used to give me when she was a little girl, I could finally haul myself into the bedroom, shut the door, stand before the unraveled woman looking at me in the mirror and ask the Lord of the Universe what the hell he wants from me.

Chapter two

You should know, my dear daughter, that I came into this world only because of a string of tragic events and shattered loves. It was Aunt Batya, my mother's younger sister, who told me the whole story during the quiet Shabbat mornings when we would sit on the porch of my grandparents' apartment; not the veranda, which was the entrance, but rather the little balcony that overlooked the alleyway where Ashkenazi worshippers with their frock coats and fur hats would pass Sephardi worshippers in their pressed pinstripe suits heading toward the various synagogues in the neighborhood or back to their homes.

It was Batya, who in her youth was introduced to the finest of young men but never married, who also taught me where, in the old wooden bedside table, my grandfather hid the battered tin box full of white peppermint candies as hard as gravel. It was from her stories, which even now I recall with the sharp taste of mint in my mouth, that I learned that if everything had turned out right, Bubbe Malka, my mother's grandmother, would have stayed behind somewhere in late nineteenth-century Russia with her first husband, who was her true love. Our family came into this world only because poor Bubbe Malka couldn't have children, or at least so everyone thought. Because after ten years of childless marriage her loving husband was forced to submit to the rule of halakha, and divorce her.

How many times have I pictured in my mind's eye this poor couple's unwilling separation, man and woman bound together in the perfect coordination that develops in ten years of love, weeping in each other's arms and then parting with only the greatest effort, like a living creature torn in two? This image has always chilled me to the bone, because I understood from a very early age that from the time they were torn apart, the two of them never stopped bleeding. The woman who would later begin our family line was, in effect, already dead.

When she returned to her father's house carrying the writ of divorce which to her was a death certificate, twenty-eight-year-old Malka could no longer stand to look at the town where she had grown up and enjoyed her ten years of marriage, or at her chosen love who could no longer be hers. Her parents felt so sorry for her that they picked up and went to seek refuge in the tiny, crowded den of poverty, misery, insanity and hard piety that was, in those days, Jerusalem.

For many months did our downtrodden divorcée journey with her parents, by land and sea, until they finally entered the city's ancient walls. There she was set up, after much time and prayer, with another star-crossed soul, who had reached Jerusalem, the city of refuge, at the end of seven years of wandering which he had taken upon himself after his first wife had run off while he served as the rabbi, mohel and *shochet* of a small village in the middle of Poland, having fallen for—the disgrace!—an uncircumcised officer of the Polish army.

So it was only tragedy that caused our forebears to come to this land, Maya, and only misfortune that brought them together. Not love and determination but ruin and shame were what led Bubbe Malka to remarry and to give her rabbi husband a daughter: my grandmother Rochel.

❧

Neither did Grandma Rochel get to live with the man she loved. When she reached the age of sixteen, her father betrothed her to a brilliant and righteous yeshiva student. But at the end of the year of their engagement, the brilliant and righteous yeshiva student suddenly broke the engagement off and married his cousin instead.

Abandoned and disgraced, Grandma Rochel was then set up with a substitute suitor by the name of Duvid Heller, a yeshiva student whose questionable lineage prevented him from being matched with any bride who was not herself tainted. Grandma Rochel, who having been once engaged was now considered used goods, married Duvid Heller with the problematic pedigree out of a lack of choice. Aunt Batya explained that from day one it was clear to Grandma Rochel that he could never fill the void left by her first husband-to-be, because she had so deeply longed for her first fiancé during that whole year that had begun with their engagement party and ended with the celebration of his marriage to his cousin. Day and night she had sat and sewn their initials in gold thread onto the linens that she was going to give him as a dowry-gift, and she now understood that this had been the first and last year of her life that she would ever be in love. When in high school we studied Agnon's *Tehila* I was convinced that the renowned author had found his inspiration for the titular character in the story of my Grandma Rochel's broken engagement, but Aunt Batya found the idea absurd. "Do you seriously think," she smiled ruefully, "that your grandmother is the only Jerusalemite in history to have suffered unfulfilled love?"

Time went by, and although she was never in love with Grandpa Duvid, Grandma Rochel bore him seven children. The third, named Malka after her grandmother, fell ill at the age of two with some terrible infection and would have died, but in the eleventh hour they changed her name to Tzipora, which means bird and she flew like a bird, as Grandma Rochel put it, from her evil fate to a better one. When the girl came of age her brother Yankel set her up with his study partner from the yeshiva, a talented and dedicated boy named Avrum Drexler, and a year later she became my mother.

At the time of their marriage my father had already begun his studies at the Hebrew University, but despite this defect my uncle Yankel still believed he would make a good husband for his demure little sister. Yankel probably regretted setting the two of them up, however, once he saw that his brother-in-law had shaved his beard and, within a few years, transformed himself from Avrum Drexler to Dr. Avraham Dror, star of the Biblical Studies department, who dressed in light-colored American blazers and florid ties, combed his black hair back under a small, colorful *kippa*, and grew a sophisticated pipe out of the corner of his mouth.

My mother's fate was worse than that of her mother and grandmother, for she was never abandoned. Until the day he died, my father remained married to her, and never fell in love with another woman but, instead, with *all* the many women who fell under his famous spell every day, from students in the Biblical Studies department, to colleagues on the faculty, to the editor at the publishing house which put out his revolutionary writings, to the journalist who once interviewed him for a provocative piece in the weekend supplement of one of the national papers. I wished I could drop off the face of the earth when I would see him humiliating my mother in public, waving his hand in disgust to silence her whenever she dared express her own opinion or tell a story, and yelling right in her mortified face, "What do *you* know? You're better off keeping quiet than speaking from ignorance." But my polite, pathetic mother accustomed herself to this man, and she served him loyally for years as his personal secretary, as typist for his academic papers, as attendant of his stylish clothes and caterer of the special meals he needed to maintain his handsome physique, the source of his pride. He never bothered to hide his many affairs, and she pretended never to notice them.

❧

I couldn't bring myself to love my parents. I couldn't bring myself to find even the slightest similarity between them and me, to the point that I found it hard to believe that this tall, vain man and his lowly maidservant were really my father and mother. Fortunately, my father spent much of my childhood traveling around the world teaching and doing research at various universities, and my mother usually went with him, ironing and typing and lending an ear for him to pour out his fury and frustration at the stupidity of the world. Thanks to their many trips abroad, my only brother Yehonadav and I were frequently left in the care of our warm and wonderful Grandma Rochel, in whose home we spent days and nights and weeks, which sometimes turned to entire months.

There were the large, old rooms with paint peeling from the ceilings, filled with heavy wooden furniture and, along the walls, yellowing books on endless shelves. And there was always the smell of home cooking—fatty chicken soup, zucchini in tomato sauce, dark brown *chulent,* and other scents which accepted you as you were, even if you were a somewhat lazy, somewhat scatterbrained, somewhat frumpy little girl whose father was ashamed of her and may even have regretted that she existed.

And there, too, Grandpa Duvid would sit in his regular place in the afternoons and evenings, humming quietly as he pored over a volume of the Talmud, with the giant beer mug he used for his tea. Whenever I came near he would dig deep in his pocket, pull out a white candy as hard as gravel, and hand it to me, smiling, without lifting his eyes from the text and without pausing in his learning and humming even for a moment, as if he just wanted to send a reassuring message: *I know you're here, I know you have a habit of taking peppermint candies from my tin box and it's really okay with me, you're really okay with me, I'm glad to have you around.*

In the mornings my grandfather worked as a scribe. After his visit to the ritual bath and morning prayers, he would immediately begin leaning over the rolls of parchment and would form with his quill rows upon rows of beautiful black letters, taking care with every precise stroke, trying not to think of the secret powers contained in every one of the letters, which constantly aspired to burst forth and disrupt the order of the universe. Grandpa Duvid knew where the line was drawn between heaven and earth, and he knew that he must never, under any circumstance, cross that line, lest he suffer what his father had suffered when *he* passed into the world of kabbalah, when he crossed that line and couldn't come back. Grandpa Duvid's four brothers and sisters died of hunger and disease when he was a child, during the hardships that Jerusalem suffered through the First World War. After the youngest of them died, his mother fell ill and passed away as well. And all this, Aunt Batya explained to me, was purely the fault of his father the mystic.

"Instead of trying to find food and medicine for his miserable children," she told me, "he holed himself up and studied the secrets of Creation. His wife was too ashamed to ask others for help. They say he even stopped collecting their ration money, and his family perished before his eyes without him lifting a finger. He spent so much time studying the hidden teachings, Shlomtzi, that his own mind was hidden from him. He saw only the higher worlds. Everything he cast his eyes on was set ablaze."

During the nineteen years that the old city of Jerusalem was under Jordanian rule, Grandpa Duvid couldn't visit the graves of his mother and brothers and sisters on the Mount of Olives. But he always kept before his eyes the image of the simple gravestones lined up together on the mountain's slope, four short stones next to one long one, the latter shielding the others in its granite grief. And he always remembered his obligation to spend his living days with both feet firmly on the ground, lest he follow in his father's path and destroy the world that the Holy One created.

❧

Yehonadav, too, preferred to be with Grandma Rochel rather than at home or at Grandma Bracha's, my father's mother, because only at Grandma Rochel's could he disappear among the people and things that crowded the dark rooms, daydream with his thumb planted in his mouth and remain undiscovered until later in the day, when he'd steal into the kitchen to sneak some chocolate rogelach or a slice of *kugel* left over from Shabbat.

As for me, I took refuge behind walls made of friends and playmates. But more than my friends at the religious girls' school or the local chapter of the Bnei Akiva youth group, more than the friends I met in the wide, newly built neighborhood where my parents lived, Shabbat-desecrators with whom I played hide-and-seek and capture-the-flag in the long evenings of summer vacation—more than all these I loved the children who lived in the old, bare stone houses with their little paved yards which surrounded Grandma's back porch with endless laundry lines flaunting sheets and white shirts and dark polyester pants and *tallitot* and *tzitziot* with their fringes flapping in the wind.

Even today I think of my grandmother's neighborhood as having been the focal point of all my happiness on earth. Though upon growing up I realized that it was in fact little more than a sad *haredi* slum, as a girl I saw it as a warm, secure womb. The center of this womb—a womb within a womb—was Grandma Rochel's apartment. And the pinnacle of all safety and security was reached on Friday nights at the beginning of Shabbat, when I sat with my aunts and uncles and cousins around the wide table with Grandpa Duvid sitting at its head, smiling warmly.

I'd try not to think about the dreary Friday night dinner table at my parents' house—my father trying to impress the guests; my mother shuttling from table to kitchen and back, smiling apologetically; Yehonadav with his panicked stammering, chastened even on the rare occasions when he wasn't being chastised; and myself listening to the sounds from outside, sounds of non-observant kids in their scout uniforms dancing together in the nearby public garden, singing passionately, as from deep conviction: *A boy takes a girl / a girl takes a boy / the rebbe said, / "They must never wed!"*

❧

Our own house was more of a museum to me than a home. My

father had filled the grand living room with the fine Judaica he had collected in his travels around the world: antique bronze menorahs, polished shofars made of rams' horns, silver candlesticks and crafted spice-towers with tiny silver flags waving from their ramparts, fancy handwritten scrolls of the Book of Esther in engraved wooden boxes set with jewels, and even two or three kosher Torah scrolls adorned in velvet covers embroidered with gold. I felt less pretty, and less valuable, than any of them.

My father was also one of the first people in Jerusalem to own an automobile. When he'd occasionally drive me to school or youth group, I'd ask him to drop me off one or two blocks away, so my friends would think I'd walked. And when we would go visit my grandmother, as soon as the sleek, sky-blue Renault '59 came to a stop in the alley near the porch entrance, a crowd of kids with curly sidelocks would appear out of nowhere and engulf us, admiring the wonder on wheels, deliberating about its nature and merits in animated Yiddish.

"They don't often get a chance to see a real automobile," my mother would defend them gently as they pressed against the fenders, fondled the headlights and taillights, kicked the tires, and stuck their heads through open windows to try and fathom the car's innermost secrets. But my father would yell at them, in their own language and without removing his pipe, as he impatiently cut a path through the crowd.

I hated his never removing the sticker with the red Star-of-David which the previous owner, a doctor, had put in the corner of the windshield. I hated it when we arrived at a place where entry was restricted or prohibited, and our car would get in because my father led the security guard to think he was a doctor rushing to save a life.

"You will notice I'm not lying," he would boast, glancing proudly over his shoulder at the audience in the back seat, namely Yehonadav and me. "Notice I didn't say a word." It was true that he never told the guard he was a doctor. He simply pointed importantly to the sticker and all the guards in the world rushed to clear him a path.

Once when I was in fifth or sixth grade, my friends and I went on a treasure hunt which our wonderful youth-group counselor Shlomit had prepared as a midweek activity. We were running around looking for the little clues she had hidden among the streets of an upscale neighborhood on the outskirts of the city, and I was shouting and laughing and searching just like everyone else, and suddenly one of the girls called out, "Shlomtzion, look—there's your father's car!" And I was about to say, *It can't be, what are you talking about?* but there it was, the familiar sky-blue Renault, lounging in front of one of the fancier buildings.

"It's probably a different car, it just looks like my dad's," I offered as everyone stopped running and gathered around the car, which itself now looked embarrassed and confused. My friend insisted: "No, it really *is* your father's car. See? It's got that red Star-of-David in the windshield."

Just then a couple emerged from the building arm in arm, talking jovially, the woman a stranger with good posture and a red coat, while the surprised man was none other than Professor Dror, who had been honored just the day before by my mother with a fancy party in their museum-like living room to celebrate his promotion to the professorate.

He was a father only from a distance, Maya, but with you he was different. With you he was "Grampa Avam," all warmth and love and hugs and gifts, and you, even as a baby, returned his affection in spades. Whenever we got near my childhood home on one of our mandatory visits, you'd start squirming in my arms, raise up your hands toward the same second-floor apartment where my wounds still remained fresh, and begin crowing, "Grampa Avam! Grampa Avam!"

Only on your account did he allow himself to visit us so often in Tel Aviv. I would open the front door and he'd walk right in without so much as looking at me, lower himself to your level as you ran toward him shrieking, take you into his hungry arms, drink in the fragrance of your curly hair as you buried yourself in his embrace and lay your gratified head on his shoulder like Noah's dove finding a perch after the Flood. Then he'd mutter, sighing, "Once again I have been forced to visit this sweaty city of yours." Sometimes he'd chalk his visits up to college business, sometimes it had to do with his books, and sometimes he'd just say he had to meet someone. And I'd think: *Daddy, why can't you just come out and say it? "I came to Tel Aviv because I love my granddaughter, because I can't get by without seeing her once in a while, because I have to get a whiff of her pure essence and bask in her sweet glow that offers me just that much comfort."*

❧

Today, reviewing my life like a videotape running backwards, I understand that in all his days on this earth, all my father really wanted was love. When I try to fast-forward past the awful episodes and the hurtful words, past the insults he inflicted on my mother and the bawling and stammering he inspired in Yehonadav, I discover a smiling, friendly father—not in the scenes shot in our grandiose, grotesque apartment, but rather in the lecture halls in Israel and around the world in which Professor Dror appears, on the dais, having the time of his life delivering one of his riveting lectures, full of twists and turns and laughs. How happy he looks in these scenes, his perfect physique upright, his charcoal hair bobbing to the rhythm of his own theatrical movements, all his energies aimed at carving up the biblical text, dressing it, and serving it up to his adoring, enraptured audience.

It was there that he got the intense doses of love he so craved. There, or at the large family gatherings and social events when someone would ask him to do his magic show. Smiling devilishly, my father would stand behind a table or other raised surface and begin producing all kinds of handkerchiefs and coins from his mouth, ears, and sleeves. When enough of a crowd had gathered, he would, for the finale, do his famous trick with the coin and hats: he'd place three hats in a row, place a coin under one in sight of the audience, and say a few magic words, causing the coin to vanish from under one hat and reappear, to gasps and oohs and ahs, under another.

At times like these he was intense and satisfied, eyes gleaming, smile wide and true and getting bigger every time he said those magic words and the coin moved from hat to hat as the adults in the audience doubled over laughing and the children left their mouths dangling open, forgetting to close them.

"What a terrific father you have," I was told by jealous friends and acquaintances, especially women. "He's amazing!"

"Amazing," I agreed. "Right."

❧

But at my grandmother's I had Friday night dinners that gave me strength, peppermint stories with Aunt Batya Saturdays on the balcony, and hordes of cousins, who, arriving with their families to visit Grandma Rochel and wreck her apartment, warmly accepted Yehonadav and me—even though we were the only ones with a tiny family of just two kids; and the only ones who were not, as they saw it, really Torah-observant but rather *mizrachistim*, liberals who thought we could pick and choose whatever commandments we wanted to observe; and even though we were the only ones who stayed behind at Grandma's when they and their parents had said goodbye with chocolate-rogelach kisses and left her sitting there, exhausted, surveying the devastation they had left in their wake, sighing with satisfaction and wishing on her enemies that their homes should always be clean and orderly.

At Grandma's I also had Estherke, beautiful Estherke with the long, thick golden braid, who lived with her family in the apartment below and who had occasionally babysat me when I was little. When I got older we became friends, perhaps I even fell in love with her a little, and even though she was five years older than me Estherke would often ask me, tittering with embarrassment, about the facts of life. She would cover her quivering lips with her hand as though giggling were a sin, and when I explained to her how it is that children came into the world, her long swan neck turned beet red and her cheeks flared like roses.

She also wanted me to teach her Hebrew, since they spoke only Yiddish in her home and school, so we sat and read together from a third-grade textbook or from the old children's reader that Grandpa Duvid bought me at a used book store. In return for every lesson I gave her in the holy tongue, she would let me brush her amazing, thick, golden hair that fell down to her thighs, and then braid it anew.

I was eleven, and Estherka was going on sixteen, when I decided that a girl with such blue eyes and a thrill for life had no business spending her days cloistered in that suffocating neighborhood as if she were Grimm's long-braided beauty Rapunzel, who was kept in a tower by a wicked witch.

"You really ought to be a star in Hollywood," I informed her one day while I brushed her hair. "Or at least a model in Tel Aviv."

Estherke grew quiet, then covered her mouth with her hand as she began to laugh, her body quivering and her golden hair flying about until she calmed down, looked at me with wet blue eyes and said, "I know what Tel Aviv is, but Shlomtzi, *vas ist* that other thing you said?"

So I, the corrupting but determined youth, explained to her in simple Hebrew where Hollywood was, what movies were, and what actresses and models did. "You deserve to be free," I preached. "You deserve to be rich and famous and to do whatever you want instead of being stuck here forever, cooking chickens and hanging up laundry for the rest of your life."

❧

Another soul-mate of mine was Shayaleh with the curly sidelocks, who lived in the apartment next door to my grandmother's. He was always coughing and congested, and so skinny and pale as to be nearly transparent, despite the best efforts of his mother and seven sisters to make him strong and healthy. When we were six or seven we decided to get married. I promised him that after the wedding I would invent a cure for whatever ailed him, and the two of us would live happily ever after.

In the meantime, Shayaleh helped me take care of the emaciated cats that wandered around the neighborhood. He and I would go door to door asking for chicken bones left over from Friday night dinner, and he egged me on as I pilfered cheese and sour cream from Grandma Rochel's fridge to feed them or when I went out to save those in distress. When a misbegotten feline got locked, one Friday night, in a fish store the next street over and yowled through the night, transparent Shayaleh was chosen to crawl in through the store's side wicket because of his size. He struggled with the ungrateful prisoner and came out only a long while later, coughing and reeking of fish, his face scratched and dripping with blood and snot, to the chagrin of his mother and seven sisters.

And it was in Grandma Rochel's neighborhood that I also met Yair. He was two years older than me and lived in Bnei Brak, but when he was eleven, his father died from "the disease"—which is what they called cancer back then, as though it might spare them if they refused to speak its name—and afterwards he spent all his *Shabbatot*, holidays and vacations with his grandparents, Rabbi and Mrs. Berman, who lived on the street intersecting my grandmother's alleyway. Rabbi Berman had a *shteible* in his home, where Grandpa Duvid prayed every Shabbat. I was very young when I first took notice of Yair while accompanying my grandparents and cousins to this *heimische* synagogue. When I got a little older, and prayed there on Rosh Hashanah and Yom Kippur next to Grandma Rochel and the five old ladies who wept into their prayer books in the bedroom which served as the women's section, I would stare at him from afar and avert my gaze whenever our eyes met.

After his father died, I began seeing Yair more often, when he was sent on errands to the corner grocery store, or when he sat, staring into space and swinging his legs, on the stone wall in front of his grandparents' house. When I walked past I'd sneak a glance at him, taking care not to turn my head so he wouldn't see, and I knew deep down that this boy belonged to me and I to him, that on the deepest level we were one and the same, as if he were my brother, as if he were my own reflection, as if he were my own, male, self.

❧

I was nine and a half on that long, hot, muggy Shabbat night in which my grandmother's neighborhood was kept awake by the desperate, bottomless wailing of the cat locked in the fish store. All night long I tossed in bed, trying in vain to block out, if only for a few minutes, the clamor of the almost-human cries.

Yehonadav, who was four and sleeping in the same room as me, made his own contribution to the ruckus, waking up twice calling for Mother. "Go back to sleep," I ordered, but like him I felt a little jealous of the free, shameless way the cornered creature voiced its anguish and fear.

At sunrise I dressed quickly and ran in the direction of the wailing. And there was Rabbi Berman's grandson, already climbing the store's wrought-iron bars. He carefully placed one foot after another on ascending bars until he was high enough to stretch one hand toward the side window of the store, while holding on with the other. I moved closer and shouted from below, "Nice work! Now try to get in and get him out."

He overcame his shyness and turned to me. "I'm just too big to get through that little window," he said, disappointed.

"Wait," I said, "I know someone small enough to fit." I ran to call transparent little Shayaleh, who would do anything I asked, and Shayaleh squeezed through the opening to go rescue the cat. After an eternity in which the wailing turned into a horrible screeching of animal and child together, Shayaleh emerged empty-handed, ragged and cut up and stinking to high heaven.

❧

Over the past few years, after the grief over losing Yair's love faded a bit—or maybe didn't really fade, but rather found a quiet place on the shores of my soul, becoming no more than a familiar, indelible pain—I have tried to look at our childhood together as a treasure that enriched my life.

For many years, the wounds were so fresh that any time I called up the image of Yair and me as children, the feelings would well up until I started drowning in inconsolable grief. Only lately have I learned to overcome my ingratitude, to stop judging the early joys in light of what came later—the cruel rupture that took place when I was nineteen. Now that I've learned to do that, not only do the memories hurt less, but I've even started finding pleasure in them—in the simplicity of our bond from our very first meeting; in the joy of roaming the narrow streets and ducking under laundry lines, running along Hanevi'im Street to the B'nai B'rith library, returning full of expectation, then reading for long hours in the house or yard, he submerged in Jules Verne and I in Charles Dickens or the reverse, pausing to share the exciting or humorous passages, to analyze the characters and their predicaments, to weave dreams; and in the sense of adventure we shared, which propelled us to explore beyond our own neighborhood, as far as our legs could carry us, trying to lose ourselves in the world and discover faraway new lands, stopped only by the *Caution! Border Ahead* signs that surrounded the little city and fanned our curiosity even more.

I remember fondly the deep discussions we had on those long walks. We were young, but our conversations were heavy and infinitely serious ones about God and man, good and evil, life and death, mostly about death but also about love, how to love God and how to love in general, what love could possibly be worth if in the end we all die, was it possible for a man and a woman to be married if they didn't love each other, or did not love their children, or loved neither each other nor their children nor God, and whether it was normal for a girl to love her grandparents more than her parents, even *instead* of her parents, and why did people even bother to have children, and how much did it depend on their own choice, how much on the souls, which force people to bring them into this world, and whether the souls really want to be brought into this world, or does God impose it on them?

Again and again I would drag him to the science museum near my parents' apartment to ogle the animals that were stuffed and posed in glass display cases, ready to pounce on their quarry. Wolves, foxes, wildcats and weasels and even a panther—all of them completely dead but with a spark of life glinting in the glass eyes that had been implanted in their perfect bodies, a spark that forced me to try and figure out what really divided them from true life.

And then I would feel, each time anew, the admixture of disgust and delight as I rushed Yair to the second floor of the little old museum, where, on a shelf, suspended in a jar of formaldehyde, dwelled a real human fetus of five months. "Shlomtzion, let's go," Yair pleaded, agitated. "Please, let's get out of here." But I could have stood there forever, staring at the fetus floating in the jar, at his face, which looked deep in thought, as though he were dreaming an endless dream about his life that had ended before it had begun; at the lines that creased his little forehead, as though he was trying to figure out whether it was for good or ill that he had never been born.

And once, hidden among a group of Norwegian tourists, we snuck into the medieval castle that was the Notre Dame cathedral, at the very edge of the Israeli section of Jerusalem. We passed through the corridors and the chilly, grand halls, shielded by the *goyim* with their large limbs and ruddy cheeks; we went with them up to the roof, by the statue of the Holy Virgin swinging her baby on her shoulder as though he too wanted to take in the view. Suddenly the country opened before us like a cloudburst and we saw that on the other side of the border, past the Old City's walls, there was a completely different reality, in which men, women, and children went to and fro, fat and skinny and short and tall, bareheaded and wearing keffiyahs, going from here to there, talking and shouting and buying and selling, sitting and standing, lugging sacks of goods on mules or in rectangular wooden wagons, gathering among the colorful stalls at the raucous market.

"We have to go there," I declared, my heart pounding. "We have to go to the Western Wall, to Mount Moriah, it's just right over there!"

For several weeks I schemed about the disguises we would wear, the tourists among whom we would hide, the Arabic we would learn so that once inside the walls we could speak without arousing suspicion. It was unthinkable that we should continue living placidly on our side of Jerusalem while over there, remote and hidden yet just within reach, lurked a different, fascinating, magical world.

"There are some things even you can't do," Yair cautioned. "Some things even you can't understand." I resented his willingness to give in, the lowness of spirit with which he resigned himself to the limits of reality, but in the end I capitulated, pretending like him that Jerusalem had no hidden, secret part. But then the Six Day War erupted, and the Old City gates opened before us of their own accord, like the treasure-filled cave of Ali Baba.

There was one scheme, however, from which Yair did not even try to dissuade me: The plan that when we grew up we would build a special orphanage called Nemeczek House, named in honor of the faultless and tragic hero created by the Hungarian playwright Ferenc Molnar in *The Paul Street Boys*. We would walk by the former Arab villages of Malha and Beit Mazmil, all the way up to Ein Karem, and the whole way I would describe to him the physical and spiritual benefits the poor orphans would enjoy in the large and inviting facility at Nemeczek House, located on the shores of the Sea of Galilee and surrounded by orchards and gardens. We would give these unwanted boys and girls unconditional love in the spirit of little Nemeczek—that lean, good-hearted boy who suffered a fatal illness and died only because he tried to make peace among his violent friends. I announced to Yair that anyone who needed love and warmth would be welcome, including the miserable Arab children who were forced to leave Ein Karem and Malha and Beit Mazmil because of the Jews' War of Independence.

At age twelve I started planning our wedding. I suggested that since we could not yet be married, we should at least take a trip together during Passover break to the big city of Tel Aviv and sail down the Yarkon River. But Yair, whom at around this time I had begun to call

Iri, said his grandparents would never stand for that sort of immodest behavior—leaving him little choice but to accept my backup plan, which was to catch a movie at the Edison. We prepared for the adventure as for our wedding, scrounging for the one-lira-and-ten per ticket, stealing through the narrow streets, and, with a rising sense of expectation, crossing the main avenue and climbing the steep hill that led to the Edison Theater, in order to see *The Parent Trap*. It had my favorite actress, the blonde and perfect Haley Mills, playing the roles of identical twins who trade places, their clashing personalities crafted by Eric Kastner in one of my most beloved childhood books, *Lisa and Lottie*.

The box-office window had bars like a prison cell. My heart pounded as I held the two rectangular slips of paper that would hurl my beloved and me to happiness. Behind the thick glass of the padlocked display there were double-images of Haley Mills, sitting next to herself, arguing with herself, even throwing herself into a pool. Yair and I entered the large theater and made our way among the rows of wooden chairs to the seats marked on the tickets, looking carefully for anyone familiar who might rat on us. The lights dimmed, the curtain rose, the newsreel began, and then finally the movie, and I almost burst into tears of shock and disappointment, because instead of *The Parent Trap* with the magical Haley Mills, there was an altogether different film—a western, full of unshaven, gun-slinging cowboys and dames in décolletage who wore lipstick even when they slept.

It was one of the worst calamities of my life up to that point. But Yair actually seemed pleased, so I had little choice but to sit with him through two hours of shootouts and dust clouds, staring at his darling face that was turned up to the giant screen and illuminated by its dancing light. Shrouded in darkness I allowed my trembling hand to move slowly toward him, until it landed softly in his young, smooth palm. Blood pounded in my veins and my heart reverberated like a gong through the crowded theater, but Yair was transfixed by the cowboys and their galloping horses, and I couldn't tell whether he even noticed I had touched him.

On our way out of the theater I saw a sign saying that *The*

Parent Trap would be showing at the Edison only on Mondays and Wednesdays.

The night before the Passover Seder, my parents returned home and informed me that my father—who by then was already known as the great Professor Avraham Dror, *bête noir* of the Biblical Studies Department and author of the best-selling book on the Bible in the Modern World which had been translated into thirteen languages—had been offered a coveted teaching position at Columbia University, and that our family would be moving to New York for the next few years.

Immediately after Passover began the "waiting period" which led up to the Six Day War, and I almost wished that the armies of those five Arab nations would indeed invade Israel as they promised, just so that my father would not take us to America. At my parents' house I helped the neighbors' kids clear out the junk from the building's underground bomb shelter and wash its gray concrete floor, and at my grandparents' I helped fill sandbags and pile them in the entryways of Estherke's ground-floor apartment, where all the tenants were supposed to gather when the shelling began. Every morning, when the teacher led the class in reciting Psalms—*Strive, O Lord, with those who contend against me / Fight with those who oppose me / Draw out your spear and battle axe against those who persecute me*—I whispered a prayer that no harm would come to Yair Berman, that he would remain forever by my side.

The war ended right after it began. I cried, protested, begged to stay in Israel and live with Grandma Rochel, but only a few weeks remained to explore the Old City with Yair before I was dragged beyond the seas. I did not return to live in Jerusalem for four long years, years that scuttled our plan to grow up together, and maybe even scuttled my life. If not for my New York period, perhaps I would have been good enough, simple enough, worthy enough in Yair's eyes to be his wife.

New York took me by surprise, you see. I had planned on living there as a wretched exile filled with longing, and instead I struck roots like a Wandering Jew, roots which burrowed deep into the alien, impure, rich soil and infused me with the energy to grow and even blossom. Yair was in the background the whole time, for just as I knew myself, I knew with absolute certainty that he was mine and I would marry him and we would live out our lives together. But I also loved New York, I loved being in New York, and I only began to worry a little when, halfway through the four American years, we came for a brief visit to Israel and I discovered a different Yair, reticent and shy, who blushed when I ran toward him on the street near his grandfather's house and who responded to my enthusiastic greeting with only a feeble "Hello."

"He is a maturing religious boy now," Aunt Batya later explained. "At this age they don't talk to girls."

When I protested that we were also religious, and that he was certainly no *haredi* like Uncle Yankel's kids, she looked at me with pity. "There are all kinds of religious people," she asserted, "and all kinds of excuses for not returning love."

My cousins had also grown older and more serious in the two years since we'd last met, and my friends were astonished at my American clothes and changed habits. One Shabbat afternoon a young couple walked toward me in the alleyway by my grandparents' apartment, the man in a new, smart black frock coat and an imposing *streimel* whose brown fur lay on his head like a sleeping bear cub, the woman with a tight, white snood covering her shaved head and indifferent blue eyes which suddenly woke as her face passed mine, and she whispered, "Shlomtzi, is that you?" Only then did I realize it was Estherke.

"I got married two months ago," she reported in a heavy Yiddish accent, "and this"—she pointed toward the smart frock coat that had drifted away from us toward the end of the alley with its curly cub on top—"is my husband Yehoshua."

I felt horrible for her. I wanted to say to her, *Estherke, Estherke! Why did you let them set you up with this nerd before you had a chance to be free, to taste life and decide what you wanted to be?* But when she saw that her husband was leaving, she just shrugged helplessly. "*Gut*

Shabbes, Shlomtzi," she blurted and ran after him like a dog keeping pace with its master.

☙

When we returned to New York, I wrote Yair the first letter. "I know it's awkward for you to be in contact with girls, but maybe in my case you'll agree that I'm no ordinary girl. I'm your twin sister, and I miss you." At least once a week I sent him five or six pages jammed with experiences, feelings, and plans for our future together, and for every three such letters, he sent me one. "Shlomtzion, how are you?" he wrote. "Sorry I have to be brief, but I'm not as good at writing as you are, and I'm also lazy. Other than touring the country and being a counselor for Bnei Akiva, I do basically nothing."

But after a few months, he began sending me long letters of his own.

> I'm going through changes, Shlomtzion. Up till now I basically never really prayed with proper intent, I never took my Talmud studies seriously, and I never really thought about the meaning of life, of my existence as an individual and as part of the Jewish people. But now I've started getting into the teachings of Rabbi Kook, and I'm attending classes with the rabbis of the Great Yeshiva, and of course with the head of the yeshiva, and the world has simply opened up before me. More important—*I've* opened up before me, my whole self has been revealed to me, and you just can't imagine how wonderful it is.

At first I read his ruminations out of consideration for him, to understand what he was going through and to make sure he wasn't pulling away from me. "It seems ridiculous to look at the Jewish people as the center of the universe," I wrote back. "Are you sure that this narrow worldview really fits you, who were once so open-minded, who used to read everything and could carry on a conversation about anything?"

❧

At this time I was deeply impressed by what my New York high school for music and the arts—which I insisted on attending despite my parents' preference that I go to an Orthodox day school—had to offer. In art class I painted out of a deep, powerful sense of longing, as though I were no less than another Van Gogh and every still-life were a portrait of my own suffering soul. I excelled in English literature, shone in history, even did well in math once I discovered a whole new way of looking at it from our Chinese teacher, Mr. Wong.

I hung out with a group of five students from my workgroup in the daily art class who became my closest friends: Lee Howard, tall and black-skinned, his giant smile revealing pearly-white teeth, his long legs doing a little jig when he walked; Anthony Sarantakis, Greek and chubby, who knew everything; Maria Santos, a gentle and talented Philippine; and Steven and David Klein, identical twin brothers, Jewish geniuses with a wicked sense of humor whom I had no difficulty telling apart despite their identical flat faces, identical piles of wavy red hair, and identical thick, square glasses.

All five had a hard time pronouncing my glorious, ancient name, and instead called me "Shelley"—that is, when they weren't calling me "Moshe Dayan" or "Israel." And they would tease me, saying I was only pretending to be Israeli, that really I was an "all-American girl." Sometimes I would even wonder what was so bad about being there after all, why was it so important to be Israeli, when I could just as easily stay in New York and keep on riding rental bikes with my friends on Sundays in Central Park, going with them to exhibits at the Met, the Hall of Science and the improvised galleries in the avant-garde lofts of Greenwich Village, attending the free concerts all over the city, dancing with them at parties, sketching the boats sailing down the Hudson together, playing guitar and clarinet in Washington Square as passersby tossed coins into Lee's battered hat, singing duets by the Beatles and Simon and Garfunkel in the subway station on the way home from school. And laughing ourselves silly at the masses of humanity who just couldn't understand that the joke was on them.

This was the late 1960s. We were decked out in striped bell-bottoms and massive, colorful necklaces with peace signs on them, and we called on grown-ups everywhere to Make Love, Not War. We didn't actually want to be real hippies. We never ran away from home, never snuck into high-school bathrooms to sit in a circle on the floor and indulge in the latest chemical substances, and never did more than French-kiss. But freedom and justice were in the air and we all breathed it in, we all wanted to be followers of Krishna and foot-soldiers of King, we all proudly carried the banner of equality and universal love. I really enjoyed the time I spent with these friends, and it saddened me to think we would soon be forever parted.

Years later, when I told Yair all about Lee and Anthony and Maria and the Klein boys, he just said: "Good thing you got out of there in time."

But imagine, Maya, that I had stayed in New York. Maybe today I would have been Shelley the happy Bohemian artist, not Shlomtzion the forlorn architect. Maybe I'd be living on the Upper West Side in a high-rise with a magnificent view of the Hudson River, mixing colors and painting from morning till night and then till morning again, answering to no one. Maybe I'd be lapping up my life. Maybe I'd be loving. Maybe I'd be.

❧

Slowly and reluctantly, however, like a trickle of water against dry sand, Yair's words began to penetrate my head and my heart.

Shlomtzion, when we were kids we argued about whether souls wanted to be born or God forced them. You argued that it would be better for souls to remain in Heaven, and I said it was better for them to come down to Earth. Now I've discovered that your opinion was accepted by the sages of the school of Shamai, and mine by the school of Hillel. For a long time they argued about it, and the whole thing appears in the Talmud, tractate Eruvin, folio 13b. In the end your position won out. But you should know that to see the Jewish people as the center of the universe is itself the most open-minded belief possible. To be a part of the Jewish people is the greatest compensation the soul can receive for being forced to come down to Earth.

Without even putting down the letter I ran over to the Talmud and opened it for the first time in my life. It took considerable effort to figure out how to find tractate Eruvin, folio 13b among the enormous and elaborate volumes, and I leapt with delight when I found it. For two and a half years the schools of Shamai and Hillel argued the matter, with one school saying that man would have been better off having never been created, the other that he is better off having been created. When finally they took a vote, it was decided that indeed man would have been better off had he never been created, but now that he has been, he should take great care to watch what he does.

That day I began searching through the dozens of rabbinic volumes which my father had brought with him for his research from our home in Jerusalem to our apartment in New York, and I looked up the sources Yair mentioned in his letters. It was as though the moment the rabbis agreed with me that man was better off having never been created, I could enter their world without hesitation. Thus I discovered *Lights and Mists of Purity* by Rabbi Kook, as well as his *Lights of Repentance*, a clear and articulated volume which explained that every individual was in fact a part of the whole, that even I was not just floating in space but connected with all of existence, that the universe was good and just, and that the goodness and justice inside of us comes as a result of our own correspondence with this All.

Towards evening my father came into the living room, his stupid pipe dangling from his mouth, and caught me curled up with *Lights of Repentance* on the couch in front of a lifeless television. With repugnant glee he called out, "Tziporale, look at the holy texts your righteous daughter is reading!" And my mother ran in from the kitchen, wiping her hands on her apron and beaming, for a moment thinking that my father, for once, wanted to share with her something genuinely joyous.

Chapter three

What would have happened, Yair, if my mother's grandmother had had children with her first husband? What if they had never been forced to divorce after ten years, if her parents had never come to the Holy Land, or if her second husband's first wife had never run away, making him come to Jerusalem? And what if my grandmother's first groom had fallen in love with her and not his cousin, or if your father had not died an untimely death, or if your grandparents hadn't lived in the same neighborhood as mine, or if that cat had never gotten locked in the fish store?

Today Maya brought your sweet, smart boy over to my place. They are so much in love, Yair. When I saw them I saw us, twenty-one years ago, and I shuddered when Ariel greeted me and smiled, for it was your smile, your bashful, brown, bespectacled eyes, your puerile red lips, your sweet dimple on the right cheek. Like him, you also didn't look that impressive twenty-one years ago. You, too, didn't cut such an imposing figure, even in uniform, neither tall nor broad-shouldered; your body also looked so thin, so unassuming and vulnerable as to threaten to collapse in on itself at any moment. But boy, Iri, how much I wanted to be in your arms! How protected and right I felt when your frail body was near mine, as though I drew my ability to live from proximity alone.

As I sat with them, Maya leafed through our photo album and told Ariel about her amazing father, about his extended, unobservant family, and about my family, our *haredi*-Orthodox side. Your son sat there, hanging on her every word, lowering his head over the pictures, the nape of his neck smooth and delicate like a gazelle's, so similar to yours that my heart skipped a beat. She told him all about her Grandpa Avam the Bible professor, and about Grandma Tzippi, who after his death tinted her hair red and moved to Florida with her new husband Bob, an aging American prankster who worships the ground she walks on.

Did you know, Iri, that my Grandma Rochel is still alive, and that she asks after you sometimes? "How is the love of your life," she asks with a smile, "the gentle grandson of Rabbi Yehezkel Berman? You were inseparable when you were kids," she effuses, "a match made in heaven. Tell me, Shlomtzileh, how come you never married him?" And I have no answer.

❧

My good friend Eden, the one who got me to tour Scandinavia last summer and who also takes me to these dance and Yoga and self-awareness classes, says there's no such thing as the life that "could have been." "This is your life," she croaks with her tobacco-stained voice, standing there with her hands pointing toward the table in front of me, as if my life were lying on a plate and I'm supposed to lick it clean.

Maybe you remember her twenty-two years ago, when her name was Edna Tzur. After her divorce she went to the Interior Ministry and formally changed her name from Edna to Eden. It made a big difference, as though it was not just her name that had changed but that everything about her had become new and different.

Twenty-two years ago, however, she had a long, thick braid that reminded me of Estherke's long lost one, and on Saturday nights she and her husband would come from their secular kibbutz in the Jerusalem hills to the Rosh Yeshiva's weekly class on the parashah in his yellowing apartment in the Geula neighborhood. I got to know her as she and I sat in the apartment next door to the Rosh Yeshiva's, squeezed among dozens of women and girls of all ages on the heavy couches and simple wood benches, concentrating in awe at the stereo speaker that had been placed on the table in the middle of the room, from which resonated, like the voice of the Lord from the clouds on Sinai, the voice of the Rosh Yeshiva, who was hidden among the men who crammed the apartment on the other side of the wall. Eden and I helped each other decipher his words, distorted and broken due to his advanced age and the poorly rigged sound system, and one Saturday night I introduced you to her husband, Tzvika, on the way out of the rabbi's house. You remember that old carob tree—the one with the giant roots sticking up out of the pavement, making everyone who passed by walk carefully so as not to be tripped by the mound of cracked asphalt that had erupted around them? We stood together right next to those insane roots—you later told me how impressed you were by this authentic kibbutznik couple whose souls longed for Torah—and from then on the four of us would meet up after every class and stand together in the street among the dispersing students, reviewing the rabbi's profundities and gathering up their falling sparks.

And then, Yair, nine years ago I bumped into her again at a photography exhibit at the Tel Aviv Museum, and she was so skinny and her hair cropped so short that I barely recognized her, and we embraced like two lone survivors of a shipwreck.

It turns out that after they got married, and after I disappeared from Jerusalem in general and the Rosh Yeshiva's classes in particular, Eden, who was still Edna, became Orthodox together with her husband Tzvika, and they started observing the mitzvot. In 1975 they left their kibbutz with their two children and went to live in a religious settlement in the southern part of the Golan Heights, where they had another child. Eden adjusted well, they worked the land above the El-Al valley, and she wore a colorful kaffiyeh over her lovely hair, took classes in the Bible and Jewish Philosophy every night, and even quit smoking.

Gradually, however, Tzvika became increasingly extreme in his observance, and his stringency became obsessive to the point that he even forbade Eden and the kids to speak about secular matters in his presence. Only the holy words of Torah could be uttered. Eden began suffocating and didn't know what to do. Then Tzvika decided they were leaving the Golan and moving to a Hassidic community in the south. That was when Eden recalled a halakhic ruling according to which a married woman who has committed adultery is forbidden to continue living with her husband.

A few years before this, she had asked their rabbi in the Golan what she should do with respect to an affair she'd had soon after she was married, long before she and Tzvika had become observant. The rabbi had cleaned off his glasses and focused intently on his lenses before advising her never to tell her husband about it. "As long as your husband doesn't know you were unfaithful, you are permitted to him," he explained without looking at her. "But if he ever finds out, he will be obligated to divorce you."

So when Eden started suffocating, she approached Tzvika among all the boxes they had not yet unpacked in their new low-ceilinged tenement in the Hassidic community in the south, looked him in the eye, and whispered, "I was unfaithful to you, with Steve Goldman."

"*Waddya mean* Steve Goldman?" Tzvika's holy lips parted, as he hauled up from the cellar of his memory the talented musician and entertainer who had arrived from America during the wave of Zionist fervor following the Six Day War; whom Eden had taught Hebrew at the kibbutz's Ulpan; who would make Eden melt with pleasure whenever he sang or played the various instruments he knew. "When could you have possibly seen Steve Goldman?"

Eden answered impassively, "November, 1967."

And yes, she got her divorce right away, but the rabbinical court awarded custody of her three children to their God-fearing father, so that they wouldn't be raised by their adulterous mother, Heaven forbid, and all her legal battles and all her pleading were of no avail. Even short visits with the kids were barely tolerated by Tzvika. It was only after four years of solitude that her son Omer showed up on her doorstep in Ramat Gan, skinny and filthy, his shoes torn, eyes sunken, and skin parched, four days after he'd vanished from his father's place and been declared missing, triggering a police search complete with media coverage. When Tzvika heard that the boy had made his way on foot all the way from the middle of the Negev to the middle of the coastal plain, he apparently allowed a sliver of reality to penetrate his consciousness and decided to permit Eden to keep the boy with her. But as for her daughter Talia, who has married a *haredi* yeshiva student and had five or six babies of her own, poor Eden has not seen her in years. Her youngest son, Elhanan, who calls Tzvika's second wife "Mom" and wears a black felt wide-brimmed hat, meets Eden only once every couple of months. This is her life, of which she tries to make the best she can, rather than getting caught up in the life that "could have been." So who am I to complain about mine?

❧

Truth is, Yair, most of the time I really don't complain. I'm generally happy: I get up in the morning, shower and brush my teeth, get dressed and go to work, plan and sketch and sit in meetings, talk to clients and chat with friends, attend classes, and twice a week make a tasty, nutritious meal for my sweet *moshavnik* Yossi whom I met on the trip to Scandinavia, go to bed with him and then spend a simple, splendid evening with him talking, reading, watching television. He never shows up empty-handed, sometimes bringing a crate of apples, sometimes apricots, sometimes nectarines, and I give them out to neighbors and make jam and compote, just like a warm, carefree, rural housewife. Saturdays I go visit him in the Hefer Valley and we ride around on a tractor among the crops, or we go on a hike with the Nature Society. We've already gone on two more organized tours abroad, to Istanbul and Paris, with the matching luggage that we bought especially for these trips, and for the many more we hope to take together.

All in all I would say I'm surviving, that I managed to save myself. But deep down I still regret what happened, Iri. It could have been you and me spending these simple, splendid evenings together. I could have been embracing *you*. We could have been in love. What was it that I demanded of you, Iri, what did I ask other than to let me be yours, to let me give you seven or eight children, to let me raise them to be wise and learned and to love and fear the Almighty, to walk true and pious with God, to cling to the Lord, enlightening the world with their Torah and good deeds, doing the work of their Creator? What did I ask, Iri—and why did you leave me?

Chapter four

When we came back to Israel I proposed marriage to Yair. I was just sixteen, but I felt strong and mature enough. Nothing was more urgent, I thought, than to quit my role in the inane production my father had been directing and starring in his whole life, and to focus on the real and true world of Yair and me. It was time to begin, once and for all, fixing this confused, misbegotten world that was just holding its breath, waiting for the two of us to get married and come save it.

But Yair had just been drafted into a special army unit affiliated with the yeshivot. He was a gracious, gutsy soldier in the tank corps just like your Ariel is today, and he bathed me with his brown eyes and carefully brought the runaway train of my heart to a halt. "No, Shlomtzion," he said. "Right now I need to focus on my training, and you're still too young to marry. Let's wait a while, give ourselves a chance to grow and improve and prepare."

I had little choice but to breathe deeply and resign myself to two years of growth, improvement, and preparation. In due course I became an exemplary student in the girls' high school. In the evening I would bring myself under the wings of the rabbis and *rabbaneot* that Yair recommended, sitting in their sparse apartments overflowing with books and students, attending classes on the teachings of Rabbi Moshe Chaim Luzzatto, the Maharal of Prague, Rabbi Abraham Isaac Kook and his son Rabbi Tzvi Yehuda, and I could tell that my soul became increasingly elevated and pure, preparing its flesh-prison to pass through this world, which is but an antechamber to the World to Come, living a proper life among the People of Israel in the Land of Israel according to the Torah of Israel, a life filled with merit and meaning in which everything is genuinely good and just, a life of *Thou shalt be holy, because I, the Lord who sanctify thee, am holy.*

I became enamored with Rabbanit Hava Schor, the wife of the assistant dean of the yeshiva, Rabbi Moishe Schor. I attended her class on the Maharal's *Eternal of Israel* Tuesday afternoons without fail. She was in her late thirties, a strong and aristocratic woman with a soft voice, long fingers, and a face like that of Athena, the goddess of wisdom whose severed statue I had seen in a museum in Athens on a trip with my parents and brother. Her torso upright and her neck wondrously straight and tall, she offered eloquent interpretations of the Maharal, expertly combing the volumes of Talmud and midrash before her. Sometimes she raised her lovely eyes, making little wrinkles in their corners when she smiled, and slowly scanned the women and girls listening to her from the beds and benches that packed her humble apartment—from the narrow living room lined with bookshelves crammed with holy works, down the hallway with its swirling bands of dust, and into the kitchen, where two sinks were permanently piled with dirty dishes.

If the Rabbanit Hava Schor had merely sat before us every Tuesday afternoon with her wise and soothing voice counting from one to a thousand, the experience would have satisfied my thirsty soul and compelled me to keep coming back for months or even years. To my delight, however, she instead taught us about *The Eternal of Israel*, its complexity, its unfathomable depths and soaring heights, and I sat among the students and imagined that she looked at me differently, that she knew I was special, that she expected great things of me and that I would never, ever let her down.

Like a special-forces soldier in training, I scrambled up the steps of the *Path of the Just* as they had been laid by Rabbi Luzzatto—from Judiciousness to Zeal, from Zeal to Cleanliness, from Cleanliness to Temperance, and so on, until I was able to see from afar the final destination, the steps of the Holy Spirit and Resurrection of the Dead. No less. Only when Yair was off on leave did I allow myself a break from my own boot camp, and then I would go everywhere with him, traveling and studying, never separating except to go to the bathroom or when we parted late at night, him to his grandparents' and me to mine, to catch a few hours of sleep before reuniting. Of course it never crossed my rarefied mind to violate any of the prohibitions written in the codes of Jewish law, so I never tried to get Yair to touch me, God forbid, even a little—even though every bone in my body ached for his. I breathed only through his lungs and saw the world only through his eyes, and in retrospect I know I may have been a burden to him, that perhaps even then he was starting to think about escaping. But I also know that this was out of my hands. Because it was only by looking through Yair's eyes that I could countenance this world, that I could see it as a place one could survive—even if I would have been better off never having been created.

On one of his furloughs we trekked up to Pekiin in the Galilee. I was eager to visit the cave where Rabbi Shimon bar Yochai and his son Elazar had hidden from the Romans, to see the dirt they had buried themselves in up to their necks for thirteen years, the fount which sprang from the ground on their behalf, and their carob tree, which to this very day still weaves its branches on the mountainside.

"They sat in the ground for so long, their bodies began to get covered in rust," I retold the Talmudic tale. "Just imagine, Iri, what it means for your body to rust. When they finally left the cave after twelve years of studying the Torah's innermost secrets, they despised everything they saw, for they believed that the people had abandoned the eternal life for the sake of this world. Everything they looked at was set ablaze."

"Yes, but in the end the Holy One put them in their place," Yair tried to temper my enthusiasm. "He asked them: 'Did you leave the cave in order to destroy My world?' And He sent them back to the cave for another whole year."

"What did God want from them?" I questioned. "Why did He create a world that is so easy to destroy?"

On the way back to Jerusalem, we stopped at a dark, abandoned gas station to put water in the radiator. There, on the shoulder of the road, I saw a large shriveled dog, old and forlorn and ownerless, its bones visible through its sparse yellowish fur, sitting and watching the cars go by, waiting for someone who would never come.

❧

"The world rests on three things," my beloved teacher Yair recited. "On Torah, on Service, and on Good Deeds." To strengthen the third pillar, we added a whole list of voluntary activities to my regimen. For months I spent my Sundays and Wednesdays reading history textbooks aloud to students at the high school for the blind, preparing them for the matriculation exams. Mondays and Thursdays I helped deaf children with their homework and speech exercises. Tuesdays I took handicapped youths on excursions in their wheelchairs. My father called me Florence Nightingale. When he saw me preparing to leave the house in the afternoons, he would raise his eyebrows and call after me, "Whom shall the white angel save today?" But the handicapped kids loved me, and their gratitude gave my life a measure of justification. I shuttled back and forth among them as if they were entirely dependent on me, as though I were charged with healing their mortal wounds, as though I had been sent by a negligent Creator to ask forgiveness, in His own name, of every single soul that had been destined to live its life in a defective body.

Amidst all the bustling about and my charitable work I eventually learned of the death of Shayaleh, pale and snotty Shayaleh, the neighbor's kid who used to follow Yair and me like a shadow back in those good old days, and who struggled all his life with a serious chronic respiratory illness. He died on his eighteenth birthday. When I went to console his mother and seven older sisters who were sitting *shiva*, now relieved of the burden of caring for him, I sat before them in silence and suddenly thought of the little golden chicks that Grandma Rochel used to buy for me in the market of Machaneh Yehuda. A chick born that same day cost five *agorot*, and oh what immense pleasure I felt when the merchant, a kid who sat in the street corner with a crate that emitted tiny chirping sounds between his legs, would pull an infinitesimal chick from the pulsating pile of golden life and place it in my outstretched palm. What total love I felt for that small creature with its beating heart, its shiny black eye-points, that new, sweet being that would depend on me alone from that moment on. What selflessness when I prepared for the chick its bedding of cotton balls in a shoebox my grandmother gave me when we got home. And what gratification as I watched it waddle across the floor and peck perfunctorily at the food I had crumbled and the water I had placed for it in an upturned jar lid, naming it Ferdinand and planning its future, how it would grow and learn, and how I would train it to be the wisest of all roosters. And oh how devastated I was when all my Ferdinands died, one after another, sometimes the day after we bought them in the market, and sometimes two or three days later. The last Ferdinand held out until his golden fuzz started to give way to whitish feathers, but then he too was found lying on his back, hunched and stiff, claws curled upright, eyes locked, beak wide open. Only when I wept and asked Grandma Rochel never to buy me another chick did she disclose to me that all the chicks that the village boys sell for five *agorot* apiece are defective birds that could never survive more than a few days anyway.

My grandmother was only trying to relieve my guilt for the death of those in my care. But I felt insulted, swindled. And as I sat before Shayaleh's aging mother and seven older sisters, who had been so happy when he was born and had spent eighteen years trying in vain to keep him alive, I seethed at the Merchant who sold them Shayaleh out of the box of defective chicks.

"You know, Shlomtzion," his sister Elka smiled warmly as I rose to leave, "he spoke about you until the end, about how when you were kids, you promised to marry him and invent a medicine that would cure him."

❧

And I was so very pure and beneficent, Maya, the first time I volunteered for the famous humanitarian, patroness of Jerusalem's poor, the Rabbanit Tzadok. Excitedly I walked through the Machaneh Yehuda market, which I had not visited since Grandma Rochel had taken me shopping there as a child, and with spiritual elation I followed Yair's instructions through the dim, covered alleyways, turning left between the counters of slaughtered chickens and the counters of dried fruit, descending among the low houses and emerging into a sun-drenched courtyard in which, along whitewashed walls, sat people waiting their turn to receive a blessing or counsel from the greatest of the mystics, the husband of the Rabbanit.

My heart heavy with fear, I crossed the yard and rapped on the blue wooden door, rehearsing how I would request of an elderly, Yemenite rabbi's wife to conscript me into her legion of girls distributing food and used clothing to needy families. But when the blue door opened, I stood before a robust woman of about forty-five, her dark hair spilling from beneath her colorful headscarf, her eyes adorned with kohl and shadow, her lips with bright red lipstick, and between her fingers a lit cigarette.

"Excuse me," I said in the small voice I used back then, "is the Rabbanit Tzadok home?"

"Sure she is," said the woman in a husky voice. "Come on in, sweetie."

She led me into a kitchen that was narrow and old but sparkling clean, and sat me at the table with three young women. At the center of the table was a tall pile of fresh parsley.

"Anything that's yellow or dry you put to the side," she said. "The fresh, green ones we'll use for the patties we're making for the rabbi's students for lunch." She placed a chain of sprigs before me, and I had little choice but to start searching through them submissively.

It was only about ten minutes later, after listening to the four of them talk about how many students would eat there today and what we would serve them, after watching the one big pile of parsley transform almost completely into two medium piles, one yellow or dry and the other fresh and green, that I screwed up my courage. "Excuse me," I asked, "do you happen to know when the Rabbanit Tzadok is supposed to be back?"

The three younger women burst out laughing, and the woman with the husky voice looked at me from under shadowed eyelids, puffed on her cigarette with red lips, and waved me over, drawing me into her warm and crushing embrace. "Nechama Tzadok at your service, my darling."

❧

It was from her that I learned to scrub floors until they sparkled, to cook rice to perfection, and to give to others not for their own benefit nor for mine, but just to give for the sake of giving.

She had no children of her own. Once, while we worked together, she told me and the other girls that when she was fifteen she became pregnant by her husband, the great Rabbi Yitzhak Tzadok, but because of the harsh conditions at the time, she became ill and nearly died, losing the baby and her uterus with it. They were married in Yemen when she was eleven and he twenty-five, for she was an orphan and he took upon himself to raise her and educate her and care for her needs. She traveled among the villages in a mule-drawn cart, together with Rabbi Tzadok, who studied the Written Torah and Oral Torah and taught the young children in the poor Yemenite villages. "They were so poor and pathetic, my sweeties," she told us, "you cannot even begin to imagine." Only when she began menstruating did they start living in the manner of man and wife.

I stopped visiting her after Yair broke up with me for good and I returned only five or six years later, when I brought you, Mayaleh, to Jerusalem for one of our rare visits to your grandparents and surprised myself by deciding to take you to see and smell the Machaneh Yehuda market and maybe, despite everything, to save—even if just for a little while—the life of a single golden chick.

The alleys of the marketplace brought with them a tidal wave of longing for Rabbanit Tzadok and I was struck with the need to bring you to her, to ask for a blessing and an embrace. I held your little hand as we turned left between the freshly slaughtered and plucked chickens and the sacks of dried fruit, and we slowly and carefully descended the stone steps to the courtyard. I remember my heart expanding as I imagined how she would be delighted at the look of you and how she would wave us in, ingathering my exiles with a mighty hand and an outstretched arm. But just as I was about to knock on the faded blue wooden door, I sensed that perhaps it was too quiet, and my eyes fell on a flier that had been pasted to the wall, and it was a yellowing, peeling, death notice. Despite the passage of almost a year since it had been posted, one could still read the black letters that shouted *Baruch Dayan Emet*, Blessed is the True Judge, and then whispered *Woe unto us for we are broken!* and spelled out the name of Nechama Tzadok of Blessed Memory.

My legs failed me, and I dropped to the floor of the courtyard, beneath the worn-out poster that crumbled together with the whitewash behind it, and I held you in my arms and cried on your little shoulder with so much grief, so much regret, so much pity for myself, for my orphanhood.

Chapter five

There are souls that know one another from primordial times, from before they ever descended to earth and entered the body. I shook with happiness the first time Yair read me that sentence from Rabbi Kook's *Lights of Holiness.* An electric charge ran between us at that moment and I knew that for his sake I would find the strength to tie back my wings and hide them under my long, modest dress, to overcome the disdain I felt for the things of this world, and to finish high school.

For it was at the beginning of twelfth grade that I went through a period of disinterest, when all I wanted was to give up the vanities of this life and form a mystical union with the pure and absolute Truth, like Rabbi Shimon bar Yochai and his son Elazar, who buried themselves in dirt for thirteen years in the cave in Pekiin until their bodies got rusty; like the monk who built himself a little hut in the crags above the monastery deep in Wadi Kelt, where he consorted with eternity all his days without suffering the company of mortals or sullying himself in the World of Lies, living only by grace of a small wicker basket dangling from the end of a long rope attached to his solitary perch, in which the other monks put whatever minimal provisions he needed to survive.

I couldn't understand why anyone would choose to live a material life on this earth, if all light and truth were to be found in heaven. When Grandpa Duvid used to take off a minute or two from crafting his holy words, and step out onto the little porch overlooking the alleyway, or stand in the corner of the kitchen making himself some tea in his giant beer mug, he often sang the soft and stirring melodies of the High Holiday services, especially the end of the Yom Kippur confessional: *Master of the Universe / Before I was created / I was already unworthy / And now that I am created / It is as though I never was created / I am but dust when alive / All the more so in my death / Behold I am before You / Oy! / Behold I am before You like a vessel filled with shame.* When he got to *Behold I am before You* my grandfather's voice would crack from within, like parched earth yearning for rain. For my part, however, I was revolted by the indignity of having to keep my body just so it could face the worms and filth that awaited it at the end of its entirely pointless allotment of days on earth.

"It's all a joke!" I would protest to Yair's reddening ears. "I know, I know, the World to Come is like a banquet hall and this world is a corridor leading to it, and so on. But don't you understand that we mortals have no real chance of ever becoming worthy of the banquet hall during the three-score-and-ten pathetic years we spend in this dismal corridor? *The One who dwells in Heaven laughs, He doth ridicule them*, and the Torah that He has so graciously given us from His throne on high is just rubbing salt in our wounds. All your efforts, Iri, are purely Sisyphean, because Torah or no Torah, you are to Him no more than a little cockroach making its way along the pile of filth that we call this world, crawling around trying to ignore the fact that it's been taken in."

Yair would get nettled. "Shlomtzion," he'd scold, "you are way out of line. I don't know whether your fanaticism is something you inherited from generations of dysfunctionality, or maybe it's entirely your own, a product of the vast difference between the true Torah you are studying and the baloney you were involved with when you were with those American hippy friends you keep telling me about with such love and longing. You need to understand that there is value to the lives of those people who do not spend every waking hour basking in the glory of God, that this world is important, not just as a corridor to the World to Come but also in its own right. Creation is not a pile of filth, Shlomtzion. It is full of beauty and majesty, full of instruments that we may use to attain the very holiness you so desperately seek—"

But then he would collect himself, apologize for losing his temper, and start saying how it was really okay, even righteous, for me to feel this way. That the suffocation I felt in the material world was really the sign of a great soul. And so I had to apologize as well, again promising to finish the matriculation exams with honors, so that I could get a good job and support my husband who would sit and study Torah, for in what may a woman merit, if not in sending her husband and sons off to the house of study?

❧

It was around then that I began to revere a woman named Darya Sela, who was the closest thing to that monk in Wadi Kelt that I was ever able to meet face to face. She was a *ba'alat teshuva*, having found religion on her own, a stubborn and hard-nosed woman of about thirty, with a male haircut and a mortified face, who had come to Jerusalem from a secular kibbutz affiliated with the Hashomer Hatzair movement and landed in the classes taught by the Rosh Yeshiva on the parashah, as well as in Rabbanit Hava Schor's class on *The Eternal of Israel.* Word had it that her turnaround from extreme-secularist-kibbutznik to *ba'alat teshuva*—one who, it is said, stands in a place where even the completely righteous cannot—was the result of losing her dear husband, who fell in the Six Day War during the battle of the Golan Heights which were then called the Syrian Heights.

Her own secret cave was a shed she rented at the back end of a backyard of an apartment building along one of the narrow streets of the Beit Hakerem neighborhood of Jerusalem. Her place was small and humble, a thin curtain separating the main room from the little alcove which held the kitchenette and bathroom. But the walls were filled with shelves upon shelves of holy books, most of them brand new. She even had a shiny new set of the Talmud, and the whole Zohar with the commentary of the Sulam, the volumes still smelling of bindery glue. It was in the midst of this world of wisdom that she sat, day and night and beyond, studying the Torah.

After my first visit to Darya Sela's sanctuary I began going to Beit Hakerem any time I felt spiritually thirsty, sometimes in the evenings or late at night, and sometimes in the morning when I was supposed to be at school. I'd get off the bus filled with expectation, climb the narrow road in a cloud of awe, open the narrow gate to the path leading behind the building, and then proceed to the back of the yard, where I would knock on the door to her shed, terrified. On the door was pinned a scrap of paper that said "Darya"—*Dwelleth the Lord*—as if this were the very passage to the divine.

She did not so much teach me as study with me from her many new books, such as *Pri Tzaddik, Sefat Emet, Em Habanim Smecha,* and the *Ein Yaakov* commentary on the legends of the Talmud. I was swept away by these study sessions, and I worked at them so intensely that my body was on fire. But the more we studied, the more dissatisfied Darya Sela became with me.

"You are still on the outside," she chided me with her metallic voice, narrowing her gray eyes. "If you want to get close to God, you will have to work a lot harder."

Only after I had sworn through tears that there was nothing I wanted more than to behold the sweetness of God and dwell in His sanctuary, did she relent. "Don't cry, my good girl," she said. "Don't cry. *The Lord's Torah is pure, and it strengthens the soul.* To study the Torah you need to turn every ounce of your being into one great ear with which to hear the word of God, a great funnel through which the truth may pass."

I was afraid of her, but again and again I found myself making the trip to Beit Hakerem and opening the narrow gate to the back yard. When I sat with her I felt weak and small to the point of dissolution, but I still kept making the pilgrimage to her inner sanctum with increasing frequency, as if punishing myself.

Years later I met a woman from her kibbutz, and when I inquired about her, she sighed. "Darya? She was the beauty of the *meshek*, a talented girl with a wonderful sense of humor. She married Alik Sela a year before the Six Day War, and when his plane was shot down, she fell too. They say she went crazy, Jerusalem Syndrome or something."

And not too long ago, I saw Darya Sela on the Nahalat Binyamin promenade in Tel Aviv. It was a hot summer day, and she really did look like that monk in Wadi Kelt, with her long, buttoned-up black garb and closed shoes, her thin gray hair uncovered—meaning she still had not remarried—and her eyes gravely surveyed the display windows.

I watched her until she went into a fabric store, the city stifling around me.

❧

The thirst for the living God ate away at my soul until I began believing that I was special, one of the righteous few who are able to see how stupid the world is, how far it takes us from our true goal—to cling to the Lord.

On the Simhat Torah holiday I went with Yair, as every year, to the festive *hakafot* at the Western Wall. But this time I felt superior as I saw him head straight for the men's section and join one of the circles of dancers, adding himself to hundreds if not thousands of other bobbing *kippa*-clad heads, joining the circling bodies, destined to decompose, that were spinning wildly around the Torah scrolls being carried in the center. I was revolted by the sight of all those fools, my husband-to-be among them, who deluded themselves that there was anything to rejoice about in this World of Lies. I couldn't stand their levity, the levity of cockroaches who have agreed not merely to run around aimlessly on a pile of garbage, but even to leap and dance and sing songs of praise to the One who put them there.

On our side of the hideous plastic partition danced the women. Among them, also jumping and singing with their screechy voices, were the girls of my Bnei Akiva chapter, who had come to the Wall *en masse*, led by my good friend Naomi Ron. She was murdered in the West Bank a year and a half ago. When she saw me, Naomi, may she rest in peace, tried to pull me into the circle, but though I liked her more than most of the others, I still couldn't dance, I couldn't celebrate, I couldn't be like everyone else. I pulled away from her sweaty grasp on my sleeve, closed myself to the sound of songs bubbling up in biblical verse from the sea of throats rising like a tide from the packed piazza, and leaned against the angular stone wall which, if you climb the path behind it, takes you up to the Mugrabi Gate and then through to that place where the earth touches Heaven, and I thought, '*Who will ascend the mountain of the Lord, and who will stand in His holy place?' No one will ascend, O King of Glory, so don't do us any favors. We're trapped here, down below, and all along You've just been toying with us.*

After a long while, Yair came over to me, mopping rivulets of sweat off his brow and neck with his plaid handkerchief and smiling sympathetically. "Come, gloomy girl," he said. "Let's go study something that the late rabbi wrote especially for you." I followed him, lost and in turmoil, through the crowd of fools who continued to charge the Wall as though they expected to find revelation right then and there, and he guided me through them like Moses leading Israel through the divided sea, and brought me to the steps that led up to the Jewish Quarter of the Old City. We climbed until we reached the building of Yeshivat Hakotel and then entered the yeshiva's great study hall, empty now because all the students had joined the dancing down below.

"Have a seat," he said, pointing to the study benches, taking in his hand the blue, thin volume of *Lights* by Rabbi Kook. "Look what he wrote here, Shlomtzion." He glowed as his hands quickly found a chapter called "Thirst for the Living God." "You'll see how well he saw what you're going through. 'When the soul yearns for the clearer light, then the world becomes reviled in its eyes.' Are you listening? 'It expands and grows so much into the world's limited expanse, that the whole world, with all its material and spiritual treasures, seems to it like merely a house of anguish, its air no longer breathable.'"

I shifted uncomfortably in my chair, finding it inconceivable that the holy, pleasant Rabbi Kook ever experienced the same disgust that I did. Yair continued reading excitedly, his gnawed-nailed index finger pointing to each word for me as though I were a little girl learning to read. "'Thus will the power of the will and the strength of life at times be weakened in those people for whom the desire for God is their inner directive.' You understand that you don't have to give up? This is you. The rabbi's talking about you! You're just suffering from a soul that yearns for the clearer light."

Yair's gentle voice contained his great excitement, his eyes looked up from the book and infused my own with hope, and I so loved him, Maya, I so much wanted to tell him to take me and we'll run together, take me and we'll run, I wanted to gain the World to Come in that single moment and bring satisfaction to my beloved. But just then, as I sat beside the decorated window overlooking the masses of people filling the plaza of the Western Wall and who seemed content with nothing more than that, as the golden mosque leered down at them, peering over the wall's shoulder in gilded ridicule, my inner directive ground to a halt. All I could say to him, weakly, was "Yes, Yair. I see it. I'll be okay. Don't worry."

❧

Most times I managed to keep going, studying the material and getting good scores on the matriculation exams, just as I'd promised, so that I could be a woman of this world for Yair's sake. But never did I forget even briefly that I was really nothing more than a vessel of shame and disgrace, a decaying storehouse of cells. I imagine it's pretty hard for you to believe, Maya, that your materialist mother—whose greatest aspirations today are a clean and orderly home, independence at work, and American movies with their happy endings—was once a girl in whom any passerby could hear an imprisoned soul crying for help.

I tried to take comfort in the Song of Songs. Yair and I studied together the commentary that depicts the book as a story of unfulfilled love between the people of Israel and the Lord of the Universe, between body and soul, between material and spirit. "Time and again the two lovers in the Song of Songs try to find each other, but time and again they fail," Yair explained. "They lose each other in the expanse and never fulfill their love. One cannot awaken absolute love before the time is right, before the redemption, and so whenever we get out of bed to answer the knock on the door, we find that our beloved is no longer there, that the moment has passed—and that maybe there never was such a moment to begin with."

I tried to tell myself: *That's just how things are, Shlomtzion, there is no perfection in this world, and even you, with all your isolation and greatness of soul, have to learn to live with imperfection.* On one occasion I screwed up my courage and, at the end of a class given by the Rabbanit Hava Schor, when the gratified women and girls had closed their copies of *The Eternal of Israel* and risen from the beds and benches to put on their coats and kiss the mezuzah with their fingertips on the way out, I stood to the side until the Rabbanit Hava noticed me, and I asked in a humble voice whether it would be too much trouble if I could visit her for a single, private conversation.

She received me in her kitchen on a Friday morning, offered me tea and cheap biscuits on a plastic plate, and gave me one of her warm smiles, the kind of smile the goddess Athena would have smiled, if she had smiled. "I hope you don't mind, Shlomtzion," she said, "if I start making food for Shabbat while we talk." So I sat on the edge of the chair as the rabbanit peeled potatoes, fried spinach patties, and mixed batter in a large bowl. I thought I should probably get up and at least wash the dishes piled up in the two sinks, but out of shyness I went on sitting, taking tiny bites out of a biscuit and offering a thoroughly honest confession of my feelings of superiority and the disdain I felt for anyone who was capable of being happy in this world, about my impatience with Creation, and also—as every few minutes a junior rabbi or yeshiva student knocked on the door, stuck his head in, and asked if Reb Moishe was home and when he'd be back—about my deep fear that such thoughts were a grave sin.

I expected her to react with a warm, emotional embrace, telling me that she felt exactly as I did, and advising me as to how to go on living my life despite being so spiritual and unique. Instead, the rabbanit poured the batter into a baking pan, covered it, and put it in the oven. She wiped her hands slowly and carefully on a towel, and then pulled a book off the top of one of the kitchen cabinets—*To the Pathways of Israel* by Rabbi Tzvi Yehuda Kook. For the next twenty minutes she read aloud and then offered her own interpretation of an essay in which the rabbi described the process of redemption of the holy people in the holy land.

When her young daughter came home from kindergarten, the smell of cake wafting through the house, the rabbanit turned off the oven and began showing me to the door. There she stood with me for another fifteen minutes, giving a rousing impromptu sermon on the powers hidden in every Jew, as her little girl called out for her and tugged, in vain, at her skirt.

I left her apartment confused and dismayed. On Saturday Yair and I took our Shabbat walk, and I told him about our private conversation in which the rabbanit did not even try to solve my problems and may not have even been listening to what I said. Yair laughed. "Silly girl," he said. "Everything she said and did was her way of answering you—including the cake and the little girl and all the other things of this world she was engaged with before your eyes. She was trying to show you that this is the way to redemption, for a people or for individuals. And that there are no shortcuts, not for a nation and not for a single soul."

❧

In our efforts both to improve and to sanctify life on earth as much as we could, Yair and I came up with a list of principles upon which we would found our ideal society. It would be a society of Torah scholars, people who worked only for subsistence, where anyone who wanted to join would be welcome. The name of the city that would be home to this ideal society, Yair suggested, would be Kfar Haneviim, "Prophets' Town"—"since everyone can become a prophet," he said, "and therefore everyone should try." There wasn't a single aspect of daily life we ignored. For the sake of healing and bettering humanity, we came up with novel ways of improving everything in Kfar Haneviim—from a unique architectural style for its homes that would be ideally suited for the Land of Israel, to new methods for economizing on fuel and curbing air pollution. Eating healthy, in our opinion, meant eating mostly fruits and vegetables, and we even had a well-grounded view of what the ideal clothes should look like. "Yes, Shlomtzion, there is importance to what mortals use to cover, as you put it, the nakedness of their increasingly decaying bodies. Therefore, in Kfar Haneviim we won't wear clothes that cling to the body and highlight our external form. Instead we'll want clothes that are roomy and soft and appropriate for the climate in the land of Israel. We should return to the old styles, dress like Arabs with their long, modest robes, or in baggy cotton pants. And up above the waist, a Jewish man should wear a long, broad shirt, with threads of azure blue attached to its four corners, just as the Torah commands us."

We planned the Kfar Haneviim school system around the values of nature, goodness, honesty and drawing closer to God, in accordance with the teachings of Rabbi Kook in his famous "Epistle on Education," which everyone always talked about but no one ever put into practice. We also wanted to gradually reduce the age of marriage, so that ultimately fifteen- and sixteen-year-olds would marry and continue to live in their parents' homes. "The good Lord did not put so powerful a flow of hormones into the bodies of sixteen-year-olds just so that they would masturbate and then hate themselves for it," Yair said, and then we both lowered our eyes out of shame. "Besides, Shlomtzion, look how wonderful it is that the two of us have grown up together since we were kids. Too bad we couldn't have married when we were younger. The world isn't ready for it, but at least we two are growing older together, building upon one another and internalizing the idea that our relationship is a natural, obvious thing."

We knew that if the world had been ready for it, we would have gotten married right away, and I slowly began resigning myself to an immature world, in which one cannot get married, cannot rejoice in the highest light, whenever one feels like it. *First we have to go out and repair the world in the kingdom of God,* I kept telling myself, *and this is exactly what Yair and I will yet do.*

❧

Now it was the night of Purim, the holiday of the "scroll of exile" and the "hiding of God's face." Yair and I went to a Purim party at the yeshiva. Hassidic music blasted from powerful speakers in the large dining hall, the sweet odor of cheap wine lingering in the air. They sat me in a corner with eight or nine young wives of the students, whose gracious and gratified countenances I was supposed to inherit in the not-too-distant future. I tried to follow the convoluted sermons of intoxicated rabbis who were called to the podium one after another, and I watched as one or two hundred students milled about the dining hall in groups, moving with the music, passing bottles back and forth, drinking and grunting in their stupor, their attempts at dance soon reduced to a stagger, lacking direction or rhythm.

"The wine goes in, the secrets come out," quoted one of the charming wives, whose name was Einat. I had met her in the weekly classes of Rabbanit Hava Schor. She now had a flower embroidered on the pocket of her denim jumper marking the exact midpoint of her pregnant abdomen. "Look how much love they have," her child-like voice effused, "how strongly they cling to the Lord. You see what secrets they hide all year long, when they're sober?"

At that moment, as if to illustrate the point, a bearded student emerged from the circle of dancers, lurched over to the side, fell to his knees and began bawling. "Master of the Universe!" he cried. "I don't know what to do! All my life I have prayed to you, and you don't answer! Oh God, I can't take it any more! Give me a sign, please, just give me a sign!" He writhed on the floor, overtaken by wine and melancholy. Another student then hobbled over to him, extending a hand to help him get up. As he passed near me I recognized the wobbly Samaritan as none other than my own Yair, his face on fire, his hair a frenzy, his white shirt stained and half-untucked. I watched him, worried and amazed, as he pulled up his comrade and slung him over his shoulder like a wounded soldier on a battlefield, then carried him until they were both swallowed up by the dancing revelers.

In this tide of grief that passed for a party, I saw one student leaning against a wall and caressing it, his hand moving up and down the whitewashed surface as he muttered bitterly, "The Temple of God, where is our holy Temple?" And at one of the tables that had been shoved to the side, there sat the reverend Rabbi Moishe Schor all by himself, stroking his long beard and rocking in his chair like one who mourns the destruction. When a group of students came over and tried to raise him from his chair, he emitted a strangled wail, and I was able to lip-read the words "I'm so ashamed, I'm so ashamed!" as he finally succumbed to their persistent tugging at his body and clothes and was dragged, against his will, to the circle of dancers.

As the evening wore on, the dining hall filled with rings of wailing students embracing one another, supporting one another, screaming at one another at the top of their lungs, "I love you! I love the Jewish people! I love God!"

From where I sat I was able to discern that this graceless dance was none other than the dance of souls trying desperately to cut their ties to the material world and to touch heaven, despite the weight of their prison-bodies, the rags of useless flesh and blood pulling them earthward and preventing them from taking wing.

At one-thirty in the morning, long after I had last seen Yair dancing with the others, wild and holding a half-empty bottle of wine, the charming Einat came over to me. "Come Shlomtzion," she said. "My husband says Yair's not feeling too well, and that we should take you home."

"Where is Yair?" I asked her quiet husband, who even now, at the end of this insane evening, seemed restrained and orderly, his clean white shirt glowing. "Take me to him," I entreated, ignoring his warning that I might be horrified by what I saw.

He escorted me, back hunched with unease, up the stairs leading to the dorm rooms. When we reached the corridor of the third floor, we heard Yair's voice, half coughing and choking, half crying, or maybe even laughing.

My guide threw me a reluctant glance, but I nodded my head and he opened one of the doors a crack, peered inside and motioned to come closer and take a look.

The room reeked. I saw Yair in the middle of it, sitting on an unmade bed, doubled over, heaving the contents of his stomach into a bucket being held in place by one of his friends, while another gripped his quaking shoulders, the two talking to him and trying to calm him while he, through the retching that ripped him in two, laughed hysterically. Indeed, the noise he made was a kind of wild laughter, completely free, a laughter I had never heard from him before and never imagined I would.

In a moment of calm, the friend supporting him raised Yair's dangling head and wiped off his chin with a towel. The one holding the putrid plastic bucket rested it on the floor and tried to remove the guffawing drunk's shirt, which was soaked with wine and vomit. Suddenly, my beloved noticed me, and his laughter increased to the point of near-suffocation.

"There she is," he blurted between gasps and snorts, the hand pointed at me wavering in the air, the syllables slurred. "Here is the supremely righteous woman… All she wants is to get to the banquet hall…just to *behold the sweetness of God and visit His sanctuary…* as though this fucked-up world is her problem alone…like I have all the answers…like I know whether man is better off…whether man is better off…"

When Yair said the word "better" it sounded like "butter." I found it hard to make out other words as well, and before he had finished rambling, he doubled over in a new fusillade of laughter and vomiting. His loyal friends quickly bent over to raise the bucket in time to meet the dark river that poured from his mouth, while I turned and walked out, disgusted, offended, but mostly saddened. Einat's husband following me in silence down to the street where, in the pure air, his wife awaited us, their baby in her belly, next to the car her parents had lent them in honor of the festive occasion.

☙

The shock of Purim set me straight once and for all. *If the Holy One put Yair and you into this world*, I reasoned, *this means your job is to serve Him in this world. Yair and you will still attain the level of the prophets, still be leaders of the people of Israel, of the chosen people rising from the dead in their own land. You will yet disseminate the light of God in the world, for this is what you were meant for. But for now, you must wait patiently, build yourself, build Yair, and build your relationship.*

During the period between Pesach and Shavuot, the festival commemorating the revelation at Sinai, my compulsive visits to Darya Sela ceased almost completely, and I focused instead on counting the days of the *omer* with extreme care, preparing my soul to receive the Torah. When the forty-nine days of preparation had passed, on the night of Shavuot, I went to the *tikkun* at the women's seminary affiliated with the yeshiva and spend the night in impassioned study. My whole being was ready to call in the name of the Lord, ready to realize together with my beloved the calling of the Jewish people in the world. "True, you are good people," Rabbi Nachman of Breslav had taught, "But this was not My intention / I had wanted you to be more like beasts / Howling in the woods / All through the night." *There are many good people,* I thought to myself, *but Yair and I will serve God like beasts howling in the woods. With all our hearts and with all our souls and with all our might we will serve Him through the night, until we have forced heaven to come down to earth, until we have awakened the divine love, until we have told it that its time has arrived.*

Sixteen months after that, when it was all finally over, I would understand that even my feelings of wonder on that Shavuot night were part of the grandiose illusion I had built around us. But that night I was convinced that I was for my beloved and my beloved for me. Through the night and until first dawn I studied the midrash concerning the revelation at Sinai and the Book of Ruth, and by the time the sun rose and I headed to morning prayers together with the other girls, I flowed like a tiny, disciplined drop of water among the rivers of Jews flowing from every corner of the city toward the Western Wall. I was fully connected, fully reconciled with reality, fully capable of living.

When we reached the ruins of the Temple, the sun crept over the Temple Mount and illuminated the plaza by the wall, which was again packed with worshippers—but this time I joined them in complete submission. I stood at the foot of the holy wall, together with Naomi Ron, who of course was there also and who had made room for me next to her, and I whispered the words of prayer in the siddur, thinking: *Yair, my Iri, we will sanctify His blessed name in the world like the seraphim and angels that sanctify Him on high.* And after the praise and thanksgiving and petition, and the promise that the Lord would be king over all the earth, Naomi and I embraced and exchanged kisses, wishing one another *Hag sameach*, a happy holiday, and I exited the plaza to meet my beloved as we had arranged. I walked by his side, content in my love for him, and he smiled at me, his face beaming as the two of us skipped up the steps toward the Jewish Quarter, united like the two lovers in the unwritten final chapter of the Song of Songs—like the Holy One and Israel at Sinai, like Moses and the Torah at the time of his ascent to heaven.

Almost as if this had been our intention, we came across a small band of happy American boys and girls with long hair and shabby clothes on one of the upper platforms of the broad steps. They were sitting on the stone-tiled floor learning a song from a man with a sweet, round face and shaggy beard, who stood with his back against the rail, singing, his hands waving at his sides, his foot tapping to the beat, his voice softer than soft.

"Come on over," one of the girls beckoned in English. "Reb Shlomo made up this song just this morning, not two hours ago," and I realized that the man was the famous Rabbi Shlomo Carlebach, who had arrived from the United States just a few years earlier and was known in Israel as the Singing Rabbi. I looked at Yair cautiously, knowing how he felt about my affinity for American hippies, but he returned an approving look. We sat on the steps, rehearsing with the groupies the new song their rabbi had conjured, to which he had attached the words of King David—*Awaken, awaken, awaken O my glory / awaken, awaken, awaken O harp / O harp and lute / I will awaken the dawn.*

The sun was already hanging directly above the place where heaven and earth touch, the place where the holy sanctuary will again be built, when we parted from those youths who had awakened the soul, awakened the harp and lute, awakened the dawn of redemption, and we thanked Reb Shlomo, who blessed us warmly, "*Hag sameach*, dear Jewish children, *hag sameach*, holy Jewish children."

"You never told me," I said to Yair as we made our way toward Jaffa Gate, "that sometimes when you get up and answer the door, your beloved is actually there, and he even comes in."

We laughed, looking into each other's eyes. I had everything. How could I have known then that in the end nothing would remain?

❧

As I was finishing the matriculation exams, Yair neared the end of his tour of army duty in the *hesder* program for yeshiva students. He wasn't sure whether to discharge on schedule and return to the yeshiva or to extend his service and enroll in the officers' academy, as his commanders had recommended, and as I believed a future leader should. He went to ask the Rosh Yeshiva his opinion and the Rosh Yeshiva listened to his arguments for both sides, thought about it a little, and then just started talking about how happy he was that Yair had decided to return to the yeshiva. "Even King David, the venerable leader," he added, "knew when to go to war to conquer the promised land, and when to dedicate himself to studying the Torah."

The girls in my class were making their own plans, some

deciding to join the National Service, others opting to enlist in the military; in Bnei Akiva everyone deliberated over which service was more worthwhile, which afforded girls the ability to give more to their country. As for me, I put on a new floral blouse and went to Jerusalem's old, rundown Central Bus Station to meet Yair on the blinding summer day he was discharged.

With a broad smile I proclaimed, "So now we'll get married."

But even as I was saying it, a strange foreboding came over me. Maybe the storm clouds had already gathered over our heads, and maybe I felt them. Yet my heart celebrated as if it was a separate entity, and I wanted to believe in my heart rather than in the curse that supposedly followed the women in my family, who lost the men they loved the way others lose socks in the wash. "Now we'll get married," I repeated, and Yair looked at me with his wise brown eyes and smiled with his fulsome rosy lips and heart-stopping dimple in his right cheek, then bent his vulnerable neck and tossed his heavy, gigantic army duffel over his delicate shoulder. "Shlomtzion, Shlomtzion," he said.

Before yeshiva restarted in the late-summer month of Elul, we took a trip down to the Sinai desert, where Yair was familiar with a number of sites and army camps where we could sleep and eat. Not knowing that this trip would be our last, I eagerly devoured the desert and sea, taking in everything voraciously, happily. Walking on clouds, I hiked and ran and climbed and dove, singing to myself, *Come O bride, come O bride!* With Yair behind me, ahead of me, all around me, what more could I wish for?

By the eighth day of the trip, I had become one of the cliffs of Sinai, a grain of sand on its blond beaches, one of the waves licking its shores, a Bedouin girl gliding above the surface of reality. "Let's just stay here," I told Yair. "Let's pitch a tent with its sides open in every direction like Abraham. You will call in the name of the Lord, and I will bake for guests."

But we had to turn north and head home. On the ninth day, as we passed Ras Burka on the way to Eilat, riding up the coast of the deep-blue Red Sea—I swore I'd return as soon as I could—Yair slowed the car. "Let's pay a visit to Rosy," he said. "He was my platoon commander until a few months ago."

He turned the wheel sharply, taking a right between the hills and palm trees, and when the sand grew deep and demanding, he stopped the car and switched it off.

"Rosy is a tremendous person," he told me. "You have to meet him. You have to see how he's lived in seclusion since he got out of the army. Okay, not really seclusion—you'll see it—just that he lives according to his own rules. He calls the place the 'Shores of Freedom.' I think you'll love it."

We left the car and walked toward the sea. Beyond a ridge we came across a small network of Bedouin tents and I followed Yair through colorful tapestries, among woven carpets laid on sand and through camels, goats and chickens, tools and implements and strong, alien odors, bronze children smiling at us with enormous eyes and waving hello in their long, faded clothes.

A dark-skinned, clear-eyed boy wearing a thick wool sweater despite the intense heat said to us "Rosy!" rolling his "r" excitedly as if announcing: "I know who you're looking for." We walked until just beyond the tent village, and then Yair pointed ahead. "Over there," he said. I looked up but was unable to see anything until we got right up close, for Rosy's earth-toned tent walls were camouflaged against the sand, the mountainside and the brush, as if he were a desert animal defending its life by taking cover in the surrounding colors.

A beautiful white dog approached us, tail wagging and head lowered, and began sniffing my legs in a rather thorough manner.

"That's Rosy's dog Lara," Yair explained. He surveyed the area, hand shielding his eyes, stood about fifteen feet from the tent, and shouted, "Hello! Commander!"

A few moments passed before the earth-tone tent flap was raised, and a great, solid figure slowly emerged. I truly loved Yair, but deep inside I felt a string I didn't even know I had being tugged, Maya, when I saw this tall, beautiful man in shorts and a T-shirt with the sleeves cropped off; whose chiseled, sun-burnished face and deep-set eyes were balanced by his wild, golden beard and the wash of curls flowing from his head like a mane.

"Welcome, Rabbi!" called the man happily as he ambled toward Yair. "I'm glad you still remember me in your civvies."

Looking back, it's funny to think that Rosy was no more than twenty-five at the time. To me he seemed like a mature, seasoned adult as he held his muscular arms wide, and he and Yair slapped each other's backs and embraced tightly as Lara barked with joy.

Then a slender young girl emerged from the tent wearing a skimpy swimsuit. "Sweetie," Rosy told her, "why don't you put on something a little more serious? We have guests, and they're very charming, modest people." He had an unusual voice, deep, monotonous and sleepy. As the girl went back into the tent, he smiled politely and welcomed me with his dreamy voice, "Good afternoon."

"Shlomtzion," Yair said, standing ceremonially between us, "I'd like you to meet my esteemed commander, Mordechai Rosenberg, one of the thirty-six hidden tzaddikim by whose merit the world survives."

"I'm honored to meet you, Shlomtzion," Rosy said in a voice that conveyed a clear warmth despite its monotonous and tired, even catatonic, timbre. "I am by no means righteous, just a humble disciple of the grand master, Rabbi Yair. And as you may imagine, he told me about you on more than one occasion. Dorit and I were about to make an early dinner—why don't you both stay? Have no fear, the Shores of Freedom Diner is strictly kosher."

Skinny Dorit re-emerged from the tent, now in pants and a shirt. I took her for Rosy's girlfriend, and was surprised to feel a bit jealous. But over the course of the next few hours, as we sat around the campfire, making Turkish coffee in a *finjan* using beans that Rosy brought from his Bedouin neighbor Abed, roasting fish that Rosy had caught that morning, and laughing endlessly, since Rosy could not utter a single sleepy sentence without sending me into peals of laughter, we were joined at the Shores of Freedom by the long-haired Shulie and the freckled Osnat, who kissed and hugged Rosy and regaled him with merriment. And when the sun descended beyond the hills and desert, with heaven and earth fusing into a single great red conflagration, as though the world were reaching its end, or perhaps only beginning, Yair and I bade farewell to the magical, hidden tzaddik, and his two new guests stayed behind, whereas Dorit took up her wicker bag and asked if she could hitch a ride to Eilat.

"You've always claimed that you came into this world by accident," Yair teased me after we had dropped her off, his hands gripping the wheel, his eyes fixed on the Arava highway unfolding before the car's headlights. "Because your grandmothers' marriages were the result of tragedy and happenstance. But if you think *you* were born by accident, wait till you hear the unbelievable story of how Rosy was born."

He then began to recount with pride—as though his former commander's convoluted story were his own creative achievement—how, during the War of Independence, Rosy's mother received word from the army that Mottel Rosenberg, her new husband, had been killed in one of the battles in the Negev desert, and was interred there in a temporary military cemetery. She went to her in-laws' house to sit *shiva* with them, and then, in the middle of the third night of the seven days of mourning, the departed Mottel Rosenberg suddenly showed up in her bed.

"Turns out the whole thing was a mistake," Yair glowed at me without taking his eyes off the road. "The guy who was killed was a different Mottel Rosenberg. Rosy's father, who was also fighting in the Negev, heard a rumor that his family was mourning his death, and he asked for leave to go home. When he reached the city in the middle of the night, he saw that the house was dark and everybody asleep, so he climbed in through the bathroom window, which was the only one without bars on it. He tiptoed through the hall and climbed into his widow's bed, and she opened her eyes which were swollen from three days of crying, and said: 'You're alive.'"

That night Rosy was conceived. In the morning, Rosy's father said goodbye to his wife and to his stunned parents, returned to his unit, and was killed again. Only this time it was for real. When Rosy was born, his mother named him Mordechai, after his father who had risen from the dead and climbed in through the bathroom window just to bring him into the world.

❧

We reached Jerusalem around midnight, and Yair came up to my parents' apartment with me to get a boost of black coffee before continuing his drive to Bnei Brak. On the kitchen table we found a note that Yehonadav had written at my mother's behest, from which I learned that while I had been laughing and dining on roasted fish on the Shores of Freedom, Grandpa Duvid had finally succumbed to the heart disease that had long afflicted him. The funeral was already taking place, following the Jerusalem custom of not leaving the dead unburied overnight.

"Grandpa died," he wrote in his childish hand. And though I understood that it was a good thing that my quiet, humble grandfather had finally passed from this world and been given leave to go beyond, had stopped having to make do with our pathetic existence, I still found it hard to be happy for him, because I could not bear the solitude in which he had lived his life. I cried internally while Yair drove me to the Mount of Olives, and continued to cry as we parked by the southeast gate of the ancient cemetery and clambered in the dark among the brambles and rocks and headstones, some whole and some broken, until finally, up ahead of us, we could make out the forms of Grandma Rochel and the rest of the family, their heads against the black sky, their feet planted around the pit into which the temporal form of Grandpa Duvid had been lowered, joining his siblings, all in a row, and his mother, whose gravestone watched over theirs in lapidary grief.

Against the pale moonlight, across from the mountain of the Temple of God which is still in the hands of infidels, the bodies standing on their feet above ground became jumbled together in my eyes with those that were buried below it. I could no longer tell them apart, and only Yair's presence beside me reminded me which category I belonged to.

❧

When the month of Elul began, Yair went back to study in yeshiva, in order to "plumb the depths of the Talmud," as he put it. Even while still in the army he had occasionally spent his furloughs there, not coming out for a whole day or even two. I understood now that if I wanted him to become a leader of the Jewish people, I would have to let him advance in his Torah studies without interference. In order to allow him to dedicate himself fully, I decided not to press the subject of marriage for the time being. Instead I would spend a year in the National Service, as most of my classmates had chosen to do as well; I signed up to teach children of new immigrants in an absorption center near Jerusalem. My declared objective—in accordance with my general belief at the time that I should always work according to declared objectives—was to continue raising my own spiritual edifice while at the same time contributing my part in the fulfillment of the prayer, *Blow the great shofar of freedom, and raise the banner of the ingathering of our exiles* through working with immigrants. I told my friends in the National Service that I would be getting married, God willing, within a year, so my stay at the absorption center would be a shortened one.

But after Elul the High Holidays arrived, Days of Awe which that year turned to days of horror. In their wake, all my plans would be confounded, and the marriage to Yair put off forever.

Rosh Hashanah offered no warning of the evil to come. Spiritually elevated, I hiked all the way from my parents' downtown apartment to the yeshiva in the city's western outskirts, where I prayed with the utmost concentration in the women's section, behind the white screen that had been put up in the back of the study hall. I was convinced that through our combined efforts, Yair and I could open the very gates of Heaven on behalf of the whole Jewish people. I was happy to see Yair praying only five or six rows in front of me on the other side of the screen—I could make out his voice among the hundred-fifty-odd other voices, and direct my prayers in concordance with his. Once in a while I was able to also make out his figure, draped in his prayer shawl and rocking to and fro, clinging to the divine. I knew he must be thinking of the words of Rabbi Kook, whom we'd begun studying again together two days earlier: When an individual's repentance is refined and free, he wrote in *Lights of Repentance*, filled with the light of the Holy of Holies and adorned with the mists of the life on high, it brings healing both to him and to the entire world.

I had no idea this would be my last Rosh Hashanah before being banished from the rivers of the Lord, sent off to search after other gods. In perfect sincerity I whispered the prayers; with all my heart and all my soul and all my might I beseeched God's mercy. I wanted to believe that the gates of Heaven were open for me, oh Maya, how much I wanted it, how desperately I yearned to enter them and praise God's holy name.

But when Yom Kippur arrived, and I returned to pray in the same spot, brimming with spiritual expectation, dressed all in white to feel pure, like the angels, the morning prayers were disrupted over and over again by pale-faced, uniformed soldiers pulling up to the building in small groups, leaving their jeeps running, climbing the stairs, entering the great hall on the tips of their army boots, and pulling aside individual penitents whose names appeared on lists they held in their hands.

God hangs the world over a void, the words of prayer reverberated through me. *He hangs the world over a void. Over a void.*

In the women's section, they had begun whispering that the army was calling up reserves. And in the middle of the midday Musaf prayer, which I had seen as our only source of hope as long as we had no High Priest to enter the Holy of Holies on Yom Kippur to atone for all our sins—in the deep quiet of the whispered *Amida* prayer, when the only sound you could hear was the rustling of pages turning in prayer books, the air was split by the sharp ring of the public telephone in the stairwell behind the study hall.

Can you imagine it, Maya? A telephone ringing in the Great Yeshiva on Yom Kippur!

A moment later we heard one of the students answering it.

Based on whatever he heard on the other end, eight or ten additional figures tore out of the hall, and to my horror I could see, through the white screen, Yair's form taking off his prayer shawl, folding it hurriedly, kissing his prayer book, and covering the distance from his chair to the door in broad strides.

I ran out into the foyer just as he was leaving. When he saw me he came over for just a moment, said some parting words and maybe also words of love, waved goodbye and then disappeared among the other reservists downstairs.

When the Musaf prayer ended, they announced a break of an hour and a half to be followed by afternoon prayers, and the hall began to empty. As I stood, trying to figure out where I would go now that Yair was gone, a great siren suddenly went off outside. Rising and falling, rising and falling like a million shofars blowing, *tekiya, shevarim-terua, tekiya, shevarim terua, shevarim, shevarim, shevarim,* unto the ends of the earth. War had started.

Stunned and frozen in place, I remained beside my chair in the women's section after the sound had subsided. A girl about my age, who had been on her way out, came back in and approached me.

"My name is Leah," she said. "I live nearby. Do you want to come over to my place for the break?"

During the service she had sat in the row in front of me, and I had noticed her smooth, pink cheeks, her perfect nose and the soft, supple chestnut hair gathered about her shoulders with a silver barrette. I had studied her that morning under the cover of the confessional prayer, watching her stand and strike her chest with her fist—*ashamnu, bagadnu, gazalnu,* We have sinned, we have betrayed, we have stolen—and I noticed how her whole being spoke of a serenity, a purity, an inner perfection that I could only dream of attaining. Now she turned to me with her soothing smile and voice as soft as her own hair, and I blushed.

"No, no," I replied. "Thank you so much. Really, I'll be all right, there's no need."

But Leah insisted, and in the end I accompanied her to her home, which really was very close to the yeshiva. On the way there

I learned that the rosy-cheeked Leah was none other than Lealeh Honig, youngest daughter of Rabbi Shmuel Honig, one of the venerable deputies to the Rosh Yeshiva.

"Oh, no," she said as we climbed the stairs to her parents' apartment on the third floor. "Look."

Thunderstruck, we stared out the stairwell window, from which we could see the western entrance of the city. Usually on Yom Kippur, the roads in and around Jerusalem were deserted. Now, however, there was an interminable flow of cars and buses heading out of the city, stopping at designated pickup spots to take on soldiers who were streaming there from all sides, fully in uniform or only partly so, shouldering duffels that had been hurriedly packed.

They were too far away for me to make out Yair, but I knew that at that moment he too was getting into one of those cars or buses, and my heart welled up in my throat.

"My fiancé was called up in the middle of Musaf," I whispered, unable to tear my eyes from the soldiers hurrying off to their deaths.

"Your fiancé?" Lealeh echoed questioningly, then drew close and put her arm around me, uttering a blessing. "*May God protect them as they go out and as they return, from now until forever.*"

When we entered the apartment, Lealeh's elderly parents received us with a sigh of relief, as though we ourselves had just returned from battle, and they caressed their daughter's cheek as if they wanted to be sure no evil had befallen her. I was immediately captivated by Rabbi Shmuel Honig, with his long, graceful white beard, and his petite, lively wife, who was thrilled to hear I was the granddaughter of Rochel Heller, whom she had known since they were children in the Old City. It was just Lealeh, her parents, and me sitting by the white-covered table, Lealeh's older brothers and sisters having all left home already.

"We have to find out what is happening," Rabbi Honig said softly. He then contorted his beautiful face like someone undertaking a colossal effort, and switched on the radio in the middle of the holiest day.

❧

The war "caught" my parents, as my father put it heroically, on one of his book tours in the United States. Yehonadav was staying with Grandma Rochel, and when Yom Kippur ended I returned to my immigrant kids. I carefully translated for them the words of Prime Minister Golda Meir, who spoke in gray and white from the fuzzy picture on the TV in the absorption center's meeting room, more or less announcing to the nation the destruction of the Third Jewish Commonwealth.

It was a terrible, hard war, and during the first few days I heard nothing from Yair. I was unable to corral the crazy thoughts that scampered through my mind, of a life without Yair, a life without meaning, a life which I really would have no reason to live. I prayed with all my strength, cried until my tears soaked the pages of my little prayer book, and said to my friends desperately, "Who knows? With all the awful rumors coming from Sinai and the Golan Heights, I may already be a widow."

On the eve of Simhat Torah, the twelfth day of the war, a message was waiting for me in the main office of the absorption center: "Please tell Shlomtzion Dror that Yair Berman has received a thirty-six-hour leave and will be spending the holiday in Jerusalem." Since the start of the war, it turned out, Yair's unit had been stationed on high alert by the Jordanian border. Only after the holiday were they to be sent to Sinai, to relieve the troops that had been fighting there since the war broke out.

I went into the city from the absorption center and saw my beloved in the little old synagogue that had once been Rabbi Kook's house, dragging his feet wearily around the altar among a circle of dancers, holding a Torah scroll up to his chest, his eyes in another world.

❧

The Yom Kippur War dealt a blow to all the messianic expectations which the yeshiva had been actively promoting since the Six Day War. In order to keep the faith, rabbis and their students now took up a palette of excuses and interpretations aimed at showing how so awful an event was in fact necessary for the redemptive process. Rumors began to spread through the yeshiva about the salvation that Israel would merit as a result of the catastrophe, which would soon develop into the War of Gog and Magog, when Jerusalem would expand unto the very gates of Damascus, as foretold in the haftarah recited on the Succot holiday.

I had a problem with such prophecies. I felt that God's hidden face was more likely to remain hidden, and there was no point in trying to fathom his mysteries. But when I said this to Darya Sela, who stood at her kitchenette with her back to me, putting up the *finjan* on an ancient kerosene burner to make tea, she turned to me with a pained expression, narrowed her eyes until they were two gray slits, and shot me a reproving look.

Just to be safe, every Tuesday I continued attending Rabbanit Hava Schor's immensely crowded class for women on the Maharal's *Eternal of Israel*, sitting in one of the back rows and trying to turn myself into a giant ear for hearing the word of God, an enormous funnel through which the truth could be poured. I still believed my studies would be a source of deep wisdom and closeness to God, for I had well absorbed what the Rabbanit Hava had taught me in our private meeting the year before—and I still believed that the day would soon arrive when I could use this wisdom for the salvation of Israel.

I felt so good and energized after Rabbanit Hava's classes that I'd go straight from her apartment to the school for the blind, where I would visit a girl named Anat, whose brother had been listed as missing in action since the second day of the war. She was one of the students to whom I had read aloud the preparatory material for the matriculation exam in history the previous year. Sometimes when I'd come home from those reading sessions I'd walk around the house for a long time with my eyes closed, trying to imagine what it was like to live forever in darkness, to know the world only through the senses of touch and sound, and never to have any idea—as one who was blind from birth, like Anat—what that additional thing called sight was, or what one missed without it. Once, as I opened my eyes, relieved of the blindness that had left me scared and dizzy, I suddenly realized that there must be other senses of which I had no inkling—that people who go through life thinking that their five senses give them a complete experience of reality are nothing but fools. There are a lot more than five possible senses, a lot more than five ways to encounter reality, and anyone who only sees and hears and touches and smells and tastes has no idea what he's missing. But he's clearly missing a great deal, since reality undoubtedly has other dimensions that are simply inaccessible to him.

When I visited Anat in the dormitory of the girls' school for the blind, she recognized me by the sound of my footsteps in the hallway. "Shlomtzion," she would cry in joy, "Shlomtzion, you came to visit!" I sat with her in her room, which she always kept clean and neat, and which she decorated with the colorful macramé works she had made. I sat on her bed, which was always tightly covered with a chrysanthemum bedspread, and listened as she read aloud the poems she had written about her brother in Braille in a special, thick-papered notebook. "Of Ilan, pure as angels' wings / and of the dream that pulls our hearts' strings / that he will yet return from battle." Then she turned on her tape recorder, and we listened to a worn-out recording of her brother's voice, faded and spotty and accompanied by the sharp strumming of a guitar, singing the "Ballad of the Field Medic," which had taken first prize in the Hebrew Song Festival four years earlier.

"I have no other recordings of him," Anat lamented, her hands caressing the sides of the tape recorder and her empty, useless eyes jumping around as though she were looking for her lost brother. "I pleaded with him, 'Ilan, make me a tape of you talking, it'll be like having pictures of you,' and he said 'Yes, Anat, sure. I'll make you a tape. I'll take the tape recorder with me to the army, and every evening I'll tape you a letter.' That's what he told me, Shlomtzion, that's what he promised. But in the end he didn't have a chance."

❧

I continued attending the Rosh Yeshiva's weekly Torah classes on Saturday nights, usually together with my new angelic friend Lealeh, and the two of us also attended the women's classes he gave Monday nights on his book, *The Flowering of Our Redemption.*

One of these evenings, Lealeh and I went, as usual, to his rustic home in the Geulah neighborhood for the class, which was to begin at eight thirty. Arriving on time, we took our seats among the other students on one of the old wooden benches that had been set up along the bookcases full of holy books, and opened *The Flowering of Our Redemption* to chapter nine, page seventy-two, where the rabbi had left off a week earlier.

But the head of the yeshiva sat quietly at his table, which was covered with layers of books and papers, leafed through the pages of his book, and said nothing.

Ten minutes passed, maybe more. Some of the women shifted in their seats or began clearing their throats to remind the Rosh Yeshiva that they were there. At length he lifted his head—he was so close to me I could make out the shape of every one of the brown age spots strewn about his forehead and cheeks—and asked, worriedly, in his stammering, Ashkenazi pronunciation that I had learned to decipher quite easily, "How far did we get in the last class?"

"We got to the beginning of chapter nine, Rabbi," someone answered.

"Page seventy-two, honorable Rabbi," added another.

Then the Rosh Yeshiva was again silent for a frightfully long time. His tall head with its big black skullcap sank into the collar of his black greatcoat, his thinning beard splayed across his chest. I was sure he had dozed off, but then suddenly his head rose, and his watery eyes, bathed in yellow and encased in a complex map of folds of skin charted with purplish veins, sprang open.

"Yes, well," he further inquired, "what page are we starting on today?"

From every corner of the room, voices tense as guitar strings on the verge of popping could be heard, saying, "We're in chapter nine, Rabbi, page seventy-two." For a moment the elderly rabbi indeed looked into the open book before him, and it seemed he might start the lesson, but then he quickly returned to his silence, shrinking into his chair like a flame about to expire. I thought he was probably exhausted, maybe even a bit senile, and I wondered how all the people in the yeshiva could justify troubling a man of nearly ninety with endless classes and meetings, both with students and with political leaders, keeping him bustling from morning until night.

But at eight fifty-eight the apartment door swung open, and a cool autumn breeze entered the room, accompanied, with brisk strides, flushed cheeks and a flurry of apology, by the Rabbanit Hava Schor, who sat down among the women. Suddenly the Rosh Yeshiva shook himself, arose like a lion, remembered precisely where we had left off the previous week and what we were to study that evening, and began reading aloud quickly, interpreting intently, from *The Flowering of Our Redemption*, chapter nine, page seventy-two.

"That's just how the Rosh Yeshiva is," laughed Yair heartily when I told him about it. "The rabbi knows exactly what he wants. You'll see that sometimes his silences are more expressive and powerful than words." Like a Hassid doting on his rebbe's every action, Yair vigorously recounted all the stories from the yeshiva about all the politicians or other VIPs who made the pilgrimage to the elderly rabbi in order to seek his counsel with regard to the fateful decisions they were about to make. "They go to him because they know what kind of public influence he has," Yair gushed, "because they know that without his okay you can't move a step in this country, and the rabbi just sits quietly or leads them on with hints until they understand, on their own, the answer to the question they had come to ask."

I had a hard time accepting this kind of mass self-effacement, as well as the idea that people needed the rabbi's approval for everything, and were not allowed to exercise their own judgment. Yair, of course, said this was because of my own volatile personality, that I needed to work on myself, and that anyone who lacks faith in the rabbis must also lack faith in God.

And when I complained to Lealeh—peppering my arguments with unflattering imitations of servile, cringing, worm-like students—she burst out laughing but then immediately pursed her lips, collected herself, and began explaining in all her sweet seriousness how "the entire edifice stands on the foundation of the rabbis."

The feminist question offered me another way of stirring her from her tranquil complacency. "It's just wrong to oppress half of humanity," I perorated as we walked together after classes. "It's just wrong to think that women were meant to choke off their abilities and to step aside as men systematically run the world into the ground. And what is it with this Bible that has almost no women in it? Did virtually *no* woman really have an impact on important biblical events—to the point that the biblical text says the men were even 'begetting' each other, as in, 'he begat him,' and so on, one generation after another, without the involvement of a single woman?"

Lealeh's silver barrette glimmered as she nodded sadly. "My dear Shlomtzion, each of God's creatures must rejoice in what it is, rather than being jealous that other creatures were given a different purpose from one's own." Her disappointment was so deep and touching that I grew ashamed of myself. I was relieved that Yair had not heard what I'd said, since he got very worked up any time he heard me say such blasphemous things, and especially when, in the heat of argument, I would call the Torah the "biblical text"—that awful term my father used when he spoke, in his arrogance, about the Torah, defiling it with the forbidden analytical tools the Rosh Yeshiva so often attacked, berating those who used them as having taken the name of God in vain.

The rare times Yair was on leave from the war, he first went to Bnei Brak to visit his mother, her second husband and their children, and from there to Jerusalem, running from rabbi to rabbi and from class to class until he had to go back to his unit. I couldn't speak to him about our plans for the future; he had just seen his own friends blasted into chunks of flesh, their blood spraying on his sweaty uniform, onto his unshaven face, into his eyes ravaged from exhaustion and horror, without his ever understanding why he, of all people, remained unharmed.

"You have to see what kind of amazing people there are in the world," he said. "You can't imagine what people are capable of doing with their fragile lives—what a heart of gold Rosy has, his courage under fire. Remember Rosy? Now he's deputy commander of our brigade. But he's so much more than a CO, Shlomtzion. He's our fairy godmother. I can't tell you what went on there, but if any of us are still alive, it's because of him."

Once when he was on leave I went with him to visit his friend Haim Denino, hospitalized in the guest house at Kibbutz Maaleh Ha'hamisha, which had been converted into a convalescent center for the war wounded. Strapping men, their flesh burned or limbs amputated, moved about the fancy new building in wheelchairs or sat in the main hall overlooking the mountains, struggling to do a puzzle or thread beads onto a nylon string, as directed by their physical therapist, while in the background a sad song played on the radio—*I promise you / my little girl / that this will be / the last war*.

Haim Denino walked out with us onto the veranda of the guest house. He was wearing a plaid shirt, and one of its sleeves was empty. When I asked him when he would get a prosthesis, he smiled apologetically and told me he wouldn't. You can only get a prosthesis when there's part of the arm left, he explained, even just a little bit. But his arm had been blown off from the shoulder. When he saw my distress, Denino laughed. "It's all right," he said. "I'm used to the reactions I get from my non-arm." He told us how a little boy had stood and stared for a long time at his empty sleeve, and then finally drew his own conclusions and announced loudly and encouragingly, "Don't worry, mister. You'll grow a new one."

"Bottom line is, I am deeply grateful to God that by some miracle the shrapnel didn't blow my head off, or hit me in the chest. I was lucky just to lose my left arm," Denino assured us.

A pretty girl pushed a wheelchair holding a boy with no legs out onto the veranda.

"And if you were at all worried that your question before was out of line," Haim added in a jocular tone that sounded like he saw it as his duty to entertain us to make up for his aesthetic deficiency, "you should see the people who tell me how lucky I was not to lose my right hand, and the look on their face when I tell them I was a lefty."

⁂

So how could I talk to Yair about marriage? All I could do when he was on leave was accompany him to the Rosh Yeshiva's classes, listen to the little he was willing to tell me on the way, make small talk about what it was like teaching the kids in the absorption center to read Hebrew and become Israelis. Yair sort of listened, half interested in what I had been doing and half still on the bank of the Suez Canal facing the Egyptian Third Army. Only occasionally would he respond with interest to what I said, smiling at my stories or asking about my work.

One evening, after we had not seen each other for four weeks, he apparently wanted to make me happy, and so he made a show of being fascinated, nodding his head when I told him what my little students had done that day and how I had overcome the challenges they raised. "You know," he said, "with all your experience and talent for teaching children, I could probably put in a good word for you with the director of Nemeczek House."

I was happy to go along, so I put on a voice of mock-worship. "Do *you* know, personally, the director of Nemeczek House?"

"Of course," Yair answered importantly. "I've known her since childhood." We laughed, almost as we had laughed in the tiled courtyard of Grandma Rochel's apartment, under the lines of clean laundry waving in the wind.

⁂

The war wound down, Yair disappeared into his yeshiva, and I tried to convince myself that I didn't really have to marry at age eighteen and a half. But Yair was still the whole world for me, he was life itself, and I felt a connection to no one else and nothing else. My barely acknowledged creeping fear that at the end of the day he wouldn't marry me was a fear of being left alone in the world, to die from grief like an abandoned dog.

One January night I slept at my parents' place, and when I woke the next morning, all of Jerusalem was blanketed in deep, fresh, wondrous snow. I couldn't restrain myself, so for three hours I tried calling the busy payphone in the yeshiva, until I finally got through. The phone rang forever, and then someone answered and agreed to run to the study hall to get Yair.

Yair sounded surprised that I had interrupted his studies, but agreed to meet me that evening on the corner outside the yeshiva. He was waiting for me when I approached, taking small steps, careful not to slip on the sidewalks, where the snow had already become dirty and icy. Together we crossed the main thoroughfare at the entrance to the city, and from there descended to the virgin snow in the valley known as Wadi Lifta. We sat on a log that lay next to a spring which was now frozen over, and immersed ourselves in the incredible, primordial white that surrounded us from all sides, together singing aloud Psalm 104: *Let my soul bless the Lord / The Lord my God is very great / You are clothed in glory and majesty / Light covers You like a garment / You stretch out the heavens like a curtain.* We were full of love for God, love for Creation, and love for each other, or so I thought at least.

I was so happy my heart overflowed its banks, and I jumped up. "Come on," I said, "let's go sledding!" I started scrambling up the mountain, as he looked on, amused, like some serious old man observing a rambunctious little girl. He didn't budge even after I had climbed a good distance away from him, the snow up to my knees, and laughed and panted and longed to live in this world, in all the beauty and splendor and bodily pleasure that the material realm can provide. Between deep breaths I yelled as loud as I could the continuation of Psalm 104, *You did cover it with the deep as with a garment / the waters stood above the mountains*, and when I had climbed about fifty feet up, I took off my parka, placed it on the snow, lay down on it and tobogganed all the way down the hill on a carpet of white, like I was flying, and then I immediately picked up the coat and ran back up the mountain, again lying down and sliding, still shouting: *He sends the springs into the valleys / they flow between the hills / How numerous are Thy works O Lord / You have fashioned them all in wisdom / the world is filled with Your handiwork*—over and over again, unable to stop, gasping for air and shouting, "Come on, Iri, come join me, look how much fun this is!" After a long while, he finally got up, but still didn't join me. Instead he just stood there, smiling, and said sweetly, "You're crazy, you know that? Totally nuts."

When we climbed back up to the main road, I was soaked and shaking, my teeth chattering. Yair took my wet, frozen parka and gave me his coat, which was warm and dry. He then managed to hail one of the few cabs driving on the slick streets and rode with me to my parents' place. I sat wrapped in his coat, enveloped in love for him, and in gratitude to the Almighty who had given me so wonderful a mate.

❧

I missed him terribly when he was holed up in the yeshiva. My efforts to take my mind off him were assisted by the immigrant children, who came to my class fresh off the plane, pale and confused, and left me a few months later tanned, free, and bickering with each other in Hebrew.

These efforts were also assisted by the blind Anat, whose brother Ilan had been found dead on the bank of the Suez Canal. He was given a military funeral, which I attended at the little cemetery in their far-off town in the South. I cut a path through the big crowd of Sephardic women that had descended upon the bereaved family, screaming and pulling out their hair. Anat's eyes were still scuttling about, as though searching for her brother, but the moment I laid my hand on her shoulder, before I even had a chance to speak, she whispered, "Shlomtzion. I'm glad you came."

And they were assisted by the Rabbanit Tzadok, whose veteran volunteer I had become. On the day before Pesach she had me training the new volunteers, explaining to each how to pack matza, wine, and the rest of the holiday goods into a box, then knock on the door of the home to which they were assigned, open the door before anyone could answer it, put the crate down on the floor inside, call out loudly and clearly "Happy Pesach from Rabbanit Tzadok!" and then run away before the family could see what had been brought, before they had a chance to demand to take it all back and tell the rabbanit they didn't need handouts.

❧

This evening you and Ariel invited me to come spend Shabbat with you out in Tirza on the fourth of November, so that I can meet the Bermans and work out the wedding arrangements. "Mom, I hope it won't be too hard for you to spend a whole Shabbat in a settlement," you said to me, and then added: "Daddy says he and Nira will be happy to meet Ariel's parents another time. As for the wedding, he relies on you to represent him as well, and besides, he and Rabbi Yair already know each other a little from serving together in the army."

And then, after you left, I saw the pictures in the news of the young settlers who have tried to take hold of the hilltops around their settlements over the last few days, and the young soldiers the IDF has been sending to kick them off. I shivered, suddenly recalling how Yair and I were part of similar scenes when we joined the first settlement efforts by Gush Emunim in Samaria back in the 1970s. It's hard to believe how we and the others hiked for miles in the dark, dodging the police and IDF roadblocks, sneaking one by one across the open terrain, and then preparing the grounds for rough living—setting up the generator, cooking up scrambled eggs in the makeshift field kitchen, and making enough tossed salad for a famished horde. At the time I was convinced, without the distraction of so much as a shadow of doubt, that we were to be part of a great historical enterprise, one that would change the world and hasten the redemption. Once or twice the Rosh Yeshiva himself even came to the old train station at Sebastia, and I remember him standing on the hilltop, an Israeli flag flapping in the wind, the sun going down behind his hunched back, its rays illuminating his tired face, as dozens of energized young men, Yair among them, danced around him in a tight circle and sang, *Lay your plans and they will be thwarted / for the Lord is with us.*

Among the girls charged with frying eggs in an enormous pan and cutting up the mountains of tomatoes and cucumbers, I usually worked with my now-deceased friend Naomi Ron, who was suffused with Zionist ideals. She took part in all of Gush Emunim's settlement operations, together with her boyfriend Shauli, whom she later married. Like me, she too believed that the Land of Israel would be for the People of Israel according to the Torah of Israel. Only she went on believing it long after I had gone off to other things, believing and believing until men with ideals of their own riddled her body with dozens of Kalashnikov rounds as she drove her car, on an ordinary day, to the settlement where she, Shauli and their eight children lived, in their big, beautiful house surrounded by grapes and figs and pomegranates, the splendor of the Land of Israel.

Sometimes, when I really least expect it, I am overcome again by the anguish over Yair leaving me, as though it's always percolating deep inside, lying in wait. But I really did make my peace with it: The first time was when I found out he had gotten married; the second time, the acceptance was much deeper, more fundamental and irreversible. It happened when I was on vacation on the Greek island of Kos, eight years after we had broken up.

I had traveled to the Greek islands with Haim, my married lover, a successful doctor, after I designed a dream apartment for him and his wife. Kos was our first stop simply because that was the destination of the cheapest flight that Haim, who was wealthy but a chronic penny-pincher, could find. His plan was for us to spend the first night on Kos and then hurry off early the next morning to one of the more beautiful islands. But that evening, as we strolled arm in arm through the alleys of the clean and neatly paved Greek marketplace and looked for a cozy place to eat, my eyes fell suddenly on a star of iron. And then another one. "Look, Haim," I said excitedly, "the bars on this fence were made into Stars of David."

"Yup," he muttered, and went on walking, tugging at my elbow.

"Wait, let's see what kind of building might have a fence like this," I insisted, retracing my steps. "Look, it's a synagogue!"

The fence, the gate of which was chained shut, surrounded a white, corner-side building with high windows and wooden double doors engraved with Stars of David as well. Three broad steps led up to the doors, and the doorframe was endowed with an ornate silver mezuzah. Along the path leading to the steps, a small, well-tended garden flourished, with bushes bearing white roses, a swath of grass about thirty square feet in size, and a bed of bright petunias.

"So it's a synagogue," Haim said, impatiently pulling at my waist. "What's the big deal, sweetheart? Come on, let's keep walking. Maybe we'll find a nice little *taverna* to staunch our hunger."

Two weeks earlier, when I had written this sinful sortie into my calendar, I had noticed that it fell on the eighth anniversary of the evening when I had seen Yair for the last time.

"It's Thursday," I said to Haim as we sat in the *taverna* he had found, and the waiter placed a platter of shrimp before him; I had a watermelon wedge. "Let's stay in Kos a little longer. Tomorrow night we can go to services at that beautiful synagogue we saw."

"You nuts?" He impaled a fried crawly with his fork and eyed me carefully, as if trying to diagnose me. "We didn't come here to daven. Tomorrow morning we're on the first ferry. Don't forget, we're aiming straight for the magical island of Santorini."

The conversation ended when the distinguished physician lost his patience, began yelling and cursing, and then left. I stayed behind on Kos, though I couldn't understand why that synagogue meant so much to me.

Late Friday afternoon I took a cab from the hotel to the marketplace, making sure to arrive before sunset so as not to profane the strange Greek Shabbat that descended on the island without its even knowing it. But the building on the corner with its Stars of David stood silent and dark until late into the night. I left, disappointed, and walked along the shore back to the hotel, conspicuous in my solitude as I meandered among the tourist couples, mostly Germans, who passed me arm in arm, talking quietly, tipsy with love and wine.

Saturday morning people rode rented bikes with their young children, splashed in the sea or lounged in easy-chairs in the sun and wind. I alone strode briskly down the beach, forsaking the day of rest, obviously irritated, demanding of the carved wooden door that it open wide this time. As I approached the alley in the marketplace I could already make out from afar that the chain was still around the gate at the entrance to the building's courtyard, exactly as it had been the night before. I felt swindled and slighted. Years ago I had walked with my grandfather on an authentic, Jerusalemite Shabbat morning, to the intimate synagogue in the home of the grandparents of little Yair, the orphan from Bnei Brak. The services took place in their dining room, with fifteen or twenty supplicants sitting and rocking back and forth around the long table that would, after services, become the Berman family's Shabbat table. When I was very little I would sit on one of my grandfather's knees during the reading of the Torah, or hide in the folds of his tallit, pretending that no one could see me, that only God knew I was there. Now the synagogue was locked, and the pathetic mistress of a shrimp-sucker was pacing back and forth along the iron fence like an animal locked outside its cage, counting the Stars of David formed by the bars and entranced by the well-tended garden on the other side, by the trimmed rosebushes and the strip of freshly mown grass.

I waited there until the sun was halfway across the sky, then wearily turned and left. I dragged myself into one of the souvenir shops on the boardwalk and asked slowly in English, "Excuse me, where are the Jews who live in Kos?" The shopkeeper, a Greek man with a wooly gray mane and a face plowed with wrinkles, stood behind a counter piled with beautiful porcelain candlesticks painted in white and blue, and looked at me with surprise. "The Jews," I pleaded. "Please, where are the Jews of this island?"

His aged eyes turned downward, as if in shame. "The Jews all gone."

"They left? Where'd they go?"

He lifted his skeletal arm and made a sweeping gesture of collecting or ingathering. "They brought them all here to the square," he explained as best he could. "Three great Jewish families were in Kos, and they were all sent there." His hand, which had completed its giant, harvesting oval, opened and waved as though it were tossing what it had gathered into the very sea that was visible through the store's display window. "To Auschwitz," he added. He looked at me worriedly, as though I might not be able to handle the news.

Only after a stunned moment did I fully realize that he was not speaking of something that had happened in the last few days. But even when I finally did understand that he was describing something his own eyes had witnessed fifty years earlier, I still felt as though I had just heard for the first time that the Jews of Europe had been murdered.

I went back to the synagogue after the candlestick man told me that the Kos municipality maintained the building and little garden as a memorial to its Jewish community. "It was the Jews who made this island," he stressed, as if this could explain why they had been wiped out. "You should know, Madame, that if not for what the Jews built and did here, Kos would not be Kos."

I stood by the chained gate and saw, in my mind's eye, beautiful, slender women descending the three wide steps in tight-fitting black dresses, high heels and wide-brimmed hats, serene gentlemen following them with their well-groomed moustaches and pinstriped suits, like the men in the alleyway below Grandma Rochel's balcony in Jerusalem, and children playing hide-and-seek among the flowerbeds, shouting to each other in Greek, laughing and running. I then accompanied them to the market square, and from there, my head lowered, to the boardwalk, where a boat had waited to take them to the death camps.

I leaned against the rail on the boardwalk for a long time, bidding farewell to the three Jewish families of Kos, for whom the Nazis had bothered to travel all the way to this little far-off island, just to find them and assemble them and send them and burn them. I gazed into the vast, empty sea, gazed at my own small and meaningless life, and knew that in the morning I would take my rusting body and set off for Santorini, where Haim would be waiting, or perhaps not be waiting any longer.

❧

As the winter of the Yom Kippur War drew to an end, the Rosh Yeshiva launched a campaign criticizing government ministers, writing pamphlets and making strident public declarations about the duty to hold on to the land and never give it over to other peoples, making a bold call to students of the yeshiva to take to the streets, demonstrating and joining the efforts to settle Judea and Samaria, our heartland.

Thus began the settlements, which solidified the conquest of 1967 until this very day. "*A land of grace longs for her children,*" Yair would quote Rabbi Kook at me. "*She holds her arms out to them in love, calling 'Return, return, exiled sons, lost sons, to your mother's bosom.*'" I found myself crammed along with him among hotheaded demonstrators at a rally opposite the King David Hotel, where United States' Secretary of State Kissinger was staying. Or going to secret rendezvous points late at night, boarding a bus that wound its way up the rocky slopes between Ramallah and Nablus. The next day male and female soldiers would descend upon our mountain, having been ordered—to their dismay and ours—to drag us off by our arms and legs, like trash whose very presence on the land was too much for it to handle. And then we'd go back up the mountain, repeating our demands that the government let us stay there.

“It’s a fetish!” My father scolded me angrily, spittle flying from his mouth with the letter ‘f’. “A fetish of sticks and stones. Sheer idolatry!”

But I was convinced that our abandoned motherland, after millennia of longing, rejoiced at our arrival. And I believed I could feel her happiness. During one of the forced evacuations, Yair threw himself onto the ground, his face in the scrub and his fingers digging into the hard soil. The two soldiers who had been sent to carry him off stood there looking at him, confused, until one of them bent down, tapped him on the shoulder and said softly, “Come on.” When he got up and was taken to the bus waiting below, I saw that his clothes were covered in clods of dirt and his face awash with tears and mud, and I loved him more than ever.

❧

By the end of the following summer, efforts at squatting on the mountaintops had given way to building real towns, and we joined the Tirza group, which was to settle a rocky ridge by Ramallah; its first families were already living on a nearby army base. Yair joined a group of rabbis and students who planned to set up a yeshiva in the new town, which would be a kind of outpost of the Great Yeshiva in Jerusalem. I went with him often to the site, and even spent Shabbat there two or three times. At night I accompanied him on sentry duty, walking in moonlight down a path through the thistles, both of us listening raptly to the echoes of the *muezzin* rambling through the mountains. We disagreed about the Arabs, the lights of whose towns twinkled brazenly in the distance. I was sure they would never make peace with Israeli rule.

“You’ll see, they’ll rise up against us,” I said to Yair. “You’ll see that these refugees will want to leave their degrading camps and come back to the land they were kicked out of when we established the Jewish state.”

"The Arabs are not our biggest problem,” he ruled unequivocally. "*Tzur Olamim* said that His people should have this land, and if we stay strong and steadfast, the nations will fall in line."

While we were arguing, he showed me the hill on which we would build the town of Tirza, and I began planning out exactly where we would one day build our house together.

Chapter six

One warm evening, Yair came to the absorption center and knocked on the door of the cabin where the girls from the National Service were staying. He invited me to take a walk with him among the pines, from which you could see Jerusalem. As we walked he turned his golden head toward me and said, in the most natural voice, as though he were continuing a sentence he had started years before, "I want to marry you, O sister bride."

Through the long years that I loved him, I had enough confidence in his love for me that I had been able to overcome my fear that he would one day abandon me. That's why what followed was so deadly, Maya, devastating to the point that everything I had been up till then just came to an end, and there was no way for me to grow again from the place where I had been, just as a new arm could not grow from the shoulder of Haim Denino to replace the one blown off by the Egyptian rocket.

Because it was only for one week that Yair would walk with

me, gaze into my soul, sail off with me to our future together, and listen to my grandiose plans of how many children we would have, what kinds of fruit trees we would plant, and of how we would pray, how we would open our home and hearts to guests, how we would steadily climb the path of the just, until we reached the levels of the Holy Spirit and even of Prophecy. Even then, during that sole week of grace, we still did not violate the halakhah and let our yearning bodies touch one another. But I bathed in his love, and in my mind I started making plans for our imminent wedding, and I listened, enraptured, to his beautiful voice repeating the words of the prophet Hosea like an ancient, eternal oath: "*And I will betroth thee to Me forever, I will betroth thee to Me in righteousness and justice and grace and mercy, I will betroth thee to Me in faithfulness, and you shall know the Lord.*"

For seven days and seven nights we basked in the highest light, the pure light. But then we went to get the blessing of the Rosh Yeshiva, and our wedding canopy came crashing down.

❧

We visited the Rosh Yeshiva in the afternoon of a beautiful day in Elul, the last month before the High Holidays, at the time set by his personal secretary. Yair had asked Rabbi Moishe Schor to prepare the Rosh Yeshiva in advance. He was to tell him that Yair Berman sought to marry the daughter of the biblical scholar Professor Avraham Dror, and that although everyone knew how dangerous the father and his war against everything sacred were, the daughter really was not like that at all; much to the contrary, she had spent most of her childhood in the home of her grandfather, the scribe and *talmid hacham*, righteous scholar, Rabbi Duvid Heller, whom the Rosh Yeshiva certainly knew from back when he and his family had lived in the Old City; that for the past few years she had dedicated herself to studying with the rabbis of the yeshiva and of course with the Rabbanit Hava, even participating in the Rosh Yeshiva's own classes, in addition to her extensive charitable work and personal character development.

I will never forget that day. I will never forget the image of myself walking with Yair to the Rosh Yeshiva's apartment—not really walking, but rather being carried on a wave of beneficent certainty that filled every cell of my body that week—carried alongside my beloved to the neighborhood of Geula, down Zephaniah Street, through the rusty gate at the end of the stone wall, avoiding the roots of the giant carob tree that burst from the bowels of the earth and which you had to take care not to trip over, approaching the narrow entryway of the two-story building that had yellowed with age, up the four steps leading to the famous apartment, floating on waves of joy, not knowing this would be the last time I would ever take this path, a path which led on that particular day to my foreordained demise.

"The Rosh Yeshiva's just finishing lunch," said his assistant, who had received us at the door of the small apartment. I was used to seeing it only in the evenings, when it was full of people who had come for his class. Now it seemed different, naked and unadorned, smelling of age like any old apartment of any old man, the midday sunlight peeking between the shutters as though it feared getting caught.

I had been curious to see the rabbi sitting in his kitchen, curious to see what he ate and whether what Yair had once told me was true—that the Rosh Yeshiva ate very little, that his meals were usually made up only of the seven species of fruit and grain that graced the Land of Israel. But instead the assistant led us to an inner room. "Please wait here," he said, pulling two chairs up to the table that I knew from our classes on *The Flowering of Our Redemption*. We were left alone, and we sat and spoke in low voices.

"This room is the focal point of all reality," Yair whispered to me, looking around with eyes filled with wonder and awe. "Here the fate of men is decided, and the future of the country is determined."

After a while we heard the Rosh Yeshiva's slippers shuffling down the hallway, approaching slowly, their noise accompanied by a muffled, dry cough. Out of respect for the Rosh Yeshiva we lowered our heads, not daring to raise them until he had made his entrance into the room, dragging his heavy legs one after the other, then leaned on the table with both his arms and emitted a small groan as he rested his weak body in the depression that awaited him in the threadbare cushion of his chair.

Yair opened after a few long minutes. "Shalom, Rabbi," he said in a cautious, exploratory tone. "We are about to get engaged, Rabbi. We have come to ask the Rabbi for his blessing."

A warm smile spread across the Rosh Yeshiva's craggy face. His watery eyes glowed at Yair from above the lattice of purple veins surrounding them, his voice bubbling from beneath his thinning white beard. It seemed as though he was about to bless us. Instead he said, "I'm so happy you came, Reb Yair, so very happy. May God shine his countenance upon you, Reb Yair, and grant you peace. Just last night," he added after a moment "just last night I saw him"—referring to Yair—"here, in our class on *Lights of Holiness*"

How wonderful, I thought to myself, as though I hadn't noticed that our host had ignored my presence, *how wonderful that despite his youth, my beloved is so rare and special a student that the Rosh Yeshiva knows who he is and recognizes his face.*

"Yes, Rabbi," Yair confirmed, "I was in the class on *Lights of Holiness* last night, but now I have come with Shlomtzion, Rabbi, with Shlomtzion Dror from Jerusalem, Rabbi, to receive the Rabbi's blessing over our engagement."

The ancient, waxen hands began to leaf through the copy of *Lights of Holiness* that lay on the table, and Yair tossed me a worried look.

The Rosh Yeshiva began giving Yair a private lesson on chapter thirty-five of the second volume of *Lights of Holiness*. "We can see existence in its spiritual form," he read slowly, "the true workings of the inner life." Yair shifted in his chair, growing increasingly nervous, and gave short, quick answers to the questions posed to him by the old man, who leaned across the table as though telling a secret. He refrained from looking at me.

At this point I began emptying out, evaporating, decomposing, uniting with the dust below. Now and again Yair would try to remind the rabbi why we had come. And then the rabbi's assistant appeared to announce that people had arrived for the next meeting and waited in the next room.

We rose to leave. I was an empty shell as I got up from my chair, quickly exited the apartment, and escaped down the four steps and out the building. How fitting that as I took my leave of that courtyard for the last time, I tripped on the roots of the carob tree that had pierced the asphalt. I would have fallen on my face had Yair not moved quickly, instinctively, to catch me. He held me for just the briefest moment, and immediately let go.

❧

I spent the next day in mourning, huddled in a rocking chair on the little balcony of Grandma Rochel's apartment, missing my dear Grandpa Duvid terribly, looking down onto the neighborhood which had become far more bleak and barren since I had been a child. Yair came in the afternoon. I saw him move hesitantly down the alleyway, enter the paved courtyard, and walk warily toward the steps leading up to the third floor. He avoided my gaze even as he came and stood beside me, then leaned on the wrought iron rail, and spoke softly, almost inaudibly. "I went to the Rosh Yeshiva. I tried to ask him what he meant yesterday."

"What did he say?"

"He...he didn't really answer. He just quoted the Talmud, tractate Moed Katan, folio 18. 'Every woman is assigned to a man by God, and every day a voice from Heaven calls out, saying, so-and-so is assigned to such-and-such.'"

"Every day? Doesn't the Talmud say that it happens just once, before one is even born?"

"Yes, you're right, in tractate Sota, folio 2, it says that it happens forty days before conception."

I began quoting rapidly. "'Forty days before the fetus is formed, a voice from heaven calls out, saying the daughter of so-and-so is destined for the son of such-and-such.' We were destined for each other, Iri, assigned to one another before we were even created."

"But there is also that passage in Moed Katan," Yair said defensively, "and the Rosh Yeshiva specifically referred me to that one—"

Silence. In the elementary school nearby a chorus of children could be heard, parroting their teacher who sang verses out loud. In the alleyway below, a sorrowful old woman carried two heavily laden baskets.

"You intend to listen to him," I said, half asking, half stating a fact.

Yair leaned his arms on the rail and buried his face in them.

Over the next few weeks, Maya, the Shlomtzion I had wanted to be slowly died. Yair had numerous conversations with friends and rabbis, in which he tried to understand what the Rosh Yeshiva was getting at, and why we couldn't make it as a couple. I made numerous attempts to defy my fate, to convince Yair that the rabbi just didn't know me, that despite being the shepherd of our generation he still did not understand the case at hand. And there were the all-night walks, when Yair and I wandered the streets of Jerusalem like two children who had finally managed to lose themselves, walking in desperate silence until dawn found us drained and mute.

At the end of Rabbanit Hava Schor's class on *The Eternal of Israel*—which I knew would be my last, since the Eternal of Israel had indeed disappointed—I approached Rabbanit Hava to ask for a private meeting. "Yes, of course, gladly," she said, Athena's sympathetic smile wrapping itself around me. "Come on Friday morning, Shlomtzion, and we'll talk."

I remembered the motivational charade that she had put on a year and a half before, and I wondered whether her husband had told her the latest about Yair and me. Friday morning she again waited for me in her kitchen, which looked like the unformed and void world at the dawn of Creation, and again offered me tea and plain biscuits. But this time she didn't prepare for Shabbat. Instead she sat with me, pulling her chair up close, her eyes looking straight into mine, genuinely sad.

I burst out in tears.

Her long fingers reached for the box of tissues on the table.

She handed me one, touched my heaving back, and said quietly, "You poor thing. You must be terribly hurt."

All the questions I had planned on asking, the arguments I was going to make, the desperate pleas for her to go to the Rosh Yeshiva, who respected her and relied on her, and explain to him the mistake he'd made—all these now melted away in tears. Right then and there, in that kitchen, among the mess left by the Schor kids' breakfast, among the plates and pots strewn in every direction, the defrosting carp that lay worriedly on the counter waiting to be cut up and cooked for Shabbat, it suddenly became crystal clear that my connection with Yair had gone dead, and there was no longer any point in praying for its return.

Between the sobs which came from somewhere I never knew existed, and which sounded to me distant and alien, like the cries of a stranger, I heard the Rabbanit Hava recite, in even and relaxed tones, the dictum that "*A man should always seek to marry the daughter of a Torah scholar*," and then say that this was probably the source of the Rosh Yeshiva's opposition to my marrying Yair, for Yair was after all a very special individual, and so it was because of this, and especially since he had been orphaned of his father, that the Rosh Yeshiva was especially concerned that Yair's father-in-law be a *talmid hacham* who could raise him and serve as his mentor, and that this reason perhaps justified what I was going through. "It's not your fault, Shlomtzion," she said, "that you're not the daughter of a *talmid hacham*. But the Rosh Yeshiva sees the big picture, and we lesser folk have to rely on his special gift of sight, for only he knows what is good for the Jewish people, even when it causes pain to an individual for a while." The whole time her loving hand kneaded my upper back as if she were trying to untie the knots of my suffering, to give my blood the strength to flow through my veins, to keep me alive.

Rosh Hashanah came around again, and instead of praying in the yeshiva I sat on the balcony of my parents' home, leafing through the prayer book in utter distraction, looking up at the heavens without seeing them. The hatred for my father thickened inside me, for it was on his account that I had lost the will to exist, on his account and on account of his iniquitous biblical criticism that challenged Heaven and reduced the holy Torah to the level of man.

But it was on that very Rosh Hashanah that my father actually tried to comfort me, perhaps sensing my anguish despite the fact that I had not told him anything, perhaps hoping that my new solitude would temper the disdain I had for him. He came out onto the balcony, sat beside me and tried to talk to me. The school year was just getting started, he said, it would be a shame to miss my chance. Perhaps I should enroll at the university. As the daughter of a tenured professor, tuition would be free. Surely I also recognized that for a talented girl such as myself, the time had come to start thinking about the future.

I didn't answer him, but instead stared at the far-off mountains of Moab, visible between the buildings of Talbiyeh. I didn't answer him, Maya. He was my father, but I was not his daughter. The Rosh Yeshiva alone thought I was the daughter of this awful heretic who dissected the words of the living God—but he was wrong, so very wrong.

❧

Towards the end of the Days of Repentance, just before Yom Kippur, Yair made one last attempt at saving me. He and a married friend of his went to the greatest of all kabbalistic masters, Rabbi Yitzhak Tzadok.

He later told me how he and his friend entered the sun-washed courtyard off of the Machaneh Yehuda market, leaned on the whitewashed wall and waited their turn. Inside the house, the Rabbanit Nechama and her girls were probably busy picking parsley or sifting through rice or sorting used clothes for the poor, and people went in and out of the house, in and out. Finally the two young men were called to cross the stone threshold and enter through the blue door, into the room where sat, at his desk covered with mystical books, the fragile Yemenite *mekubal*, his glowing face lighting up everything around him.

Yair and his friend sat where they were told to sit, and the friend handed Rabbi Tzadok a slip of paper, on which were written two names in ballpoint pen. "Yair Menachem, son of Rabbi Shlomo and Hana" was written first. Below it was written "Shlomtzion, daughter of Avraham and Tzipora Malka."

The mystic took the piece of paper, his lips moving as he read the names. Despite his advanced age, he did not need reading glasses. His hands leafed through the books in front of him, forwards and backwards, until Yair grew terrified, holding his breath.

No birds sang, no fowl took wing, no ox bellowed, the angels arrested their flight, the seraphim did not say "Holy, holy, holy," the sea stopped churning, and humanity ceased its speech. The world remained silent as the verdict was pronounced by Rabbi Yitzhak Tzadok, who, after completing his inquiry, his quest, his journey beyond that which is revealed to us and to our children, beyond that which ordinary people can grasp with their five limited senses, beyond the letters of the names Yair Menachem son of Rabbi Shlomo and Hana, and Shlomtzion daughter of Avraham and Tzipora Malka, lifted his eyes and said to the quaking Yair, "Heaven rejoices, but the hand of a righteous man holds back this match."

When he saw that Yair sat expressionlessly, the great mystic raised his voice and repeated the diagnosis.

"Heaven rejoices, but the hand of a righteous man holds back this match."

"Yes," Yair said to me later, "I also don't understand how it's possible. If Heaven rejoices, why does the hand of the righteous man hold back our match? On the other hand, Shlomtzion, what counts is not in Heaven. If the Rosh Yeshiva's hand is so important that Rabbi Tzadok was able to see it, that's a sign that 'holding it back' is unavoidable."

❧

We broke up the night after Yom Kippur, a year to the day after the war had started.

We had been walking for a long time, until we neared my parents' place, in what is today the parking lot of the Jerusalem Theater but at the time was part of the Yareach Woods, and we sat on a flat rock beneath a pine tree that we had known since we were children, when we would weave long, green chains out of its needles and a brilliant future out of our dreams.

His throat was dry, his words abrupt as he spoke. "Maybe," Yair said, "it's possible to say, after the fact, that it's all for the best."

"What's all for the best?"

"The Rosh Yeshiva's opposition, the fact that he made us recognize that we were really never meant to get married."

"He didn't make us do anything," I seethed. "It was you who decided to ask his opinion and then follow it, even though it wasn't even clear when he gave it. And anyway, it's a fact that Heaven rejoiced, only he got in the way."

"I think," Yair continued as though reciting lines that he had rehearsed well, "I think that maybe what is between us might not exactly be love."

The sky fell on my head in a single thrust.

"What I mean to say is that maybe it's not really the love of husband and wife, but maybe...maybe it's the love of brother and sister, and the Rosh Yeshiva, in his great and deep wisdom, simply saw that. You and I grew up together from the time we were very little—we're so used to being together, we naturally assumed we'd end up getting married. But apparently this isn't it, Shlomtzion, apparently we weren't meant for each other, and for the past few days I've been thinking about all the different signs throughout the years that were telling me we shouldn't really be together, that we couldn't be right for each other. So, with all the—"

I needed air. I stood up, and Yair stood as well, trying to continue his speech. "So, with all the pain that we feel right now, and despite the fact that we—"

He was in the middle of speaking when I collapsed on him like someone drowning, taking him into my desperate, crying arms, holding fast to his frail body as though my life depended on it, smothering his face in kisses, sobbing into his shoulder, "Iri, Iri—I can't live without you. Don't leave me, Iri."

At first I felt his whole body stiffen, recoiling in shock over how freely I ignored the halakhah which forbids physical contact between unmarried people, but as I kissed him I also felt his tears mingling with mine, his hesitant hands carefully taking hold of my trembling shoulders, his cracking voice pleading with me quietly, as if to save his own soul, "It's okay, Shlomtzion. It's all right, dear. It's all right."

Chapter seven

What signs were you talking about, Iri? What were those hints you said were scattered across our childhood, signs that should have told you we weren't meant for each other?

Maybe you were talking about the time when we were kids and I dragged you to the movie theater—the scandal!—and, under cover of darkness, put my lustful hand over your innocent one? Maybe you should have already figured out then that I was too depraved for you, too deeply affected by the cultural poison to which I had been exposed in the home of my father, the arch libertine?

Or maybe it was the stories I told you about that weird group of friends I hung out with in my two years at the high school for music and the arts in New York? Maybe you thought that you, who never did like to hear me reminisce about those happy years, should have understood that any girl who spent the best years of her youth together with *goyim* of various races, singing, laughing, painting, and goofing off with them in the streets of that great, corrupt city, could never be a proper, kosher daughter of Israel who would build a genuinely holy home with you?

Maybe it was something about my character—my capriciousness perhaps, the crazy ideas that suddenly got into my head, or my exhortations about women's rights, free will, and man's duty to lead his own life rather than being remote-controlled by rabbis?

Or maybe you just never really loved me. You finally figured out that you had lived your life with some sort of tick on you, one named Shlomtzion Dror, that had dug into your skin just because it had no other way to survive—and you, out of kindness or cowardice or both, neither protested nor tried to remove it, but just got used to living with its legs dug into your veins, its mouthparts sucking your blood one drop at a time, until the shepherd of our generation, our great master and teacher the Rosh Yeshiva, *shlita*, came and saved you.

This unbearable realization—that you never really loved me, never wanted me at all—struck me that last night in the Yareach Woods. Since then, to this very day, I have not enjoyed a single moment of joy, not a moment of inner peace, not a moment without burning injury, the injury of your having rejected me.

❧

I assume you heard that my father died four years ago, just after his sixty-first birthday. The virtuoso lecturer with the deep baritone voice, who took such pride in his ability to string together words in seven languages before captive audiences all over the world—he, of all people, got cancer in his throat and vocal cords and went mute, suffering horribly until he was no more. Within six months, the arrogant, flirtatious charmer with the flowing black hair and the slick, quick mind was reduced to a bald, withered old man who communicated in grunts and hand motions, his searching eyes like those of a hunted animal. It was awful, Yair. In his last few weeks, my father couldn't even control his own functions. He was a bag of bones, lying in the hospital wearing a diaper and being fed through a tube, his hunted-animal eyes jumping around, and I, who always hated hearing him, who always wished he would just shut up, found myself praying for him to speak. Suddenly I desperately longed to hear his words and to answer them, to have a conversation with him, but all that came from his mouth were gurgles and grunts. He couldn't write either, his muscles were so atrophied. When I gave him a pad of paper, the pen fell from his hand, and my father cried like a baby, face contorted, and I cried with him.

My mother stayed by his side most of the time and slept at his feet at nights on a mattress. But Yehonadav visited only occasionally and briefly, for he was now an accountant who wore a necktie, who spoke almost without stammering and was called Yoni by his friends, and he must have feared that any sympathy for his dying father might turn him back into the meek little boy he once had been. For my part, during those last weeks I left work early every day and went up to Jerusalem in the afternoon to try and purge myself of anger before my father died.

Four days before he passed from the world, I came into his room at the end of a labyrinth of hallways in the oncology ward and found a note attached to the cabinet next to his bed. "Shlomtzion, they took Daddy for radiotherapy. I went home to freshen up. Mom."

I took the elevator down to Radiology and Chemotherapy and asked where I could find the patient Professor Dror. Gingerly I opened the door they showed me, and at first I thought no one was in the room, that I was in the wrong place, but then suddenly I saw my father.

He lay on a high, narrow metal table, his eyes closed, his fragile, withered hands lying by the sides of his gray, *muselman* body, his lower half covered by a sheet. As I drew a little closer, I saw the bold strokes drawn in red marker on his forehead and neck, apparently to show the technician where to aim the x-ray. I choked, Iri. A powerful desire coursed through me, an urge to embrace this decrepit human creature, to caress his wasted cheeks, to tell him, "Daddy I'm here, Daddy I love you, Daddy I forgive you, please forgive me too." But I couldn't go to him, Iri, I just couldn't do it, and he too was unable to whisper the magic words that would transfer him, like the coin of his long-lost magic trick, from this hat to another.

I stood a few feet away from the altar on which my father Avraham was bound, knowing he was awake despite his closed eyes, knowing he was utterly alone, needing contact, needing love, needing me, understanding this was my last chance. But I couldn't do it.

Only the earth piled over his fresh grave—that I was ultimately able to embrace. Only to the dirt that lay between his body and mine could I finally whisper, "Forgive me, Daddy, forgive me." Only when we sat in mourning in the great living room filled with his collection of fine Judaica from around the world, the menorahs and shofars and candlesticks and spice-towers and scrolls of Esther and even Torah scrolls with their velvet covers and golden embroidery did I feel, perhaps for the first time in my life, truly at home.

Less than a year later, my mother met a happy, wealthy American retiree in a restaurant, married him, and went off to Miami where she became a young redhead, fulfilled and in love. But during that *shiva* week of mourning, she still thought that my father's death necessarily meant the end of her life as well, for what was she without him. "You know, Shlomtzi," she said, again and again, "I gave your father everything I had, and I don't regret it."

❧

What does life want from us, Iri? How long can a person meander through the maze that existence puts him in? And what profit is there in all the toil that he toileth under the sun?

After you left me, I said goodbye to Grandma Rochel, loaded up my backpack with books and clothing, and took a bus to the Arab village of El-Azariya, where the road heading out of the city toward the Dead Sea used to be. From there I hitchhiked all the way to Eilat, and the next morning I went on down into Sinai, for I had been exiled from the rivers of the Lord, saying, "Go, take unto thee other gods," and I determined to wander for forty years, without manna or quail, without water from the rock. I even resolved that if someone were to try and send me manna or quail or water from the rock, I would turn it down politely but firmly, that I would walk for forty years among the Bedouin and the Scandinavian tourists and the other young Israelis who, like me, sought to throw themselves down on those long, far-off shores.

The whole way there I could hear a voice from Heaven, proclaiming, "The daughter of so-and-so is *not* for such-and-such, the daughter of Professor Dror is not for Yair the Pure." Soon I arrived at Dahab beach, which I remembered fondly from that magical trip we had taken fifteen months earlier, and I ended up working for Sammy and Annika in the little tourist village of Di-Zahav: as a waitress in their restaurant with the bamboo tables right up to the water; as a valet in the little straw huts they rented out (one of which I lived in myself); as a receptionist; as the coordinator of their entertainment and cultural programs; and, after six months, as a salesperson renting out snorkels to individuals and groups and as a diving instructor at the coral reef where schools of multicolored fish swam about, inviting me to join them in their infinitely colorful silence.

If you had known what I was doing then, you certainly would have felt that you had been saved from disaster. Boy, how right the Rosh Yeshiva was, you would have thought to yourself. How different this girl is from what I'd thought!

But what did you expect, Iri? Had we been joined in holy matrimony, had you married me in grace and mercy, righteousness and justice, I would have known the Lord and lovingly fulfilled my role as the good and charming wife that I had always dreamed of being for you, a proper wife who does her husband's will. Once you dumped me I went to Dahab, once you and the Lord spurned me I no longer cared what the two of you thought. Truth is, even then I didn't do anything terrible. I just went around in light, revealing clothing, threw myself into work from morning to night, and spent time with Annika, with Sammy, with their enormous, frightfully ugly dog Paul, and with the exhausted human beings who came from the four corners of the earth seeking refuge like people escaping a hurricane.

As time passed, I would increasingly find myself chatting with the guests in their different languages, singing their songs with them, dancing their dances with them, doubling over in laughter with them. Little by little, like a child nibbling on a chocolate egg, slowly revealing the prize inside, I came to understand how enslaved I had been to you for most of my life. I understood how much of my own self, my own desires, I had given up for you—and that this was, in effect, my first vacation from you since I was nine and a half, perhaps with the exception of that semi-vacation during the years in New York with my free-wheeling, peace-and-beauty-loving friends who were so different from you that you couldn't stand it.

I understood that my whole existence had been built around you, that on account of you I had never had normal relations with girls my own age, with my parents, or with myself; that my entire being had come into the world as an indivisible part of you, Yair Berman. And that, after all this, you had just crumpled me up and tossed me in the trash like a bad first draft.

And then one day, after I had understood all this, I went up into the mountains of central Sinai, and briskly climbed all the way to the peak of Moses' mountain. I stood there against the wind, against the desert that spread out below just as it spread out before Moses when he descended from heaven back to earth, and I filled my demoralized lungs with the air they so desperately needed, and I said to the firmament above and to my imprisoned soul, "Here am I, here am I."

❧

I would phone my parents once every month, and on our fifth conversation my mother said hesitantly, "You know, Shlomtzion, a letter arrived for you from Yair Berman. I'm so sorry, but I opened it—it didn't look like a personal letter but some kind of card, like an invitation or something. When I opened it I discovered it really was a wedding invitation."

Silence. A fresh, crisp evening had painted the Sinai sky a deep purple. In the tourist village of Di-Zahav, a sun-drunk Norwegian couple headed in from the beach, the man's arm draped across the woman's bare back. Lying at my feet, Paul picked up his ugly ears at the sound of laughter.

"Yair's getting married?"

"And you know the bride," my mother answered.

That's how I found out, Iri, that it was you and Lealeh. That you hadn't wasted any time. You went and snatched the perfect daughter of a *talmid hacham* and then headed straight for the wedding canopy, as though at any moment I might show up, blocking your path with a spinning, fiery sword.

On the day of your heart's joy, I marched into the center of the Bedouin town of Dahab and bought myself some presents: light cotton pants, an embroidered shirt and a necklace of tiny beads as blue as the sea, as blue as the sky. Back in the village the tourists, each in their own language, told me how pretty I looked that night, and I sat with them on the open beach, drinking their bitter beer until I was able to see you in my mind's eye, standing there in your bright white shirt, smiling with such grace and kindness at your pure, delicate bride, her eyes a-sparkle, her cheeks flushed, her soft hair gathered under a veil crowned with a wreath of the daintiest rosebuds—until I could see you as the loving couple in whom the Creator of Man rejoices as he rejoiced in his own Creation in the Garden of Eden of old, until I could say to the two of you, in all honesty and from the depths of my broken heart, *Mazal tov, mazal tov.*

Chapter eight

So there it is, Maya. Once Yair and Lealeh were married, I had a mind to stay in Sinai for a very long time, maybe forever. It was good for me there, far-off and right.

I now understood the true meaning behind the Song of Songs. All the verses about love and longing suddenly came together for me, and I realized that everything I had been taught was wrong: The passion of the two lovers remained unfulfilled not because they could not find each other, but because they deliberately refrained from doing so.

I mentioned the discovery to Annika one morning, as we sat in the office of the tourist village, sorting invoices and receipts into big file folders. She was forty-something, a big, tan Swede who had come to Israel as a volunteer fifteen years earlier and ended up "volunteering," as Sammy put it, to get him back on his feet after he had divorced his first wife and left the big city.

She knew the Bible well, from classes at a Christian Sunday

School when she was a child. "If the lover and his beloved are avoiding each other on purpose," she asked in her Swedish-English, "then how do you explain his begging for her to open the door? How do you explain her getting up to answer, and her awful disappointment when she sees that he had just then given up and left?"

"But that's just the point," I said excitedly. "She doesn't open the door so long as he's there, because she knows they're not allowed to fulfill their love."

"Not allowed?"

"Not allowed. So, only when she senses that he's about to give up, when his pleas of 'Open up for me, my friend, my pure one' grow weak, only then does she start getting out of bed. She knows that her lover won't wait until she opens the door. Not only that: when he hears her getting up—maybe he even sees it through the keyhole—he leaves. He, too, knows they mustn't meet."

"So why does she look for him in the streets?" Annika asked, troubled. "Why do they keep pining away, searching for each another?"

"They can't help themselves," I explained sadly. "That's just who they are. It's like the Jewish people and God—they can never meet, can never really be together, but they still keep looking for each other all the time, Him saying 'Return unto Me, O Israel,' them pleading, 'Bring us back unto You, O Lord,' but both of them know it won't happen."

❧

When I headed north in early summer I planned on staying briefly in Jerusalem and then turning straight back to Di-Zahav. But this was, apparently, just around the time when your wonderful soul, Maya, left the treasury of spirits kept under the Divine Throne and began making its way down to earth. A few miles past Ras Burka, as I stared out the window of the tanker truck I had hitched a ride with, something called out to me from the bluffs and the palm trees, and I heard myself telling the astonished driver to let me off.

The tanker slowed to a halt, puffing heavily, and I jumped down from the cab, pack on my back and sandals in hand. The sand got a good taste of my feet as I made my way around the mountain on the other side of which still lay hidden the Bedouin tent village. I passed among the colorful tapestries, over the woven rugs spread out on the sand, among the camels, goats and chickens, the pots, tools, strong scents and brown children smiling at me with their enormous brown eyes and their long, worn-out clothes. From one corner there emerged a woman dressed entirely in black, and only on second inspection did I see that she was scarcely a woman at all, but rather a girl no more than sixteen. I pointed north and, smiling warmly, said "Rosy," explaining both to her and to the rest of her tribe why I passed among them.

I didn't know if he had gone back to the Shores of Freedom after the war—and I had even less of an idea why I was following him if he had. But I kept on walking, until just after the Bedouin tent-village I was able to make out Rosy's place in the distance, even though the yellowish walls of his tent were still well camouflaged among the sand, mountainside and brush, like an animal blending into the scenery to protect itself from predators.

As I drew close I almost hoped he wouldn't be there. I nearly convinced myself that the war had changed him, that it had shackled his vast inner freedom, that he was now back in the city, studying in university and making a living as a night watchman, reading long, heavy theoretical treatises by lamplight in order to take his mind off his war medals and the strapping, handsome young men sent to their deaths by his command.

But then suddenly the white dog Lara appeared from nowhere and trotted up to me, her pretty head bowed in friendship. With a strong shake of her body she sent sand and sea water flying in all directions. I coughed a couple of times, trying to get attention, then called out to Rosy. Once it was clear that no response was forthcoming from the tent, I cautiously lifted the cloth door and peeked inside.

Nobody was home. Atop a colorful Bedouin carpet were piled some pillows, clothing, and a few other things I couldn't make out in the shadow of the tent's heavy walls. It reminded me of the little hiding place my brother Yehonadav used to make for himself when we were kids, building a tent out of blankets, clothespins, and string that he tied between our beds. He would crawl in and out of it all afternoon, bringing in toys, paper and crayons, books, a turntable with his favorite records, a tray of cookies, a little candy jar, a bottle of juice, but before he had even finished his exhaustive preparations, Daddy would come home, and Mom would make him take down the blankets and string and put everything back where it belonged because it was evening and time for bed.

I sat along the shore in dumb shock, the waves creeping up to my bare feet, and tried to figure out why I had come. Suddenly the dog stood still, looked intently out to sea, and began wagging her tail wildly. From the advancing maelstrom of foam, Rosy emerged before me like Neptune in all his glory, dripping and shaking water from his hair and eyes, blinking from the salt, and stared at me in disbelief.

"Shlomtzion!"

"I hope I'm not bothering you. I just thought… I've been in Sinai for six months… I work in Dahab… So on my way up north I stopped here for some reason… I hadn't planned on it…"

"No need to apologize," he said in his sleepy, monotonous voice, sending a shiver of pleasure through me. "I'm delighted you've come."

You have to understand, Maya, that this was, all in all, a desperate attempt on my part to get over the trauma of Yair. It was the first time since he left me that I'd spoken with anyone who had known us as a couple. I stayed at Rosy's hideaway for three weeks. At first I just tried to get used to being near him. I walked after him, swam with him, competed with Lara for his attention, and studied how he lived.

On the fourth day, I asked him, "How long do you think you'll be living here all by yourself, Rosy?"

He gave Lara an amused look as she sniffed at a chameleon, stiff with fear by the yellow tent. He thought for a long moment and said softly, "Don't know. Maybe forever."

"What are your plans for the future?"

"No plans. Haven't decided yet if I have a future."

"Why isn't Dorit here?"

"I'm done with that. No more Dorit."

"And Shuli?"

"No more Shuli."

"And Osnat?"

He laughed. "I'm finished with all that, okay? How come you remember them? Were they the three who happened to be here the day you came to visit with the Rebbe?"

"How many others were there?"

"I no longer remember."

❧

When the sun set, the heavens and earth would merge into a single, great red conflagration, as though the world were coming to an end, or maybe just beginning. At nights Rosy would set up a makeshift bed for me in the tent by putting pillows on a mound of sand, while he slept outside under the stars. When I arose at dawn, he'd already be hard at work, pulling fish from the sea, mending nets, or helping his Bedouin neighbor Abed tend his camels and sheep. Sometimes he went off for long walks on the beach with Lara running ahead, waving her tail like a flag. Sometimes he'd sit and read the writings of Kierkegaard in English translation, pausing after every paragraph to think long thoughts. And sometimes he went swimming in the sea, his arms beating against the waves at an even pace, his head bobbing up and down, rising and falling, getting smaller and smaller until he disappeared in the distance, as my heart skipped a beat out of worry for him.

You must be wondering whether we truly loved each other the first time our bodies came together, on the seventh night of my visit. To this day I still don't know exactly what love is, but I can assure you that we both desired each other very much. I can assure you that we both needed each other to survive. I can assure you that even now, as then, I am convinced that this was the kind of desire and need that God had in mind when He created man and woman.

I seduced him. He had not been with a woman since the war, and he would never have touched me either had I not first asked him to—and had I not first immersed myself in the sea in accordance with the ritual law, both to purify myself and to prove that I was doing this in a clear-minded, premeditated way. Seven days earlier I had still been convinced that no man would ever know me, that until the end of my sad days I would remain a virgin in order to punish Yair and God for what they had done. But before dawn on the eighth day, by the light of a crescent moon hung over a forsaken world, a world whose own Creator repented of making, a world that awaits its own imminent destruction, I, Shlomtzion the daughter of Avraham and Tzipora Malka, took one of the ribs of man and closed up its place with flesh; and I breathed into my nostrils the breath of life; and I was called Woman, for I was taken out of man.

❧

And when twenty-one days had passed, Rosy accompanied me, in heavy silence, to Eilat. We said farewell at the Central Bus Station, standing beside the bus as it was about to leave. "I wouldn't dare ask it of you," Rosy said to me, "but you know how happy I would be if you came back."

The whole way back to Jerusalem I mulled over his words, asking myself whether I loved him, but receiving no answer.

When I reached Jerusalem, I was unable to find anything for myself, not even that little bit of space I'd had in the past. So I stayed just two weeks, shuttling between my parents' house and Grandma Rochel's, praying I wouldn't bump into Yair, into Lealeh, or—worst of all—the two of them together. After two weeks I fled for my life back to Dahab, where I tried to return to a routine of working and forgetting, until one morning I was unable to drink Annika's excellent coffee—even the smell of coffee made me sick. Once the moon had waned, waxed, and emptied for a third time, I was lost, and the only idea I could think of was to go back to the Shores of Freedom and seek the advice of the father.

❦

There are souls that know each other from primordial times, from before they descended into the world, into the body. Rosy and I were married in the playground of an orphanage in Jerusalem's Katamon neighborhood. My parents did what they could to reassure their friends and relatives and themselves that everything was fine: "After all, the boy's an army officer, a decorated veteran of the Yom Kippur War, and our Shlomtzion—she is full of surprises!—met him while traveling in Sinai and insisted on a modest wedding."

After the mandatory ritual, my husband rented a small, old, Jewish-Agency-built house on a tiny moshav just outside of Ramla, and it would be fair to say things were good. "You'll make a man out of me yet, Shlomtzi," Rosy often would say when he came home from his work driving a tractor for different farmers in the area, ducking his head under the peeling doorframe as he came in. Then he would hug me and my increasingly round belly, and praise the wild paintings I had conjured on enormous canvases and the meal I had struggled to prepare despite the nausea that never left me, even for a minute.

But how forlorn he looked when he stood under the wedding canopy in the playground of the WIZO orphanage, his freshly washed curls tied back with a brown rubber band, his beard trimmed, his white shirt newly ironed and pulling against his broad chest! How out of place he seemed in our rented flat on the moshav without his yellowish tent, his Bedouin buddies, the sand and sea and open sky. How disconnected, how pathetic, a fish pulled from the sea and left to flap around on land until it dies.

"Let's go live at the Shores of Freedom, Mordechai," I offered. "I think even Lara wants to go back."

"Have no fear," he smiled, caressing us both. "I'll get used to this. We really do need to ground ourselves in reality, to try to behave like normal people. And don't forget, mother dear, the responsibility we're going to have soon," he teased in his monotonous, sleepy voice as he laid his big, warm palm on my abdomen, waiting patiently until you gave him some encouragement of your own.

❧

Maybe we would have gotten used to it all. Maybe in time I would have found a way, Maya, to stay with your father forever, and to give him more children, as I truly wished to. But if there was such a hope, it was dashed on that autumn day when Rosy convinced me to go to Jerusalem without him. One of my friends from my National Service days had sent me an invitation to her wedding, and even added a handwritten note begging me to come. Rosy pressed the point. "Go, kid," he said. "You can't hide in your dark little shell forever. Go see your friends, and have a blast."

"Come with me, Mordechai," I pleaded. "I'm afraid to go on my own." But Rosy convinced me that he would be too tired after work, that he wouldn't know anybody there, that he would only get in the way of me having a good time. I ended up finding a shiny black blouse big enough to fit over my eighth-month belly in the shopping center in Ramla, and in the late afternoon Rosy arranged a ride for me with some neighbors who were driving to Jerusalem. And so I strode, blinded by the bright lights, into the wedding hall with its gold-colored plastic chandeliers hanging from the ceiling and its mirrors lining the walls. One look in the mirrors made me realize my mistake: showing up there in a long skirt wasn't enough; I was supposed to have covered my hair, as well.

But then I was swept up by my old friends who danced around me, yelling at the top of their lungs to drown out the ear-piercing band, choking me in their mirth, saying "Blessed is He Who raises the dead!" whenever they saw me, and giving each other scandalized looks that encompassed my uncovered hair and all the questions they so much wanted to ask. What month is Shlomtzion in? How's she getting along with that secular hippy deputy-brigade-commander she married after the sudden break-up with Yair Berman? Is it possible that she, who went to all those classes, who was such a righteous girl, has now completely stopped being observant? Suddenly I heard one of the throatier girls call out, "I don't believe it... there's Yair Berman's wife!"

Into the pulsating circle was dragged Lealeh, red-cheeked and even more beautiful than I remembered, her hair wrapped in a long, green silk scarf that lent a deep green hue to her pure eyes—eyes that filled with terror when she saw me, as though I had caught her in mid-crime.

"Shomtzion," she said with a twisted smile, "How are you?" But I ran away, escaping from the coil of girls as from a furnace, and pushed through the crowd amid the bleating clarinet and pounding drums, out to the foyer, where a stupid-looking fountain drizzled water down a slope of Styrofoam rocks. I leaned against the stair rail, breathing deeply.

"Please listen to me," pleaded a soft voice behind me, the breathless words pouring from Lealeh's mouth, faster than I'd thought possible for her. "It never occurred to me that you would be at this wedding, but now that you're here it's really good we're meeting. I need to speak with you, Shlomtzion. I've been wanting to speak with you for a long time."

I wanted to flee, to disappear, to cease to exist at all, but I let her get close and lean against the rail beside me. Both of us stared at the fake waterfall, our backs to the foyer where people were entering with presents in hand and smiles on face, walking two-by-two like the animals to Noah's ark. My swollen belly intruded between me and the rail, and the contrast to Lealeh's trim figure beside me added another layer to the ungainly awkwardness I had always felt when comparing my own convoluted character with her pure soul.

"I didn't know you'd be here either," I said in a choked voice. "If I had, I swear I wouldn't have come."

She swallowed with effort. "I understand if you're angry, Shlomtzion. I wanted to visit you before I married him; I wouldn't even agree to announce our engagement until both of us had had a chance to talk to you in person. But we couldn't find you. We were told you had left the country, that there was no way of reaching you."

"It's fine, Lealeh."

"No, it's not fine."

"He was never really mine. You were free to take him without my permission, and I wish you all the best."

"I want you to know, Shlomtzion, that it's almost a year we've been married, and not a day goes by that I don't think about you, that I don't feel awful about the way everything worked out… and I miss you. You and I were so close…"

What else does she want from me? I wondered. *Is it not enough that the man I loved, who didn't love me and who didn't want to spend his life with me, loves her and chose to spend his life with her?*

And then, from among the babble of voices behind us, I heard Yair, and all my senses woke. How didn't I realize that if Lealeh was here, her husband would be too?

"Ariel and I have been looking for you everywhere," his voice said, in the tone of a child wanting to be comforted. Out of the corner of my eye I saw her turn to him, their faces glowing at one another like the cherubim atop the Ark of the Covenant of God. Their hands met around the small, soft bundle wrapped in a blue blanket that he was lovingly passing to her. *They have a baby! They have a little baby and I didn't know.* Then I heard the baby coo. Yair looked at Lealeh. Suddenly, he noticed me. A shadow fell over his face, and he shuddered as if he had seen the Angel of Death.

"I have to go," I blurted, fleeing to the dark parking lot and then out to the road, where I shivered from the cold and the humiliation. I hid in a shadowed corner for an hour and a half until my neighbors finished their business in Jerusalem and came to take me home.

❧

After that everything fell apart, and Shlomtzion the doll could no longer walk and talk no matter how much you wound her up. Early in the morning Rosy would go to work, leaving me lying in bed with my face to the wall, and in the evening he'd come back, exhausted and sour-smelling after ten hours on a tractor, and find me crumpled on the couch, barely able to muster the strength to ask how he was doing and to apologize weakly. "Mordechai, I'm so sorry. I don't know what's happening to me. I'll try to pull myself together."

I wanted to keep playing the game. I knew that was what everyone did, that only people who kept playing survived. But you have to understand, Maya, it was not in my hands. From the moment my eyes were confronted with the connection between Yair and Leah, I could no longer find myself. I was missing in action, like the blind Anat's brother during the Yom Kippur War, suspended between life and death, the baby inside me cut off and futureless, just like its old friend in the jar of formaldehyde at the science museum in Jerusalem. Until I had seen them together, I had really believed that the rescue operation I'd conducted on myself had been a success. *You've chosen life*, I'd flattered myself, *You have a good and honest husband, you are learning that this is good enough, and it's all working out for the best.* But the moment I saw them together, the edifice collapsed. The dam burst. All I could think was that the Rosh Yeshiva had sinned against truth when he said we should break up, that Yair had sinned against truth when he had chosen to follow that opinion, and that I, the idiot, had sinned against truth when I gave in and accepted the verdict.

The thought of Yair and Leah in love drove me insane. The image of them coddling their baby boy between them opened a deep chasm inside me. A single truth stood before me now, sharp and clear as day, its rays breaking through the windows of our rented home, through the branches of the old poplar in our yard. *Yair is for me and I for him, and anything else is just a terrible lie, an unforgivable distortion, no less than an absolute betrayal of my destiny in the world, of my raison d'être, of the redemption of all reality.*

After two weeks of this I forced myself to get up, get dressed, leave the house once in a while, and even cook a little for my forsaken husband. But I could not regain my former energy. A deep melancholy smothered me like a scratchy gray wool blanket. Rosy, worried, sat beside me one evening, following my gaze as though trying to see what I saw, and said, "I just can't get to where you are, my love. You're mourning and I don't know how to comfort you."

"Mourning," I repeated after him, tasting the word that so perfectly described my feelings.

How much guilt I felt about this amazing man. How sorry I felt for the King of the Shores of Freedom, who had abdicated his throne on my account. So many beautiful, intelligent women had fallen for him, each of whom would have been thrilled if he'd chosen to spend his unusual life with her. And here was I, having won his love, slowly falling apart over his stupid friend who had enslaved himself to the whim of an old rabbi.

"Nonsense," he chided me as he wiped our floor with its cracked tiles. "I didn't abdicate my throne, and I didn't give up a single thing on your account. You just happened to come into my life at the right time, you and our sweet little Armstrong." That was his nickname for the baby: he would alternate depending on what sex he had decided you would be that day. Sometimes you were Armstrong, after the first man on the moon, sometimes Shraga, sometimes Dulcinea.

As Rosy bent to rinse out the floor rag in the bucket, he turned and saw I was biting down on my lip. He let the rag drop into the water, washed his hands, and then came over to me. He kneeled at the foot of the couch where I was sitting, like the great lovers in the old movies when they ask for their beloved's hand, and said, with infinite softness, "You did me an enormous service, my wife, my love, when you saved me from my game of Robinson Crusoe, and gave me a once-in-a-lifetime opportunity to start a family and rejoin the human race."

❧

I'm glad you love my *haredi* cousins, Maya. I'm glad you feel deeply connected to them. When you were little you always wanted to visit Grandma Rochel and our family in Jerusalem for Shabbat and holidays and vacations, with or without me, and I understood then that you weren't just looking for an infusion of their sense of family, like an IV drip, but also of their dedication to God, which lends meaning to this world.

I'm glad your inspiration comes not from me, but rather from people like Hayaleh, Uncle Yankel's beautiful daughter, the one who was injured in a car accident and had her leg amputated from above the knee. I remember that when the two suicide bombers blew themselves up in the crowd of soldiers at the Beit Lid bus stop, Hayaleh heard that one of the soldiers had lost his leg and was in a state of deep depression. She packed up her four little children and asked you to join her, since you were a soldier and could act as a mediator, and you all went to the hospital at Tel Hashomer with balloons and candy. "Only because of Hayaleh did Yaniv come back to himself," you said in awe. "She visits him at least once every two weeks—first at the hospital, then at the rehab center, and now at home. She makes him walk and run, and gives his family support—and just imagine, she does all this while she's pregnant with number five and works full-time as a kindergarten teacher."

I imagine it, but as for myself I believe that I'm no longer bound by a divine command to take care of others. It's been years since I stopped playing Florence Nightingale, and even as an architect I am known for my extreme preference of partitions and closed rooms to give people privacy. Most of the famous designers still cling to the modernist style, to the open spaces. For them, the kitchen has to be in the living room, the living room in the bedrooms; the whole apartment has to be one big open space, where everyone has to see each other all the time. Anyone who wants an apartment you can actually live in, what I call a post-modern apartment, where the kitchen's a kitchen and the living room's a living room and a bedroom's a bedroom and a wall's a wall, comes to me and gets a plan that offers convenience and aesthetics, and also affords them the right to hide inside themselves, to think about others only when they choose to.

Nor did I take care of myself, Maya. I had a good man, and I left him. True love was granted me, and I threw it away.

I was in the beginning of my ninth month, still deep in mourning, when Rosy was called up for twenty days of reserve duty. I remember how he stood there with his old rucksack, smiling with embarrassment, all clean and handsome in his IDF uniform, and how we embraced around the sides of my enormous belly. "Mordechai, don't go," I begged. "Ask them if they can get by without you just this once."

And he answered in his sleepy monotone, "It's a brigade exercise, Shlomtz, I have to be there. But you've got my direct phone number, and the moment you tell me you're in labor or need me for any reason, I'll be there in two or three hours."

My face buried in his shoulder, breathing in the scent of the uniform he had washed for himself the night before, I said to him, "I want to love you, Mordechai—only you."

Rosy wrapped his strong arms around me and placed his lips in the middle of my forehead for a long moment. "I really need your love, Shlomtz," he said. "I don't think I can live without it."

Then he tried to persuade me not to be so stubborn about staying in the moshav by myself, but to instead spend the last few days before the birth at Grandma Rochel's in Jerusalem. And again he promised he'd come as soon as I called, and again he kissed me.

Lara and I stood by the door as he left, ducking his curly head under the peeling doorframe, walking down the four concrete steps and out the gate, waving goodbye against the gray late-January sky. Why did I let him toss his pack into the back of the old pickup? Why didn't I stop him as he slipped his body into the front seat and drove off? To this day I am convinced that were it not for that tour of reserve duty, I might have recovered; I might not have insisted on destroying with my own hands the only opportunity I'd ever have of finding a trace of happiness in this life.

With Rosy gone, without his great, comforting body next to mine, I resolved to leave him. He was dear to me, and precisely because of that I decided that I could not do him the injustice of letting him live his life with me. "Your father deserves a wife who really loves him," I told the baby in my womb. "There's no reason why so wonderful a man should play surrogate to the husband I really wanted. If not for this pregnancy, your father and I would never have married. So the end of the pregnancy will be the end of the marriage. I will no longer bind Rosy to me. I will set him free for his own sake. I will set him free, even though it'll be really hard for me without him. I will set him free, because that is what the truth demands."

❧

I was alone when you were born, Maya. I didn't call Rosy's battalion until they had transferred me to Labor and Delivery. Poor Rosy got to the hospital only when you and I had finished nursing you for the first time.

"What a miracle," he whispered when he saw you. And when he put his enormous, tan hand on your soft head with its heart-rending, light-colored downy hair, the tag of your underclothes, which had been put on backwards, peeked from under your chin, and we read the words on it together, "100% combed cotton."

I didn't want to tell him, but I had to.

"This is your daughter, Mordechai, but I am not your wife. I was never supposed to be your wife. We have to get a divorce. You can see the baby whenever you want."

His face, which had been caressing you, rose to look at mine, hurt. He turned pale. My heart broke for him, but I had no doubt that I had done the right thing.

❧

I had thought that after the initial shock, he'd be happy that I'd set him free, but it didn't turn out that way. For three months Rosy tried to change my mind, promising me that he was happy with me, begging me to stay married. I cried endlessly, cried until I melted, my tears mixing with my milk when I sat to nurse you.

"We can't stay together because I'm in love with another man," I sobbed when your father tried to reason with me. "We can't sleep together because I always imagine you're him. I always imagine him with Lealeh. I'm always grieving for the life I can't have with him."

"But you'll get over it," he said, ignoring my brutal assault, swallowing his pride. "You'll get over it, and you'll see what a wonderful life we'll have together, what a wonderful love will grow between us..."

❧

It's completely okay with me that you decided to become observant, Maya, and it's completely okay with me that you're marrying Ariel Berman, despite the fact that my good friend Eden says it's unreasonable to tempt fate in such a drastic way, and despite the fact that I really never considered such a possibility, and even took careful steps to make sure it could never happen.

After the divorce I invested all my energies into building a nest for you, the safest, most well-defended one I could, far away from the holy world that had vomited me out. I wanted you to have the best possible chance for a happy life, one without the anguish I had known, and for this reason I was willing to live in Jerusalem—near Grandma Rochel, who helped care for you—only for the first few years of your life. When you turned three I smuggled you out of the perilous city where Heaven meets Earth and Earth doesn't know how to handle it, and with my parents' help I bought us a charming apartment in north Tel-Aviv, in a pleasant neighborhood where people live their lives without fruitless messianic pretensions. For your sake I studied hard at the school of engineering, and for your sake I became one of the most sought-after interior designers in the Dan region, with people waiting in line to be counted among my clients, and paying accordingly.

Not a morning passed when I didn't think about how I should have been waking up in Yair's and my home in the settlement of Tirza, nursing a newborn and sending the other children off to school. Not an evening passed when I didn't think about how Leah Honig, not I, was welcoming Yair home from another day at the yeshiva filled with Torah and the divine embrace; how she, not I, was making dinner for him and all his merry children, sharing in his spiritual world instead of me, and taking my place in his bed.

But I learned how to douse the flames, Maya. I learned how to quell the pain, how to rejoice in you and be satisfied with that. And Rosy, who searched in vain for an opening through which to re-enter my locked garden, also rebuilt his life, and ended up even giving you the kind of family, complete with a dad and a mom and little brothers, that I so desperately had wanted for you but never knew how to provide.

Don't think that I cannot understand what you are going through. Don't think that I have forgotten the overwhelming thirst for light and truth, the quest for the divine countenance. I, too, once longed for complete union with the Eternal. My soul, too, craved the courtyards of the House of the Lord; I, too, whispered in His ear a personal vow to praise His name on Earth just as His name is praised on high.

And though it has been twenty-one years since I last crossed the Green Line, I have never erased from my memory the intoxication of returning to the land of our forefathers after the Six Day War. I haven't forgotten the thrill of the groundbreaking, historic deeds that were our calling after the Yom Kippur War, or the pride that filled me as I took part in the miraculous redemption of Israel, which was the redemption of the universe. I haven't forgotten the heart-stopping encounter between the young Shlomtzion and the biblical landscape that had awaited her for thousands of years, and I cannot deny the searing pain she felt whenever she looked at the Arab villages that wrapped themselves around the mountains of Judea and Samaria as though these hills had been theirs forever. Nor can I deny the fathomless voice she heard whenever she passed through the streets of Nablus or Ramallah, the voice of the earth calling to her from beneath the wheels of the bus, pleading for her to redeem it from captivity.

Do not judge me for ill, my Maya. I wanted your life to be better than mine, happier than mine, and for this reason alone I tried to keep you away from the supernal heights. I wanted for you a life you could handle without crumbling, and for this reason alone I taught you to disdain and despise those overly-confident settlers, always so sure that all truth lies with them.

I was glad that there was no higher authority, no God or rabbi, no father or husband, within the four walls of the apartment in which I raised you. I was glad there was nobody who made you keep quiet when he spoke, nobody whose word was law, nobody who expected to sit at the head of the table, nobody for whom you might have destroyed your childhood and girlhood in an obsessive need to please.

Only occasionally did I ask myself whether I did you wrong by divorcing your father, whether it really was better for you in our tiny, lopsided family, a stump of a family too small for a prosthesis. I wondered how your outlook on life might be affected by the fact that most of my friends were divorcées like myself, and that whenever we ate or went out together with them and their kids, we became a bizarre mass of humanity made up only of women and children. Once I watched TV with you, and we saw a nature film about elephants, and discovered that a herd of elephants also usually consists of only females and children. Adult elephant males tend to show up only during mating season, have their way with the females, and then immediately disappear again into the jungle. I even almost started to worry that one day you'd adopt the vision of a male-free world that Eden enjoys toying with, a world where men aren't needed even for reproduction, where women reproduce themselves by cloning their own cell tissue with that of another woman. "That way, women would have girl-babies only," Eden crows, "and they'd just keep cloning their own eggs until the male sex became extinct. A female messianic era!"

I do not hate men, and as opposed to Eden I'm not glad I'm divorced. Sometimes I'm awfully desolate.

❧

I tried to raise you the way I wished I had been raised, Maya. And I hope you are not angry. All I wanted was for you to be happy and carefree, a girl who doesn't have to be an intellectual superstar just to prove to the world that she exists; a girl who knows she is loved and alive and has no problem with either—happy to be loved and happy to be alive.

Maybe I shouldn't have worried so much. Whatever you lacked in our Tel-Aviv elephant pack you made up for on your own, through Grandma Rochel and our extended family. By the age of three you had invented an imaginary friend for yourself, Shuldig, with whom you would tie a silk kerchief to your head and pretend to light Shabbat candles or dance with a Torah scroll. "Shuldig wants you to pour grape juice into the cup," you'd announce every Friday night, and then make me sit at the little table where you had spread a white cloth diaper and set down three little plastic plates and two wood blocks representing loaves of bread. "Now Shuldig will say the Kiddush and we will say 'Amen.'"

Ten and a half years passed before Rosy remarried, and during that time I made every effort to avoid seeing him face-to-face. On the day he was to hand me the writ of divorce, he stopped in the stairwell of the rabbinate building and looked me in the eye, saying one last time, "Let's not do this, Shlomtz." I pressed my lips together and continued up the stairs.

"We have to do this," I told him as we entered the hall of the rabbinical court. "One day you will thank me."

After we divorced, he changed jobs and apartments frequently. I tried in vain to get you to tell me about the women in his life.

"No," you'd said when I interrogated you after you returned from visiting your father, "Daddy doesn't have a girlfriend. Just Daddy and Lara live in Daddy's house. Mommy, did you know Daddy took me to the desert? He and Lara have a tent there by the sea. Let's ask them to come live with us, Mommy, please let's ask them."

I cried with you when his white dog died of old age.

I was deeply relieved when he married Nira, a thirty-one-year-old divorcée with a doctorate in Political Science. I was even more relieved when they had their first child and named him Gal—wave—and a year later had another boy whom they named Suf—reeds. When she had their third son, Ofek—horizon—I said to myself, *That's it, three's a* hazaka, *an unbreakable presumption. He belongs to her, she loves him, they are held fast by three anchors, and my boat can set sail and be carried wherever the wind takes it.*

❧

We had a good life, you and I, a really fine life, Maya. And then—in the army of all places!—you started wearing skirts instead of pants, lighting real Shabbat candles, and eating only raw vegetables and yogurt when you came to visit. One evening I came home and my breath caught, for there, on my coffee table in the living room, lay a red hardcover book, and I knew without even getting close enough to read its black letters that it was *The Eternal of Israel* by the Maharal of Prague. I could not understand how it had come back to me of its own accord, twenty years after I had packed it in a cardboard box along with its friends, left it on the sidewalk outside a second-hand bookstore in Jerusalem, and took off like I had abandoned a box of newborn puppies. Yet I was convinced it was the very same book, its tattered binding just as I remembered, reddish strings fraying from buffed edges, spine worn in the places where my sure hands had once held it, way back then. I crept toward the table as though afraid I might waken it, my hand shaking as I reached out, and I jumped out of my skin when I suddenly heard your happy voice behind me: "Hey Mom, I got here in the afternoon and crashed in my room. Just woke up now. Why's the light off?"

When you saw the terror with which my eyes fastened on the book on the table, you laughed.

"That's my *Eternal of Israel*," you said, picking it up so naturally. Reaching out to flood the room with halogen light, you tried to understand. "Mom, why are you so pale? Sit down, I'll make you coffee."

"Where did you find it?"

"I didn't find it, I bought it in that little old bookstore on Allenby Street."

"Whatever for?"

"There's a wonderful teacher in Jerusalem, Mom. Her name is Rabbanit Hava Schor. She gives classes for women on this book, on Tuesdays in her home, and I've already gone a couple of times."

By this point I realized it wasn't really my *Eternal of Israel*. But a creeping fear had begun to erode the inner peace I had struggled so hard to cultivate since you were born. Is it really true that one can never escape the wretchedness dictated by heredity? Must fate really always come around and strike in each and every generation?

I still wanted to believe it was all temporary, a passing phase. But after being discharged from the army you went to quench your thirst for the living God in the seminary at Tirza, and then you fell in love with the son of Rabbi Yair Berman and left me no choice but to give in to fate. It's all right, my sweet, it's really okay. I hereby surrender.

Chapter nine

Surely you remember the lovely Estherke, who lived in the ground-floor apartment of my grandmother's building. When we were kids, Iri, you used to get all flushed whenever she spoke to us in her mixed Yiddish-Hebrew, trying her best to improve her knowledge of the holy tongue, erupting in self-deprecating laughter any time we corrected her mistakes in diction or grammar.

You and I both hoped that Estherke would be too much of a free-spirit to remain among the ultra-Orthodox, and we waited for the handsome prince who would come to her rescue. But when she came of age, she remained caught in the tight net of tradition. I came back from New York on a visit and found her married, wearing a tight kerchief that prevented any alien ideas from entering her shaven head, and an invisible collar tied to a leash held by her especially irksome husband, a skinny, sorry soul named Yehoshua Grazenstein, with a great fur hat and a poker face.

I kept hoping she would snap out of it, that she would get

up one day and walk out on him and on the dark alley that her life would become in his company. But a few years later her mother visited Grandma Rochel in the retirement home, and she reported that Estherke had moved to the *haredi* neighborhood of Sanhedria and had four children.

I had almost completely forgotten about her when, one Shabbat not long ago, I was going through the weekend paper and my eye fell on an article about this ultra-Orthodox man who had left it all, become non-observant, and started an organization to help people like him who had fled from the dark side. "These young people need help breaking the bonds of religion," he was quoted as saying in the caption under a big picture of him with an intellectual-style shaved head and round glasses. His name was Shuki Granit, and as I read on I learned that he had once been one of the star students in a *haredi* yeshiva in Jerusalem. They had set him up with a wife, and at nineteen he married a *haredi* girl who was more sophisticated than he. They were divorced now: she wound up staying in that world while he, who had never even known of a life outside of the *haredi* neighborhoods in Jerusalem and Bnei Brak, gave it up, along with religion as a whole, in favor of a life of enlightenment and cultural advancement.

The pieces of the puzzle came together, and I suddenly realized that Shuki Granit was Yehoshua Grazenstein, his ex-wife none other than our own Estherke.

The next day I tracked down her address, put on a long skirt, drove up to Jerusalem, and parked the car in Sanhedria next to a big apartment building whose stairwells were filled with old strollers and rusty bikes. Every entrance to the building had its own bunch of mailboxes, which I scoured for the name Grazenstein. It was in the third entrance, way up on the fifth floor, that the angel of my youth opened the door and her fleshy body embraced me feebly. She was wearing a faded, laced housedress, and when she looked at me she wiped a tear from her doughy face.

We sat on heavy couches in her diminutive living room and drank tea from old glass mugs just like the ones her parents had when we were kids. Estherke told me that at first Yehoshua had been an introverted guy who was one of the most solid, superb students in the *koylel* where he studied, but that one day, when she was pregnant with number five, he just walked out the door and never came back.

For a long time she had been unable to extract a writ of divorce from him—at first they didn't even know where he was, whether he was even alive, and only after huge efforts did the representatives of the special rabbinical court somehow manage to track him down in India. "Can you imagine, Shlomtzi?" she said. "In *India* they find him, living on some kind of commune for people from all over the world who have decided to leave everything. A long time passed before he would even admit that it was really him, and he finally agreed to grant me a divorce."

"What a jerk," I seethed.

But the woman sipping her tea on the old couch smiled and shook her head. "No Shlomtzi," she said, the old spark suddenly back in her eye. "You don't understand, and I had hoped that you of all people would. There was freedom here. I brought it into our home when I married Yehoshua. I brought freedom with me but never had the courage to use it—I just kept it here under the bed, like some mail-order gadget that collects dust for so long that nobody remembers what it's for. Finally Yehoshua decided that it was a shame to waste that freedom, so he took it and ran off."

Only when Maya was about six or seven, did I allow myself a boyfriend. He was a famous Tel-Avivian doctor, and I had designed a stunning renovation of his and his wife's Arab-style home in Jaffa, with grand windows overlooking the sea. She insisted on an open Jacuzzi in the middle of their bedroom, whereas he was an old-style arrogant chauvinist. I cooked for him the delicious meals that his wife wouldn't make for him, I laughed at his dirty jokes and I even went with him on a luxurious vacation in the Greek islands, but it never once occurred to me to fall in love with him. When I saw he was getting in over his head, I sent him off to look for another mistress.

In the years that followed I limited myself to a few short-term gigs, since I knew that no man could relieve my inner loneliness. Only recently have I found some release in Yossi the *moshavnik*, with his tractor, with the preserves and compotes I make from his produce, with our trips together with the matching luggage.

"Yossi's such a sweet guy, why don't you just marry him?" my friends ask, belching smoke from between their pursed, wrinkled lips. "You'd actually make a great housewife, you know?"

All of them really want a lifelong love, but all of them have been burned at least once by the hot coals of marriage, and all of them laugh out loud when Eden expands on her vision of a wonderful world for women only. Haviva, whom I also met when she was divorced and raising little kids on her own, remarried nine years ago but sometimes still prefers our company over that of her husband Oded. "I like being with him," she says, "but I also like being without him sometimes, and he doesn't get it."

"Men are all dependent types," Eden declares.

"No, really," Haviva continues, "you just have to see how Oded falls apart every time he gets home and I'm not there, or if he calls me during the day and I don't answer. He whines at me, 'Where were you? I couldn't find you, I was so worried!' I can't talk on the phone more than five minutes when he's around, because he gets all insecure. He starts hovering around me like a beggar, making these impatient noises, like he has to have my full attention. Even when he's not home, he can't take it when I talk on the phone with somebody else. If he calls and gets a busy signal, he complains later on, 'Who were you talking to for so long? I tried to call and it was busy for hours.' And when I ask why he called, what was so urgent, of course he can't remember."

"Thanks a lot, but I don't want to get married," I retort to my friends. *But neither do I want to break up with wonderful Yossi*, I then say to myself. He is my third serious relationship, and you don't break up a third time. For it says in the Talmud that a woman who is widowed three times in a row is considered a "deadly" woman, and I, who have already driven away two potential husbands, mustn't drive away the third, lest I officially become a rejecter of men.

The truth is, I take some satisfaction in the fact that both you and Rosy are set, both married to stable and dedicated women. You've probably lost touch with Rosy since you were transferred out of his reserve unit into the military chaplaincy. But Maya doubtless told you that he built a house in Rosh Pina, that he now owns a big auto repair shop, that his wife Nira is a professor at Haifa University, and that they have three sons named after his Shores of Freedom. I see his family once in a while. They come out in full force for the important events in Maya's life—last time I saw them was at the graduation ceremony of the final group of officers trained by Maya, just before she was discharged. Rosy carried a basket full of goodies he had prepared for his daughter the officer, and Nira smiled at me courteously from behind her sunglasses, as if to thank me for passing this wonderful man on to her. And their children, Gal and Suf and Ofek, light-haired and beautiful and wearing colored sneakers, laughed and shouted and climbed happily on their father's broad back, never showing the slightest awareness of the fact that if I had not made him divorce me, they would never have been born.

Chapter ten

Until Nira snared him, Rosy's eyes would lock on mine in sad supplication every time we'd meet. After he married her, however, our eyes became our own. Now we lock eyes, not on each other, but on our daughter.

"Daddy loves his garage," Maya tells me. "His face lights up when he greets his customers, and he fixes engines with such joy, it's like he's fixing the world."

Maybe he really is one of the thirty-six hidden tzaddikim that the rabbis said the whole world depends on, I think to myself as I imagine him rummaging through the guts of a car or lying on his back exploring its underside, with just his legs in their blue workpants sticking out from below, his face and hands as black as a tire with motor oil, his body soaked with gasoline fumes, but his eyes rejoicing at everyone who enters his garage, his monotone voice brimming with warmth and generosity.

Rosy fixes the world, and I too am throwing everything into my work. I never stop coming up with new, surprising ways for mortals to pass their fleeting, pathetic lives in their temporary dwelling places on this earth. I am considered a leading interior designer, and am often invited to lecture on my post-modern method of restoring the notion of privacy to our culture. Photos of my work appear frequently in design magazines, both here and abroad.

But now and again, like Old Faithful, a desire erupts in me to return to my first love and become a painter, to invent wild, colorful worlds. Two years ago I even dragged my friend Edith to the Old City of Jaffa for weekly art lessons. In a spacious studio—which Edith, a rabid leftist, didn't forget to remind me had, until fifty years ago, been the basement of a beautiful mansion owned by a wealthy Arab family which was now probably living in some hovel in the refugee camps of El-Boureij or Jabalya—I sketched cracked pottery, rusty teapots, disinterred tree roots, and once in a while a tired female model who bared her limbs for us while her entire demeanor said that she just wanted to get dressed and run out of there. After thirteen classes I decided that the time had come for painting—among other old loves—to pass out of longing and into memory. Edith continued without me, painting in the underground studio, graduating from teapots and models to flowers and fruit and urban landscapes, and recently her work was even exhibited in a gallery alongside three other novice artists. I went to their exhibit together with Yossi, who feigned interest for my sake. We walked from one work to the next, arm in arm, and I mused about Shelley, the bohemian artist living in New York, who had lived a life of free creation since childhood: Without hurt, for she had never been about to marry you and had never been rejected by you; and without guilt, for she had never trapped in her net a man named Mordechai Rosenberg, and had never crushed his spirit.

But if you didn't love me, Iri, what am I supposed to make of your behavior all those years? Who forced you to say all those words, do all those things, make all those promises? Who was giving you stage directions, for example, on that day that I am now recalling so vividly, my seventeenth birthday, when you waited for me in the afternoon outside the religious school for girls in an orange Beetle you'd borrowed from a friend, and drove me to the Jerusalem Forest? There you spread out a tablecloth, and like in the movies, laid it with a whole picnic you had planned meticulously in advance. Then you ceremoniously presented me with an easel, paper, and watercolors, positioning them against the verdant spring vista, saying sheepishly, "The whole world was created just so you could paint it." You stood next to me studying my confident brushstrokes in silence, and when I glanced at you I noticed that your gaze was fixed not on the paper but on me, and your expression was of longing.

❧

It was seven years after I sent Rosy away that I rented out our flat, quit my job at the architectural firm, packed up Maya and Shuldig, and moved to New York. I told myself I was returning to the place where I had spent the best years of my life, that I could replace my fake life with a real one by transplanting myself far away from you and Lealeh, far from the flowering of the redemption, far from the Heavens rejoicing above while I suffered below. The plan had been in the works for some time. I hatched it in secret, like a prisoner planning a daring escape from a well-guarded fortress. One day when visiting a friend, I met her sister who had just come in from New York, where she had lived for many years, making a good living marketing Israeli food products.

Her name was Rona, and she was short, blond, and full of energy. When I casually asked her about the job market in New York, as though I was just curious, she saw through me immediately.

"Come work with me," she said eagerly. "The work-load's gotten too demanding for me to handle on my own. I've been working insane hours and barely get to see my kid."

Late that summer we landed in my alternate universe. We rented an apartment in Queens in a red brick high-rise whose twenty-three floors housed mostly Chinese, Indian, and Israeli families, refugees like us. Though we were not greeted by my old friends from high school— at the airport I had searched in vain for Anthony Sarantakis, Lee Howard, Maria Santos and the twins Steven and David Klein—I was determined to find happiness and believed I would succeed. In utter freedom I walked the length and breadth of Manhattan, as through the skeletal innards of a giant fish that had swallowed me up as I ran away from the Lord. Along the broad avenues I found peace and tranquility, the skyscrapers protecting me like walls to my right and left, the flowing masses of humanity inviting me to get lost among them, as though I really were one of them. Among the high towers I could make out the sky, but it was sullied and irrelevant, while I found the blessings of prosperity by pushing Israeli soup mix, soup nuts, chocolate spread, and even Israeli floor rags, which I had suggested that Rona add to our inventory, and she had readily agreed—a decision she has not regretted to this day.

The first time Rona invited us to her place in Queens for dinner, a dark-skinned youth tailed us from the subway station, and followed us into the lobby. I panicked. Someone had just told me that same day how her handbag had been grabbed by black teenagers, and I was already preparing to hand over my purse in the hope that he would leave me and Maya in peace. I shielded Maya with my body as he followed us into the elevator, and when he pressed the button for the seventh floor where Rona lived, I pressed six. On the sixth floor I got out with Maya, and after waiting a full ten minutes, we crept upstairs.

When I rang the doorbell, it was the dark-skinned fellow who answered the door. "Hi!" he welcomed us with a victorious grin, his teeth gleaming from among African features.

"Hi Shlomtzion! Hi Maya!" Rona appeared by his side, a head shorter than him. "This is Leroy, my son."

Leroy was fifteen, and in time became good friends with Maya. He was the product of a one-night liaison with a gentleman who had bought Rona a piña colada in a bar. I raised an eyebrow when she told me this story, and she snapped "What? Why didn't I get an abortion? First, because Leroy is the best thing that ever happened to me. And second, because I only found out I was pregnant when he started kicking me, and by then I was already in my fifth month. I always got my period only every few months, and the doctors told me I wasn't likely to have children."

❧

Within six months of our arrival in the United States, Maya spoke fluent English and her Barbie collection had swelled beyond capacity. Rona had offered to make me a full partner, and another new friend had offered to set me up in an architectural firm.

I loved New York. I loved how it was a city of so many nations trying to live their earthly existence far away from *here*; and I loved how it gave me the chance to turn over a new leaf.

My happiness reached its height one evening as I sat with a few friends in a little restaurant near NYU. There was something familiar about the way the black jazz pianist bounced around while he played. Lee Howard, my beloved friend from the high school for the arts, had been a skinny, gangly kid thirteen years earlier, but this chubby pianist had the same amused look, the same complete merg ing with the music he played, and I approached him, moved, and asked quietly, "Lee?"

The other patrons swerved toward us in surprise when he leapt from the piano, gave me a huge hug and exclaimed in a big, deep voice: "My dear Shelley! My beloved Israel!"

I told him how badly I'd missed him, and he told me he was teaching musicology at NYU and played in this restaurant once a week for the fun of it. His chocolate eyes shone as they drank me in, and he kept saying, "I can't believe it, I can't believe I'm seeing you again."

It is hard to describe to you, Iri, the sense of security I got out of this chance encounter, how vindicated I felt that, in spite of everything, I am a creature that can be loved.

❧

It was Aristotle, the homeless man who lived across from my apartment, who caused me to return to Israel despite all this. Throughout the entire six months we had been in New York, I found myself enthralled by the homeless, people of all stripes and ages and colors who loitered in public places, camped out on sidewalks, blocked subway entrances. Millions of passersby with their suits, briefcases, fancy shoes, and clouds of deodorant wafting in their wake had trained themselves to ignore the human trash, but I just couldn't *not* see them, couldn't not feel for them, couldn't not be struck by the sense that I, too, was living on the margins of society. I was particularly troubled by one filthy man whose tall stature had been brought low, his broad shoulders hunched forward like those of a battered child, a man roughly my age who lived on a traffic island near our home.

I named him Aristotle because of his philosophical gaze and his fine Greek nose. His hair was long, tangled, and formed a single hair unit with his beard, unwashed and uncombed for years. He wore a heavy, putrid coat down to his knees in all weather. His pant legs were so frayed that he dragged strings behind him as he walked, and his feet were covered in rags. His little island, which had two or three benches surrounded by oleander bushes on it, was flanked on one side by a broad thoroughfare with cars and buses barreling down its six lanes twenty-four hours a day. On the other side was a service road, beyond which stood the local supermarket and our red-brick apartment building. I couldn't come home without seeing Aristotle among the oleander, and sometimes I imagined that he looked back at me.

Early mornings before dawn, before the sealed skies attained their murky light, before the deluge of busy, ordinary people flooded the streets, I would lie awake in bed thinking about his hunched figure scampering across the silent service road to scavenge garbage cans in the sleepy neighborhood. Whatever scraps of food he found he would later share, this I knew, with the pigeons that assembled at his feet as I passed by the traffic island on my way to work, their feathers coated with a layer of soot, their cooing lost in the din of six lanes of traffic.

Pesach came, marked only by Rona coming back from Israel with a duffel laden with leaven-free soup mix, and Maya being sent to Israel to spend the holiday with her father. In the elevator of our building I ran into two Israeli neighbors, their hair bleached and coiffed, their purple eye shadow lording over lashes drenched in mascara, their nails long and blood-red.

"But if you want to make meat kosher for Passover," one said to the other as I entered, "you have to use coarse ground salt."

"Nah," the other answered. "You don't need special salt to make meat kosher. I'm definitely doing it with regular salt."

"Is it true you were once observant?" the first turned to me. I was baffled as to how one could handle a slab of meat with dagger nails like hers.

"It's true," I admitted. I had been outed, it was fair to assume, by another neighbor in the building whose husband, a man I knew from our youth group days in Jerusalem, was now an emissary of the Jewish Agency in New York.

"So, what can you tell us about where to get coarse ground salt?"

I had a hard time explaining, as we stood by the fountain outside our building, that the size of the salt doesn't matter, and that there is no way on earth to turn the non-kosher meat they bought into kosher meat. "Meat can be kosher," I lectured, "only if it comes from a pure animal and is slaughtered properly."

As I finished the disquisition, my eyes fell on Aristotle, who sat on a bench bundled in his overcoat and adjusting the rags around his right ankle.

"So awful," neighbor number one clicked her tongue as she followed my eyes. "And to think that he's the son of Dr. Feingold!"

"Who's the son of Dr. Feingold?" I asked, shocked. Mark Feingold was Maya's gentle grey-haired pediatrician. His brightly lit clinic took up the ground floor of his beautiful house in a fancy part of our neighborhood, and on Saturday afternoons we'd bump into him and his wife as they walked home from the Orthodox synagogue, of which he was president.

"Him over there," answered neighbor number two, pointing with her chin at Aristotle, who was now wrapping his left ankle.

"Years ago he cut all ties with his wonderful parents," number one explained. "He'd rather live on the street than enter their home or let them take care of him."

From that day on, I could not find a shred of peace for my soul, until I parted farewell from my beloved Shelley and landed back in Israel with Maya and a suitcase full of Barbie dolls. As I stepped off the plane onto the tarmac, I was suddenly struck by the great blue skies and the unimpeded Israeli sun, the rays hitting my head with neither hesitation nor mercy. But I knew I was home, I knew I was walking on the same earth that you walked on, and I knew I would never escape my own destruction unless I learned how to look back without turning into a pillar of salt.

❧

How far apart we have grown over the years, Iri, how distant my people are from yours. Sometimes it feels like we're speaking different languages, breathing different air, seeing a different reality. Most of the people I know are thrilled that the Oslo accords are signaling an end to the occupation, and cannot understand why anyone would continue to support the settlements—which, you must admit, have brought nothing but trouble after all. In this surrogate life I've led ever since you tossed me out, I've mostly come across those you would call leftists, and you should know that they're good people who love this land no less than you and your friends do. For years I actually got along just fine with both them and their opinions, until recently when Maya restored to me Rabbi Kook's Land of Israel, wrapped in its inner spiritual graces and the existence of the nation. Just imagine, Iri, she goes to Jerusalem and attends Rabbanit Hava Schor's classes on *The Eternal of Israel*, and has a whole shelf dedicated to the works of Kook, *Pri Tzaddik*, Luzzatto, and all the rest in her room. Every time she comes home and empties out her enormous backpack, it's as if in addition to the clothes and other things she's dumping on the floor, I also get a whole pile of *the sanctity of this nation originates in the sanctity of the land,* and *the land of splendor longs for her children,* and *the fourth in Nahmanides' list of 613 commandments, is that we are obligated to conquer the land and not leave it to the other nations.* Today I know you can't run a country based on these things, even if they are beautiful, even if they are true in theory. But something in me starts to come undone when I see her confidence. Something pulls me back to when I used to believe these ideas, just as Maya does today.

I sometimes think I'm the only one in this country who doesn't know exactly where they stand, whether on the Left or Right, for the Oslo accords or against. My friends can't stand your people. They blame you for endangering both your children and theirs, and they're convinced you're simply allergic to all that is good and enlightened. And to be honest, I cringe as well whenever I hear you being interviewed on the radio, so cocksure, so self-confident, and I really want to ask, *Why not just give the peace process a chance? If it doesn't work out, we can always go back to this awful endless war, which I often think has become so familiar to you and your friends that you're not willing to give up on it, even a little.* You just look *bad* in all those wild demonstrations of yours, Iri, waving around those blood-soaked posters and castigating the government after every terror attack, as though Rabin and Peres weren't themselves trying to bring an end to them through these peace agreements that you so despise.

Sometimes I really can't stand you and your side, and find myself longing to see you all removed from your godforsaken settlements so that you can stop bringing evil upon our country. But I also feel Maya's pain in all this. It kills me to see my daughter wandering her ancestral homeland like an abandoned vulnerable exile, and it's hard for me to listen to her talk about how she felt on the night of the first demonstration against Oslo. "A quarter million people, driven mad with fear, filling the government plaza in Jerusalem, Mom, including people who never go to rallies, from all over the country. Some of them brought their young children, even their babies—whatever it takes to get our country off the dangerous path it's taken. We assumed," she adds, chuckling bitterly, "that Yitzhak Rabin was a good Jew at heart, a loyal Israeli, that maybe when he saw the size of the rally he'd have second thoughts. But then he gets on the radio and starts talking about all the wonderful progress they've made toward peace, and the interviewer asks what he thinks about the huge rally happening that night in Jerusalem, and what does the Prime Minister of Israel say, slapping a quarter million demonstrators right in the face? He says, in derision, 'I couldn't give a hoot.' He really said that, Mom. I heard it with my own ears on the radio, when I was on the bus coming back to Tel Aviv after the rally. 'I couldn't give a hoot.'"

❧

With last spring's murder of Ariel's close friend Yenon Gur and his bride-to-be, Hagit, whose beautiful smile beamed from the front page of the daily paper the next morning, I began to understand that the Oslo accords were not very much of a peace agreement. "Do you see now, Mommy," Maya shouted between sobs, "your government can't say that its hands didn't shed the blood of Nonny and Hagit."

She wouldn't let me comfort her; in fact, she recoiled from me as though my own hands were dripping blood. In time I would learn that the same Yenon Gur was the son of Shlomit Gur, who lived in Tirza, and who many years earlier had been my much-beloved Bnei Akiva counselor. I wrote her a letter sharing my condolences as best as I could.

But at the same time, you should know that I blamed the murder of Naomi Ron more on your people than on Oslo. For if you hadn't been so committed to establishing a de facto situation in the territories, Naomi wouldn't have lived there, and thus wouldn't have died there. When I learned of her horrible and needless death on the news, I spent the whole night looking for my photo album from high school, as if by tracking down the old photos I could somehow turn back the clock to a time when Naomi and I were girls, before you and your friends had turned Israel into an impossible place to live. Feverishly I burrowed through the boxes and bookshelves. I couldn't remember where in my Tel Aviv hideaway I'd put the green album with the sticky cardboard pages covered in clear plastic. I finally found it in the early morning hours. Square photographs, mostly in black and white, were attached to the pages, some straight, some slanted, with pieces of colored paper in between, on which I had written in the loopy handwriting I had back then incandescent lines of verse by the poet Rachel.

"*Perhaps it never really happened*," it said on a greenish slip next to a picture of Naomi, my classmate and fellow Bnei Akiva member, standing on an ancient stone step at the top of Masada. In the photograph, her gorgeous face is distorted with laughter, she's wearing an old-style Israeli *tembel* hat, and she has her arm around another girl, one with a distant gaze. Me. I was never a very social type, because as long as I had you, Iri, my world lacked nothing. But Naomi was dating the cute counselor Shauli, and she was friends with everyone, myself included, and even though my mind was preoccupied at the time with Torah and Service and Good Deeds, I also let myself get carried away in her river of youthfulness sometimes.

"*At the mountain peak I'd roar with song / I'd give a cheer to youth*"—these words I had written on a light blue slip lodged between a picture of Naomi and me picking cucumbers on a kibbutz and another in which we were outside the clubhouse, dancing the hora together with her kids from the youth group. I never knew anyone who believed in the sanctity of the Land of Israel more than she, or in the sublime obligation of every child in Bnei Akiva to become a leader and an example for our generation. She was the only person whom I told about my megalomaniacal aspirations to leadership, and she, in her modesty, chided me with her smile. "Now you see why I'm investing in my relationship with you, Shlomtzion. The day will come when you and Yair get married, with God's help, and so will Shauli and I, and the two of you will be the rabbi and rabbanit of the great movement in which Shauli and I will be loyal foot-soldiers."

Both of her parents lost their entire families in the Holocaust. They met each other as partisans in the forests of Poland, and brought Naomi into the world in order to prove to the *goyim* that Jews, too, have a right to live. I remember her going around in her blue Bnei Akiva shirt, teaching the kids to sing in their tweety-bird voices: "*We'll rebuild the land of our forefathers / For this land is ours, is ours*"—and now I'm wondering whether whoever it was that sent her off to build her life on the outskirts of Nablus wasn't just taking her for a ride. Tell me, does the fact that this land "is ours, is ours" really mean that we must never, under any circumstance, give up on any of it? Or maybe is it possible that by holding so tight onto every inch we are just causing more and more Jews to be slaughtered, just like when we were in exile?

Broken-hearted I took the album out of the closet where I'd finally found it, and seating myself on the floor, leafed back and forth through it, searching in vain for answers, until I reached the last page. Under a picture of our Bnei Akiva group on our last evening together, right before we set off for the army or National Service in order to give of ourselves for the benefit of the People of Israel in the Land of Israel according to the Torah of Israel, I saw a pink slip of paper upon which the girl I had been had written, "*An eternal covenant is between us / A bond that cannot break / Only that which I have lost / Is mine forever.*"

My bond with Naomi was broken after I attended that wedding in which I learned about the existence of your son Ariel. I didn't even respond to the invitation she sent me a few months later, to her own wedding to Shauli. But I did go to her funeral opposite Mount Eval a year and a half ago, boarding a bulletproof bus that left from her elderly parents' house in Jerusalem. She had been murdered on her way home, the trunk of her car still packed with the groceries she had bought after work. She was right in the thick of her life, in the thick of raising her eight children, in the thick of a great love she shared with Shauli, the champion of her youth who had become her husband. But at the intersection between Nablus and their settlement, three men with automatic weapons opened fire on her Peugeot station wagon as though Naomi had been sentenced to death by firing squad, and there was nothing she could do but collapse and contort at the steering wheel, immersing herself in a mikvah of blood until her soul departed, in purity.

Chapter eleven

Friday, November 3, 1995. I'm going down to the car with a suitcase in one hand and a black jacket in the other, because Maya says it might get chilly in the evening in Tirza. She arrived last night, so excited and happy that I feared for her, and gaily announced that she had come to escort me to Tirza, so that I wouldn't get lost and end up driving around in the middle of Ramallah. "Yeah, sure, Mommy," she laughed as she stood beside me before the open wardrobe, picking out clothes for me to wear on Shabbat. "I know you were there long before me, and that you know the territories well from your days as a founder of Gush Emunim and all that. But still, a few things have changed since then, and it's a good idea for me to help you navigate the roads."

If she's so excited about my coming for Shabbat to meet her future in-laws, imagine how she would feel if she knew about our shared past. I was considering telling her the whole story. "The girl will hear the truth sooner or later," Eden, ever wise and pragmatic, said to me. "Better she hears it from you and not someone else." But I just didn't have the guts to do it, and didn't know how. So now we're getting out of the elevator, walking toward the car, putting our bags in the trunk and sitting in the front seats like Abraham and Isaac on the way to the Binding, with Abraham knowing exactly where the road leads, and Isaac seeing the fire and the wood and still hoping he's not the lamb.

Yossi came over Wednesday evening with a crate of green apples, the tart ones I really like. We ate my fabulous squash soup, the recipe for which I got recently from Haviva, a creamed soup with lots of crushed dill and black pepper, and Yossi told me sadly about his son Shai, who was about to celebrate his ninth birthday and asked that his dead mother return home, if only for one day.

Then the phone rang and my heart screeched to a halt. I thought it might be Rosy calling from Rosh Pina to apologize for not accompanying me to meet the groom's parents.

"Hello, this is… Yair Berman speaking."

"Hello."

"I'm calling about this coming Shabbat. That is, I'm calling on behalf of my wife Leah."

"Yes."

"She asked me to just say that… What I mean is that up till now all communication between us regarding the arrangements for Shabbat have been through the kids, and I just wanted to say that we…"

"It's fine. Thanks."

"I also wanted to ask…"

A pause.

"If Maya knows…if you told her…"

"…No, not yet."

"Ah-huh."

"And Ariel?"

"No, Leah and I both thought there was no reason to rush…"

"Yes."

"So…good, we'll see you on Shabbat, God willing."

"Thank you for calling."

The telephone weighed a ton as I slowly placed it back on the hook. Yossi, who was scraping the remains of the thick soup from his bowl, fastened worried eyes on me.

"What happened?" he asked. "You've just gone white."

"I turned white?" I asked mechanically, putting a hand to my forehead as though to check the color of my skin. "No, I'm fine. I just heard a voice I haven't heard in twenty years."

I stood beside him as he washed the dishes, and then rested my head on his shoulder as he watched the raucous TV talk-show he so loves. Then I kissed him passionately, peeled off his clothes, and made love to him with utter devotion—precisely because he is unable to recite even a single line of the writings of Rabbi Kook, precisely because he does not know that souls sometimes expand to the point where there is no room for them in this world, precisely because he has never once aspired to be a prophet.

"You know," this gift from God said to me afterwards, lying on his back and looking at the ceiling, "sometimes I think that when you're with me, you're really the most with yourself that you could possibly be."

"Does this bother you?" I was concerned.

"No, just the opposite," he smiled, turning his farmer face toward me and brushing some hair out of my eyes. "It just shows me how much I mean to you."

❧

As we drive out of Tel Aviv I'm reminded of my journey two days ago to pay a *shiva* call to Eden, whose mother passed away this week on their kibbutz at the foot of Mount Gilboa. Her mother had been an introverted woman who dedicated her life to working long and hard; to hear Eden tell it, she had never enjoyed anything, anytime. "Trying to get a good word out of her is harder than drawing water from the rock," she used to complain to me. "I've been trying since I was a child, and it's no use."

As I entered the small and sparse apartment, the design and furnishings of which had not changed since the 1960s, Eden got up to greet me and we hugged for a long time. Then she introduced me to her father and sister, who said Edna had told them all about me. As I sat beside her, she leaned over and whispered in my ear, "You should congratulate me on the birth of my brother."

"You have a brother?" I was surprised.

"So it seems. My mother left a letter, sort of a will, where she says she wants to be buried next to her first-born son. When we asked Dad to explain, he says, 'Yes, we had a son. We named him Giora, and he would have been fifty-one years old.'" Eden, whose father and sister still call her Edna, lit a cigarette and drew on it until her cheeks nearly touched each other from the inside.

"How did he die?" I asked.

"Giora? Diphtheria. You know how old he was?"

"How old?"

"Five weeks, Shlomtzion. Do you get this? Giora would have been fifty-one, but in reality he was only five weeks old. She devoted her entire life to mourning over a five-week-old baby, instead of giving something to her two daughters. Our only crime was having stayed alive."

"Don't you think you're being a bit harsh?"

"I'm being harsh? Don't you think *she* was being harsh? It took till now—till after she asked to be buried next to her first-born son, her *beloved* son—for me to finally realize that all these years it wasn't my fault."

❧

Maya and I are driving to the settlement of Tirza, and Maya pulls out of her duffel bag a tape of songs by Dedi Ben-Ami, a singer from Nahalal who used to top the charts when I was her age. Back then he sang the tortured words Othello says to Desdemona as he strangles her to death; now he's got a beard and sidelocks and sings the lilting songs of Breslav Hassidim. "Is it okay if I put this on?"

Maya asks politely, then puts the tape into the car stereo and hits the switch.

"Sure, why not?" I reply. "Might as well get into the spirit." I am reminded of the foolish girl who used to quote the words of Rabbi Nachman of Breslav to her beloved. "*True, you are good people / But this was not my intention / I had wanted you to be more like beasts / Howling in the woods / All through the night.*"

Have I also dedicated my entire life to mourning? What will Maya think of me when she finds out that all my behavior toward God and man has been a response to one ever-open wound—the pain of losing my first love?

But immediately I regret the comparison, ashamed at having drawn a parallel between myself and Eden's poor mother. She lost a living, breathing baby, pink and warm, who entered the world from her womb and drank her milk, and I lost nothing more than a megalomaniacal fantasy and a love that was never born.

❧

This morning I suggested to Maya that we make a detour to Jerusalem on our way to Tirza, so that we could stop at the retirement home and tell Grandma Rochel about the engagement. As we drive past Ben-Gurion Airport, Othello's voice fills the car, "*Rabbi Nachman of Breslav says thus / Never give up hope / We must never give up hope / If harsh times come / We must only rejoice.*" Maya gazes with satisfaction at the view of the plains flashing by the window, whereas I'm trying to understand what exactly happened to me this Tuesday, during the self-awareness class that Eden drags me to each week.

I get the feeling that there is nothing that Jeanine, the tall, lanky instructor, likes more than to make her self-awareness class do social exercises. The first few times it struck me as insipid, and I demanded that Eden explain why I'm all of a sudden supposed to start playing games like I've gone back to kindergarten. But after a while I got used to them, and this time Jeanine promised us a special, feminine experience. She divided us up into groups of three, and instructed one person in each group to stand with her eyes closed while the others drum with both hands all over her body.

"You should bang on her like a bongo drum, ah? Just like a bongo!" Jeanine announced before hurrying to the corner of the room to dim the lights and put on some African drum music at high volume.

The music shook the air, *boom-pa-ba-da-doom-pa* making our blood rush in our veins, and I got on my knees and started pounding with Eden on our friend, a stately and refined attorney named Ora. After being a bongo for five or six minutes, big tears began to flow from her closed eyes, cutting rivers into the rouge on her cheeks. Her body started shaking desperately like someone trying to break out of irons, and the transformation she underwent at that moment was so moving that Eden and I just started beating faster and harder, until our stately attorney fell into her own internal abyss and started wailing like a child, begging, "Mommy, Mommy! I need you Mommy!"

We hugged her and comforted her according to Jeanine's instructions, and after she had calmed down, and we took a short break, it was my turn. I stood between Eden and Ora, closed my eyes, and relaxed my muscles in the way I had learned in previous sessions. At first the drumming was soft and hesitant, but then Jeanine came and told the two drummers that for me they'd have to work especially hard. "Like this," she said, demonstrating. "Hard, ah? So that she feels it real good, because our Shlomtzion knows how not to feel anything she doesn't want to feel, isn't that right?"

I don't know how to explain what happened next. Until that moment I thought I had grown used to the weird fact that my Maya was marrying Yair and Lealeh's Ariel. But out of nowhere, out of the rapid pounding on my back on my stomach on my shoulders on my thighs on the back of my neck on my chest on my hips on my butt, out of the wild African drums that shook the air around me and went inside me and flooded my blood and pounded my heart *boom-pa-ba-da-doom-pa*, my soul could no longer handle it, and it suddenly rose up, tall and hungry like a bear waking for spring.

"Don't want, don't want," I suddenly wailed, the words erupting on their own like the words of God from the mouth of a prophet, my head swinging back and forth, and the music wasn't loud enough to drown out the awful words that came out of me as though they had been waiting just for this moment, like I was Job—yes, like Job yelling at God in his anguish amid the storm. "You can't play with me like this, you cruel God with your twisted sense of humor! You can't! Why did you send his son of all people to steal my only lamb? You're a cruel god, a sadist! O tell me why you fight me—how abominable are your works, O Lord! I hate you, hate you, hate you..."

But God didn't answer, only Jeanine rubbed my back and shoulders with deep sympathy, her long arms embracing me in her mercy and loving-kindness, longsuffering and full of grace and truth. Then we got ready to pound on Eden.

Chapter twelve

"Jerusalem is so wonderful," Maya sighs as we descend Mount Castel, the city's western outskirts coming into view on the mountaintops. *Yes,* I think to myself, *so wonderful that when Grandma Rochel goes the way of all flesh, I never intend to show my face here again.*

And yet the pleasant autumn sun shines on us as we get out of the car by the retirement home. It's a handsome building in the neighborhood of Katamon, its face speckled with little private balconies, on several of which sit aged men or women, alone, looking over the street as if watching a movie they already know well. We approach the gate, and from within a group of four or five elderly women who have gathered in the entryway to sun themselves we hear the still-lucid voice of Grandma Rochel. Then she herself emerges, rising and walking toward us happily, but with the support of a walker that she's been using since she fell a couple of months ago and broke her hip. In honor of our visit she is wearing a pink tailored outfit, a stiff brown wig on her head, and a pearl necklace around her neck. Even after all these years it's still strange for me to see her here and not in her home, the home I loved as a child, the home from which she is, in my eyes, inseparable, and without which she seems like a tortoise without a shell.

In her room on the third floor of the retirement home, which we got to by way of a tiny, sluggish elevator that smells of urine and cleanser, this eighty-nine-year-old pushes her walker back and forth between the refrigerator and stovetop and serves up tea and cookies while chatting non-stop with Maya about how our extended family is doing and what each of its members is up to. This great-grandson got married, that granddaughter had a baby girl, another great-grandson is about to have his bar mitzvah—the two of them getting caught up in all the details, their conversation punctuated every few minutes with "*Baruch Hashem*—Thank God,—*bli ayin hara*—No Evil Eye, may there be only good tidings for our family, *Be'ezrat Hashem.*"

We sit around a little table which is covered with a floral oilcloth. Maya takes one cookie after another from the plate, wolfing them down and telling Grandma Rochel how great they are. I am getting ready to tell the old woman about the engagement, but suddenly she claps her hands and cries out, "*Nu*? I understand you get a mazel tov, Shlomtzion?"

"What mazel tov?" I'm taken aback.

"Mom," Maya laughs, "I already told Grandma Rochel about it on the phone."

"Really?" My voice cracks and I can't conceal the jealousy I feel over the relationship the two have developed behind my back, which has revealed itself yet again. If I didn't love Grandma Rochel so dearly, I would resent that she has drawn my daughter too close, stealing her heart and seducing her into religion.

"Of course she told me," the old woman confirms. I restrain myself, and the three of us begin chatting gaily about the upcoming wedding; we laugh at the bride's expense; at the great-grandmother's expense who would soon, No Evil Eye and With God's Help, see her descendants unto the fifth generation; and at the expense of the mother-in-law-to-be, meaning me.

"What about the boy's family?" Grandma Rochel turns to look at me once she has finished her tea. "Are they related to the Bermans we know?"

"He is the great-grandson of Rabbi Yehezkel Berman from the shul," I answer quietly, and add quickly, "But I haven't yet told Maya about the family."

My wise and wonderful grandmother is shaken by the news, but she also understands the hint and so changes the subject. "I told Maya about my first engagement," she reports.

Maya, who of course was about to ask me what I knew about Rabbi Yehezkel Berman and what I had failed to tell her about her groom's family, keeps quiet and gives my grandmother her full attention.

"You told Maya about your first engagement?" I am a bit surprised by this. She had never told *me* about it; I had had to hear the story from Batya, my unmarried aunt.

"They betrothed me at the age of sixteen to a genius of a Torah scholar," Grandma Rochel says, "and when I was seventeen he called it off."

"How can you call off an engagement?" Maya vents her outrage. "They say it's even worse than getting a divorce. Just think, Mom, Grandma Rochel was in love with this genius, and not only that, but in those days the bride would spend the entire year of the engagement embroidering a dowry-gift of bed linens for her groom. And then, after all that, Grandma finds out she did all the work for nothing."

"Back then they used to introduce the bride and the groom by bringing them together on the Mount of Olives on a Shabbat afternoon,"—Grandma Rochel becomes misty-eyed as she speaks—"in order to make sure first of all that the bride and groom found each other attractive. My mother and aunt took me there, after dressing me up like a princess and pinning my hair up with big pins. At three-thirty we started walking down the path on the Mount of Olives from the top, while at the same time the boy started walking with his escorts up the same path from the bottom. When my party and I got to the middle of the mountain we saw them approaching. I looked at him and right away I knew I liked him. He was a handsome boy, not tall but impressive, with powerful, dark eyes. When they saw us approaching, they slowed down, and my mother and aunt started walking slower as well, so that he and I could have a good long look at each other. I remember that when he looked at me I blushed—boy did I blush! I felt my heart pounding like a dove caught in a cage, and I was so shy I looked down."

"What happened next?" Maya asks.

"I fell sick in love with him, *that's* what happened next," Grandma Rochel smiles and looks down, flushed now as then. "When I got home my father asked me, 'Do you want to meet the boy they showed you today on the Mount of Olives?' And I answered, 'Oh, yes.' How scared I was that the boy would say he didn't want me! I couldn't wait until we got the answer, but Saturday night, right after Shabbat ended, we received word that he had agreed to meet me, and I was in heaven. A few days later he came to our house together with his father and they sat with my father in the living room. I waited in another room until they called me in, and then I entered together with my mother. Just imagine how nervous I was! Then they set up another meeting, and at this one they left the two of us alone for the first time. With the door open, of course, so that we wouldn't violate the halakhah by being alone together."

"What did you talk about?"

"What did we talk about?" Grandma Rochel tries to recall. "To tell the truth, Mayaleh, I was so shy that I probably didn't say anything at all, and he, I think, talked about the weather and other important things. Next was the engagement party, and for the occasion they made me the most beautiful dress I'd ever seen, and they put makeup on me—a little around the eyes and on the lips—and the house was full, so many people came to celebrate with us, and my mother made a meal fit for a king. The groom sat with the men and I sat in another room with the women, but I felt that our hearts beat as one. That we were bound together."

When she says the words "bound together" Grandma Rochel clasps her old, transparent hands, looks at them, and turns sad.

"By that point he was already in love with *her*, with his cousin," she mumbles. "But I didn't know..."

"His cousin?" I pretend to be surprised, so as not to let on that I've known this story since childhood.

"The guy called off the engagement so that he could marry his cousin," Maya updates me, and the two of us watch with concern as the old, stoop-shouldered woman rises from her chair with great difficulty and shuffles, with the help of her walker, to the china closet by the wall. It is made of dark, carved wood, three wide drawers on the bottom and shelves with glass doors on top, a fancy antique that had stood in the living room of Grandma Rochel and Grandpa Duvid's house for many years, but which now, standing next to the raised metal bed and the little table with the floral oilcloth in her narrow room in the retirement home, looks like it is sick with longing for its proper home.

On one of the shelves of the cupboard, alongside the silver, there are a dozen books—the few that Grandma Rochel could salvage from among the hundreds that had surrounded her for most of her life. She opens the glass doors, takes out a book bound with a crumbling gray cover, and plods back to the chair. The book is *Tzena Urena*, in which she has read stories from the parashah in Yiddish translation every Shabbat from the time she was a girl. She pulls out an old photo from between its pages, her hand shaking as she shows it to us.

"This is him," she says, and I am astounded by the longing which shines from her face. In the picture is a boy of no more than nineteen, his cheeks and chin bearing the downy beginnings of a beard, standing behind a book-stand on which rests an enormous volume of the Talmud. His arms lie on the book as though he were engrossed in study, but his serious countenance is turned upward, his dark, fiery eyes aimed straight at the camera.

"They took the two of us to a photographer on the day of our engagement party," my grandmother says. "Each of us separately. That's what he looked like then. And this is what I looked like."

She pulls out another photo from between the pages of *Tzena Urena* and shows it to us, causing my heart to skip a beat, and Maya to exclaim, "Grandma, you looked incredible!"

A slender, perfectly poised girl, sitting on a carved-wood chair behind an ornate desk, holding in her delicate hand a quill dipped in ink. There is no resemblance between her and the Grandma Rochel of today, nor between her and the Grandma Rochel that I knew from other photos. Only when I study her young face closely do I realize that it is the smile that makes the difference, the smile of a girl in love on the day of her engagement party, wearing a dress made especially for the occasion. A smile that full, that faithful, that heavenly, she never would smile again once that glorious year was over.

She puts the two photos back into the book, and sighs from deep inside.

"He did you such injustice," Maya tries to comfort her, but Grandma Rochel stops her.

"He did exactly what he had to do. If he had married me despite being head-over-heels in love with his cousin, then he really would have done me great injustice."

Maya raises her eyebrows.

"The worst thing anyone can endure," Grandma declares, "is to live your whole life with somebody who wants to be somewhere else."

After a long silence in which the three of us let this sink in, she rises from her chair and pushed her walker again back to the cupboard. Slowly and carefully she returns *Tzena Urena* to its place among the other books, and closes the glass doors. Then she bends over to reach the drawers below. Her hand pulls at the golden handle of the middle drawer, but the metal legs of the walker are in the way and she can't open it.

"Maya, could you help me with this drawer?" she asks, moving herself and the walker out of the way as her great-granddaughter comes over to open it. "Please," she adds hoarsely, "take everything out."

Maya rises from the open drawer with her arms full of starched, ironed, and perfectly folded white linens. Grandma Rochel looks at them protectively, her withered body trembling.

"Come, Mayaleh, put them down on the table. I want you to see how beautiful they are."

The dowry is placed before us, as clean and bright as on the day it was rejected. Grandma caresses every sheet, coverlet, and pillow case with her veined, age-spotted hand. She stands at attention as she unfolds a pillow case, and Maya and I gasp as the exquisite lace comes into view, gracing the edges all around. On one corner there is embroidered pink rosebuds that look so alive it seems they could open at any moment. And next to them, in gold, are the Hebrew letters *yod, resh, bet.*

"So you sat for a whole year and embroidered all of these?" Maya asks in astonishment, "

Grandma affirms it. "A whole *year*. Day and night."

Maya unfolds a sheet, to check if it has the same roses and lettering, and indeed it does, leaping out from between the starched folds as if trying to escape so they could bloom in freedom. "Amazing," we both say, and Grandma nods in agreement as if to say "Yes, I know."

If the letter *resh* stood for her name, Rachel, then the *yod* probably stood for the groom's first name. What was it? Yaakov? Yehoshua? Yisrael? Who was this Y.B., between whose initials Grandma's *resh* was forever imprisoned?

"You've preserved this beautiful dowry of yours very well," I say admiringly. "These linens look good as new."

"That's because I've never used them," Grandma explains in a weak voice. "And because every year before Pesach I wash them and starch them and iron them carefully."

"You spent an entire year on this incredible embroidery," Maya tries to understand, "And then the guy just shows up and says the wedding's off?"

The old woman's hand reaches out to fondle some of the lace that sticks out of the pile. "He didn't show up to tell me. He sent a messenger to our house, and after the messenger left my father called me over and told me to sit. Then he told me they'd find me another husband."

Another husband. That's how she saw Duvid Heller back then, and would continue to see him through forty-nine years of marriage. Forty-nine years during which, every year before Pesach, she washed and starched and ironed the linens meant for her first and only love.

And what linens did she and the "other husband" use? Did she ever embroider pink rosebuds and golden letters on sheets for my Grandpa Duvid?

Well, at least in my case the groom came and called off the wedding to my face.

"They never had children," Grandma Rochel says in awe, her eyes gazing afar. "And he died young, at the age of sixty-five, while his poor cousin survived him another sixteen years."

❧

"*But now that I am created / it is as though I never was,*" so my dear peppermint grandfather would sing to himself, his voice cracking as he stood in the kitchen to make himself a strong cup of tea in his thick-walled, oversized beer mug. As we make our way from the retirement home through heavy traffic to Jerusalem's northern neighborhoods, I feel more sorry for him than ever before.

When Maya asks me what Grandma Rochel and I know about Ariel's family, I assure her that it isn't too important and that I will tell her all about it over Shabbat. After sinking deep in her own thoughts for a while, she draws her own conclusions.

"Tell me, Mom, have you never met Ariel's father or mother before?"

I knew this was coming, but I can't say I'm ready for it.

"After all, you were active in Gush Emunim at exactly the same time Rabbi Yair was there," she presses the point. "And you and Leah Berman might have met at the weekly Torah classes with the great Rosh Yeshiva. Once I asked her if she remembers you."

"What did she say?"

"She said she does."

"I remember her as well. Tell me, sweetie, did you bring any other tapes besides this one of Rebbe Nachman of Breslav?"

Maya understands that this line of inquiry had come to an end for the time being, and she slips into the tape deck a collection of Naomi Shemer songs that she has been listening to since childhood.

❧

The car moves at a crawl as we drive up Route 1, which divides Jerusalem's eastern and western halves and leads to the city's northern exit, toward Ramallah. I try to guess what the Rosh Yeshiva would have said about the Oslo accords and the anticipated withdrawal from the territory he so deeply loved.

It was shortly after the Purim holiday in 1982 that I came to Jerusalem together with seven-year-old Maya to visit my grandmother, who still lived at home back then. We got stuck in a horrible traffic jam downtown; nothing was moving in the entire city center. When I asked other drivers I found out it was because of the funeral of the great Rosh Yeshiva, who had passed away at the age of ninety-four. I parked in an alley off Haneviim Street, since we wouldn't be getting anywhere anyway until the procession passed, took Maya's hand and walked briskly toward Zion Square, joining the human river of tens of thousands of others who walked to honor the deceased leader of the generation as it flowed from Harav Kook Street to Jaffa Road, toward the building of the Great Yeshiva.

I stood with my daughter behind a group of passersby watching the procession, and we looked at the thousands of people as they slowly walked, heads bowed, lost in their own thoughts or speaking quietly to one another. I searched among all the men with their beards and the women with their covered hair looking for Yair and Lealeh, since I had no doubt they would be there, but I did not find them.

I wondered whether the Rosh Yeshiva had known before he died about the withdrawal from Sinai, as it had taken place just a few days before. He had always instructed the faithful to settle in every part of the promised land, and now it seemed that at least as far as Sinai was concerned, his teachings had been to little effect. From the day Prime Minister Begin signed the peace treaty with Egypt, the Rosh Yeshiva had promised that there would be no withdrawal, had even sent his students to rally against the evacuation of settlements. But now his students had been summarily knocked off the rooftops with water cannons and carried away in big metal bird-cages built specially for the occasion, or lifted away by cranes as giant bulldozers came to crush the walls of the houses, the town square at Yamit, and the greenhouses where flowers and tomatoes had been cultivated, and the Rosh Yeshiva had passed away, and the Jerusalem sky hung low and gray over the heads of his mourners.

Maybe that's how the settlements in Judea and Samaria will meet their end as well, I thought to myself. *Maybe the settlers awakened love before it was desired, before the time was right, before it could be consummated.*

❧

At one minute to one, Maya pops the tape out of the deck to listen to the radio, her face tightening as she hears the opening tones of the news broadcast, as though preparing herself for the worst. This morning a car bomb had exploded next to a bus at the entrance to Gush Katif; tomorrow night, after the closing of Shabbat, the huge peace rally that everyone had been talking about for the past two weeks would be held at the Malkhei Yisrael Square in Tel Aviv. My friends had told me that this time they thought it was really important for them to go, even though they were not the demonstrating type. "To tell the truth," Eden admitted, "it's really not so much a peace demonstration as a rally in support of Rabin, who's been dropping rapidly in the polls in comparison to Netanyahu. But Rabin's trying to bring peace, and it's important to show our support." I was glad that the trip to Tirza meant I wouldn't have to decide whether or not to attend the rally. "Who knows what time we'll be back," I said to my friends. "They'll probably want us to meet Saturday night to go over technical issues for the wedding." Eden gave me a sympathetic look and let it drop.

"What kills me is how they keep calling it a peace agreement," Maya is now fuming. "An agreement that brings us Arafat from Tunis and gives the PLO a military base in the middle of Israel, is going to bring us nothing but a horrible war."

Now on the radio they are reporting that all the streets leading to the rally would be closed as of tomorrow morning. There would be no parking allowed on the streets surrounding the square, nor would cars be allowed on them.

"There's so much peace," Maya mutters, "that the police are more worried than ever about terror attacks."

And all I could think about was whether, after the exhausting Shabbat this was bound to be, I'd be able to drive down my own street when I got back to Tel Aviv, whether I'd be able to get home.

Chapter thirteen

Twenty-one years ago, the route from Jerusalem to Tirza began in the Sheikh Jarrah neighborhood, climbed up Mount Scopus on a road on which dozens of people in a convoy heading for Hadassah Hospital had been murdered during the War of Independence, and from there turned northward. Now Maya is telling me to go straight up Route 1. After stopping at the last traffic light at the bottom of French Hill in order to pick up three hitchhikers from among a crowd of settlers looking for rides, she says to head straight into the neighborhood of Shu'afat, from there to Atarot and then on into El-Bireh and Ramallah.

"Not so good to drive here without reinforced windows," she states quietly, as though hoping I wouldn't hear, and then adds more loudly, "But let's not worry about that. Since Oslo they've been throwing a lot fewer rocks."

"So maybe," I challenge her, smiling, "maybe that means the Oslo accords weren't such a bad deal?"

Maya sighs impatiently as if to say I am beyond hope. "Where do you come from, Mom? They're only biding their time, holding off on throwing rocks at Jews only as long as they think they can get more land and a better deal out of Israel. The moment they've gotten everything they can through diplomatic means, they have every intention, according to their Phased Plan, of returning to the armed struggle."

I shiver. How decisive my daughter sounds, how sure of her own righteousness.

"Only next time," she continues fiercely, "they won't use rocks. They'll have all those guns we're giving them now as part of the accords, and they'll have all the weapons and bombs they've smuggled in now that we're not looking, and they'll have their bomb factories which we can no longer monitor like we used to, thanks to the *peace* agreement."

She starts the tape again and we hear the light, carefree voice of Naomi Shemer: "*I'll go for a stroll / Across the Land of Israel.*" I know that in theory Ramallah and El-Bireh are part of the Land of Israel, but I can no longer hear the earth calling out from beneath the wheels of the car as I did twenty-one years before. Maybe it is still calling out, maybe it is just that I can no longer hear it pleading, *Save me, redeem me, return unto me since I am yours.*

"Soon they'll open the new Ramallah Bypass so we won't have to take this whole long route," my daughter tries to comfort me.

I nod my head, not telling her that I rather enjoy driving through the streets of Ramallah, filled with men reveling as they flow out of the mosques after the Friday prayer; or that it is really nice to think that maybe there is finally a modicum of peace after all, however fleeting. I like the yellow taxis the Palestinians have now, remarkably similar to the cabs in New York; and I am pleased to see that the private cars which pass us have spiffy new white license plates with green numbers signifying the Palestinian Authority, instead of those ugly blue plates which the Israeli occupation authority had in the past issued to residents of the territories, with a Hebrew letter written to signify which city they were from—*resh* for Ramallah, *het* for Hebron, *bet* for Bethlehem. The streets are clean and well-maintained, studded with grand marble houses adorned with balconies and verandas with wrought-iron railings and crowned with miniature Eiffel Towers on their rooftops. The PLO flag, which had been banned until recently, now waves everywhere, and every once in a while we pass by one of the joint security patrols where Israeli soldiers and Palestinian policemen keep the watch as one man with one heart.

Twenty-one years ago we traveled in a bus that huffed and puffed and belched diesel fumes, and I watched the crowds in the streets and tried to explain to Yair that you can't conquer people and leave them forever without a national identity. "So what exactly do you suggest?" he would answer without bothering to take a serious look at Ramallah's residents, and I would look out the window at occupied Arabs walking down occupied streets and going in and out of occupied stores, and I would say to them in my heart, *Rebel already, rebel already, rise up against the military regime already, against the neglect and the whitewash. One day this will all blow up anyway. You can't remain occupied and without an identity forever, so what are you waiting for? Force the State of Israel to stop putting off the reckoning, force the Jewish people to make clear once and for all whose land this is.*

Eight years ago they finally started rebelling, but when the Intifada erupted I could no longer remember why I had ever believed that an Arab revolt would force the Jews to understand that the Land of Israel was their own. And I no longer understood why I had been so sure it would be such an awful, terrible thing to divide—for the sake of just a little peace and personal security—this seething strip of land between us, so that it might cool off just a little.

Maya is chatting with the hitchhikers in the backseat, and I take advantage of the moment to focus on my breathing, slowing and lengthening my inhales and exhales in a way that can, according to my yoga teacher, prepare me for stressful events like the imminent encounter with Yair. "Breathe like a flute," she says. "Mouth closed, the air enters the nose and passes down the throat as through a flute, into the lungs and then back out again." Thirty years before, Yair and I had discovered, on the roof of the Notre Dame church in Jerusalem, that thousands of real people lived and breathed on the other side of the Old City wall. Now I see a strip of auto repair shops at the northern outskirts of El-Bireh, and then, after a steep incline, there suddenly appear on our right rows and rows of red-roofed stone houses, climbing the hills off the side of the road.

"That's it, Mom," Maya announces. "There at that gas station you make a right."

But where is Tirza? I want to ask, as if I've been expecting to find the little troupe of pallid trailers that had rested on the bare hillock the last time I was here. My heart pounds like that of a girl in love. *Why have I spent the last six months studying yoga if now I am unable to breathe?* So here I am, following my daughter's instructions, turning the wheel to the right, dropping off the hitchhikers at the seminary, driving past pretty houses with luscious gardens, pulling over in front of one of the houses, which has a beautiful swing made of Scandinavian wood decorating the front yard, as though this were a resort and not an invader colony in the heart of enemy territory.

This is where they live? I want to ask, but as in a nightmare I am unable to make a sound.

"This is the Arbivs' house," Maya says, opening the car door, and I recall how Maya had explained to me the day before that we would be staying in the house of a family who were going away for Shabbat to a bar-mitzvah. "They were worried you wouldn't be able to handle their pets," she laughs as a little brown dog and three cats welcome us at the door, "but I told them you actually like animals."

Inside we discover a large Dalmatian that has reached grand old age, an iguana frozen on the branch of a giant indoor fig tree, its expressionless eyes narrowing every few seconds, and an aquarium filled with tropical fish. I am filled with reverence and jealousy when I hear that in the backyard they raise rabbits and tortoises—and that the Arbiv family also raises humans. They have six children of their own, plus three more they took in for foster care.

When we finish getting ready—which includes putting up water to boil in the electric urn, making the beds in which we would sleep, feeding the dogs and cats, and changing to Shabbat clothes—we leave the house and make our way to the Bermans.

Before we go, I hole myself up in the bathroom in order to look in the mirror over the sink and see what *they* would soon see, Yair and Leah. An average-looking woman stares back at me, neither fat nor thin, nor sad nor happy, not stupid but not smart either. I've recently started putting reddish highlights in my brown hair, and it still curls about my face just as it did when I was a girl. My eyes are still big and bright, though now they sink a bit deeper in their sockets and dark shadows have gathered below them. My skin has not yet begun to wrinkle, and I remember how when I was sixteen I would stand and grumble in front of the full-length mirror at Grandma Rochel's house, using two fingers to assault the red pimples that had erupted on my chin and cheeks, and Aunt Batya would tried to comfort me, "Don't worry Shlomtzi, it's good to have oily skin. At the age of forty your oily skin will be smooth and wrinkle-free."

I thought she had gone mad. "I want to be pretty at sixteen. Who the hell cares how I'll look when I'm an elderly forty-year-old hag teetering on the brink of death?"

But now here I am, and here is my oily skin, the pimples forgotten and with them all the lofty dreams of a girl who wanted to take the world by storm, and in the bathroom of a stranger settler family stands a mediocre woman, a grown woman whose stitches are unraveled and whose face has finally come to resemble those of the man and woman who had brought her into the world. Now I could finally disclose that those two seemed to have been my real parents, after all.

❧

Maya is marching me down a paved path through a shady thicket burgeoning with flowers. I feel like Alice, who went for a walk near her home one day and then plunged into a wonderland with rules of its own. I would give anything at this moment to drink the potion she received, the one that makes you so small you can barely be seen.

At the entrance to a two-story house made of stone and covered with rich, colorful bougainvilleas, a thin man wearing a large knitted *kippa* stands hunched over an old bicycle. His hair is graying about the back of his thick, rough neck, but his beard is still dark. The man is trying, unsuccessfully, to put the bike's chain, which is now dangling around the pedals, back on the gears. A boy of about eleven, who stands watching him tensely, says, "Okay, enough, Dad. You don't know how to fix things, and I can just run there on foot." The graying man who doesn't know how to fix things sees Maya and me as we enter the yard, and upon recognizing us he quickly straightens himself. I can see that his eyes have not changed. His face has, but I can't make out exactly how.

"Maya," he says in a happy tone of voice, "I'm so glad you're here. How were the roads?"

"No trouble at all," Maya replies. "I'd like you to meet my mother, Shlomtzion. Mom, this is Rabbi Yair."

"Hello," Yair and I say in unison. I smile politely, wondering whether he's noticed that I have grown taller, finding it hard to believe that I am I and he is he and that this is our meeting in the middle of our lives.

"And this is Hananel," Maya adds warmly as she puts her hand on the shoulder of the eleven-year-old boy, who is smiling at me with Lealeh's pure, modest smile.

As I enter the living room I am introduced to six more children of varying ages, not including my future son-in-law Ariel, who knows how sometimes I really need a cup of coffee, and rushes into the kitchen to make me one. Among the children I am able to quickly identify Ziv, a girl of seven with Down's Syndrome, whom Maya had told me about, ceremoniously declaring her to be the embodiment of love. "I swear to you, Mom, in your whole life you have never met a human being who knows how to love the way Ziv does."

The bustle of Shabbat preparations allows Leah and me to hide our emotional turmoil. Leah has grown chubby, but the extra padding only adds a soft, magical, angelic effect, and her green eyes shine as before. Her head is covered with an ethnic kerchief, its corners meeting at the top of her high brow, and my heart contracts as she and Maya run toward each other and exchange easy kisses, like this is something they do regularly, for I know that Maya wants to be like her, not like me.

I sip my coffee and take in the room: Books and plants and more books and an enormous dining room table and more books and large windows looking over the mountains—all exactly as I had imagined it all these years. Rabbi Yair Berman answers the telephone, sets up the candlesticks, and speaks to his children, his eyes anxiously avoiding mine. His wife the rabbanit places pots of food on the electric hotplate, directs one of the older girls to start setting the table, and asks us politely how the trip was, whether the traffic was bad on the way out of Jerusalem, did we have everything we needed at the Arbivs' house. Maya and Ariel sit beside me, pining for one another and oblivious to everything. Yair's and my past is crouching in the room like a clumsy dinosaur with enormous legs folded on the floor, a gargantuan head brushing up against the ceiling and a long thick tail filling the hallway; but the lovebirds don't notice it. I suddenly realize we will have to tell them everything during the course of the Shabbat, and a sense of dread begins to spread through me.

❧

Leah declares that she's exhausted and would rather stay home and go to synagogue the next morning; I choose to attend evening prayers together with Maya and Ariel's sisters. I still don't have the strength to be alone with my replacement, who seems disappointed that as soon as the Shabbat candles are lit I wish her *Shabbat shalom* and head out into the twilight with the girls. Had she wanted to speak with me alone? Had she wanted to work out together how we would tell our story to my daughter and their son?

The main synagogue of Tirza, a large, hexagonal building with long stained-glass windows, sits in the heart of the settlement atop its highest hill. Basing myself on its views to the West—the Ramallah suburbs, the Jilazun refugee camp, the village of Gofna—I gather that this is probably the very hilltop that Yair and I stood on together on that promise-filled night so long ago. *The thoughts of man are many, but the designs of the Lord prevail*; if the Rosh Yeshiva had not scuttled our plans and done everything he could to thwart them, today there would be no Maya in this world, and no Ariel, and then what would have become of us?

In twenty-one years I haven't entered a synagogue, even on Yom Kippur; in twenty-one years I haven't prayed from a siddur; but now my fingers run through the pages of their own accord, quickly finding the Shabbat evening service. *Let us go and rejoice in God / Let us sound the trumpet for the Rock of our salvation / We shall welcome Him in thanksgiving...*

❧

When the services end and the congregation begins leaving, I make my way down the stairs from the women's section, caught in a throng of women chatting among themselves and smiling their pleasant Shabbat smiles. I had guessed that Maya and her sisters-in-law-to-be were behind me, but when the river of women spits me out into the chilly air, Maya does not follow. I stand and wait by the edge of the plaza, but the stairwell empties out, and still no sign of the girls. I figure that they probably hadn't seen which way I'd gone, and went out one of the other exits. I circle around the building's six walls, but no Maya; she probably assumed that I had set off to the Bermans' on my own, and then ran ahead to try and catch up with me. But where is the Bermans' house? I can't remember which of the paths running to the synagogue from six directions we had taken to get there. After some deliberation I pick one and, hesitatingly, start down it.

The path is deserted, as everyone has already reached their homes, and through the windows I can hear families gathering for their Shabbat meals, choruses of voices singing, *Peace unto you / O*

Angels of Peace / Angels on High! I remember how much I had wanted to have Shabbats like these, how much I had wanted to greet the angels in a Shabbat home full of light and children and joy.... Then suddenly a dog jumps out of someone's yard, barking at me fiercely. In my fright I leap aside. I collide with a woman who just then appears on my right, stepping on her foot. "Pardon me, I'm so sorry," I say. And to my surprise the woman is Shlomit Gur, my beloved youth counselor from my days in Bnei Akiva, to whom I had sent a condolence letter six months before, upon the murder of her son Yenon and his bride-to-be.

"Shlomit?" I cry, and as she turns to me, I see her eyes are misty and her expression distant. She needs a few seconds to bring herself back from wherever her thoughts have taken her in order to understand who I am, and when she finally recognizes me, her mouth bends in sort of a smile, while the rest of her countenance remains sad and lost.

"What are you doing in Tirza, Shlomtzion?" she asks hoarsely, and then remembers. "Ah, yes, Leah told me that your daughter got engaged to their son. You know, they were both very close with my Nonny."

Shlomit offers to show me the way to the house of Leah and Rabbi Yair, which she says is in the opposite direction, on the other side of the synagogue. As she walks with me I notice her belly is large and protruding, like that of a woman at the end of her ninth month of pregnancy. Following my eyes, Shlomit says bitterly, "No, I'm not pregnant, I can't get pregnant any more. But from the day my Nonny was butchered, my stomach just keeps growing, getting bigger and bigger. Maybe my womb just wants to give birth to Nonny all over again."

As soon as I get my bearings, I tell Shlomit that I can make it the rest of the way on my own, and that she should hurry home since surely they are waiting for her to begin the meal.

"Don't worry, Shlomtzion," she replies, her voice dead. "They won't wait for me. They're used to my wandering around outside and showing up late. Since my Nonny was butchered, I can't be inside the house more than half an hour at a time, night or day, and certainly not during Shabbat dinner."

It seems like she means to continue walking with me forever, throughout the generations, or at least for the rest of her mournful days, walking and walking without end, but then Ariel runs up to us, breathing a sigh of relief when he sees me. "Hey, there you are. Maya said you'd gotten lost." And my counselor Shlomit turns and walks off, disappearing together with her enormous abdomen and phantom fetus before I have a chance to thank her and say goodbye.

❦

In the Bermans' house the giant table is covered with a white tablecloth and set with beautiful dinnerware, and they begin singing *Peace Unto You, O Angels of Peace* the moment Ariel and I enter, as though we are the angels they're singing about. Yair stands at the head of the table, rocking back and forth to the rhythm, his voice pleasant, his wife like a fruitful vine, his children like olive saplings around the table, and here also am I, twenty-one years after being discarded like refuse, called upon to hand over to these blessed people the miraculous gift that was given to me and dear Rosy, my only daughter whom I raised with what little strength I had left.

After Kiddush, all the children line up according to age, each in turn approaching Yair, who places his hands on their heads to bless them. My Maya, too, stands in line and receives a blessing like the rest, as though she is theirs, as though Rosy was just some anonymous sperm donor and I a surrogate mother, as though from the moment of her birth Maya legally and truthfully belonged to this good and proper family. Everyone washes their hands and sits for the bread. Maya and the two oldest girls begin to shuttle back and forth to the kitchen, serving the dishes the woman of the house has prepared in honor of the Shabbat, in honor of her family, in honor of my Iri, for whom I was supposed to be making Shabbat meals and having children and smiling across the table as everyone sings a soft, sweet melody, *Rest and happiness / A light unto the Jews / The sabbati-*

cal day / A day of delights. I am Menashe-Haim, of S.Y. Agnon's *And the Crooked Shall Be Made Straight,* who returns to his home after an arduous journey and finds that his wife has taken him for dead and married another.

Yair and Leah keep stealing glances at me, probably wondering how I am holding up, how my life is going, what I think of them, and whether I have gotten over the past. For their sake I do my best to sit straight, smiling, chatting warmly with their children, and hugging Ziv, the wonderful little girl who, despite being mentally disabled, still excels in love and who wants to show that love by cuddling endlessly with me—which makes Yair and Leah worry that she is bothering me, but I insist she isn't. The older kids take turns wiping the drool off Ziv's chin and taking her off my lap every so often, so that I can eat as well. Towards the end of the meal, after the vegetable soup, the roasted chicken, the rice, the sweet carrot salad, the baked potatoes and the steamed cabbage, after the songs and a few words of Torah and more songs but before dessert, Ziv goes to cuddle with Maya, and her place on my lap is immediately taken by four-and-a-half year-old Tzofia, a darling child with hair in pigtails and pink ribbons.

Yair and his older children share their experiences of that morning, when they had been among the dozens of people from the settlement who'd stormed a hilltop on which the members of Tirza intend to start a new neighborhood.

An argument ensues around the question of whether it was really appropriate to make the soldiers evacuate them from the hill by force, or better to leave as soon as the battalion commander issued the order, thereby sparing the poor soldiers all that toil and trauma.

"The government doesn't understand that the hilltop is right next to our settlement," Maya tries to explain to me. "And that if we don't settle it, the Palestinians will set up shop there, and then they'll be able to come down here and enter our houses at will."

"Rabin is wicked," little Tzofia suddenly announces in a loud and very serious voice, and everybody's eyes turn to me uncomfortably.

"Oh, no need to worry," Maya laughs. "My mom already figured out that we don't really worship Rabin."

Yair, however, is not comforted. "Doesn't matter," he shakes his head, agitated. "In this house, under no circumstances are we to use harsh words to describe the prime minister of Israel. Come to Daddy, Tzofialeh, and tell me where you heard people talking like that."

Tzofia slides off of my lap and approaches him slowly, her lower lip jutting forward and her head down. Yair holds out his arms and draws her to him.

"Where *doesn't* she hear people talking like that?" Benaya, the sixteen-year-old, says to his father. "'Rabin is wicked' is nothing compared to some of the things people say around here."

"If my mom's friends were here they'd take it hard," Maya says, and I try in vain to imagine Eden and Haviva and the rest of my elephant pack sitting at a Shabbat table in a settlement. "She has friends who think peace is at the door," Maya explains, "and that it's only the settlers who stand in its way."

"It's Rabin's fault that people think of us that way—Rabin calls us enemies of peace," the children begin shouting angrily from all sides, upbraiding their father as though he were the prime minister's defense attorney, and they the witnesses for the prosecution.

"He says we're not real Israelis."

"He says he's responsible for the security of only ninety-seven percent of the country's citizens, but not for ours."

"He hates us."

"He 'couldn't give a hoot' about us."

"He says we're a cancer in the body of the state!"

"Even if all that is true," their father insists quietly, "Yitzhak Rabin is still the prime minister of the Jewish state, the prime minister of our holy and beloved State of Israel, the first blossoming of our redemption, which the Holy One granted us the privilege of building and living in after so many years of being a dispersed people, exiled among the nations. Even if the prime minister is wrong, he's still the prime minister, and we, in *this* house, will speak of him with respect and honor."

Leah ladles fruit salad from a large bowl into saucers, but things do not quiet around the table. The children keep exchanging evidence of the revulsion that Rabin feels toward them, and the comparison he often draws between the settlers and Hamas terrorists. Yifat, the nineteen-year-old who is every bit as beautiful and perfect as Leah was at her age, declares unequivocally that Rabin and Peres are traitors. Leah chastises her, "You can't speak like that about the leaders of the State of Israel, Yifati, for even they have a great deal of merit." And Ariel says, "I'm really worried about the terrible hopelessness that more than half the nation feels because of Rabin, Dad. It's creating a rift in Israeli society that may never heal."

Yair kisses Tzofia on curls done up with pink ribbons, gently lowers her to the floor, and sends her back to her chair to eat her dessert. "Yes, there's a whole lot of hopelessness and frustration," he agrees with his eldest, "and this obligates us to do whatever we can to calm people down, to channel their energies to positive things like study and education—"

"Study and education!" Yifat snorts. "Who's got time for study and education when those leftists are destroying the country? Soon there won't be anything left of it."

Her father concedes a little. "The anger and frustration can be channeled to lawful demonstrations against the government's policies. But we must make sure," he cautions, finger raised warningly, "we must make sure, that under no circumstances do we *ever* allow things to turn violent."

"I'm worried as well," Leah says, glancing at me sidelong as though she hesitates to speak her mind in my presence, but then continuing nonetheless. "There are many stupid people going around saying that Rabin and Peres can be put in the category of a *rodef*—a person who is actively endangering others, and needs to be killed. They quote it in the name of rabbis, claiming that a halakhic ruling was issued about it. Lately I worry that these rumors might reach some crazy extremist, who will do something horrible."

This causes me to tremble. "Do you really think anybody would do something to harm Rabin or Peres?"

"A crazed political assassin, an extremist? Yes," she replies sadly. "I think somebody like that would."

"That's what we have the Shin Bet for," Ariel says dismissively. "You can count on them having a file on every nutcase and extremist."

"And don't forget about the Shin Bet's security guards," Benaya adds. "They make a tight security cordon around Rabin and Peres and don't let anyone get close to them."

"Okay," Leah sighs. "I don't mean that anyone could ever actually succeed in harming Rabin or Peres. But can you just imagine what would happen to this country if someone even tried and failed?"

The attempt to envision what would happen casts a pall over the whole room.

"The Left would never forgive the Right," Leah says, moved by her own question. "It would start a civil war that would continue for generations."

"And they would use the assassination attempt as an excuse to evacuate all the settlements," Moria, seventeen-and-a-half, adds to the doomsday scenario, using her spoon to push aside the raisins in her fruit salad.

The disturbing conversation comes to a close as Yair declaims a few words of Torah, calming the atmosphere a little. We all then say the *birkat hamazon*, grace after meals, clear the dishes and remaining food with alacrity, and place a clean tablecloth on the giant table. Leah asks Yifat and Moria to put the younger children to bed, while we adults stay in the living room with herbal tea, cookies, and nuts, which the young couple serve in style before joining us themselves, triumphantly plopping themselves down.

"So, what do you think of Tirza?" Ariel turns to me. "Is this what you thought a settlement would look like on the inside?"

"It's beautiful here," I answer, suddenly entertained by the way Yair's son has become a twin of the young Yair I had loved, whereas Yair himself has become a grown-up rabbi, with gray hair, rough skin, and a faded expression. "Truth is," I hear myself answering the second half of his question, "I never imagined that the inside of the town would look the way it does today. So many years have passed since I was last here with your father."

Both couples lurch back in their seats, as if I have thrown a bomb into the middle of the room. I myself am shocked by what I have just said. I wonder whether the lemon verbena tea I have just drunk is known to be an intoxicant.

"What do you mean, since you were last here with—" Maya gasps.

She and her groom look from me to his father and then back to me and then back to his father, and I regret with all my heart that I have never told her anything, but I do not regret beginning to tell her now.

"Ask Ariel's parents," I propose, in the face of the horrified expressions they have fastened on me.

Maya and Ariel look expectantly at the champion of my youth and his Torah-scholar's daughter, as though praying that they would say I was only kidding.

"You want to tell them about it now?" Yair asks hesitantly.

"Why not?" I answer coldly, taking another sip of the verbena tea in order to warm up a bit, but not too much.

"Tell us about *what*?" my daughter demands, as their son raises his voice impatiently. "What is going on here?"

"It's fine," Leah interrupts, folding her arms, "I mean, the two of you would have had to tell them about it sooner or later." As though the burden were only on Yair and me, as though she were not part of the story, as though she had not stolen him from me under the cover of her saccharine righteousness.

Seeing that Maya is on the verge of tears, Yair clears his throat and tries to calm things down. "It's not some awful secret, Maya, Ariel. Nothing terrible happened to anybody."

"Nothing terrible happened to anybody," I repeat, smiling cynically. "Just one stupid girl's life was destroyed."

"Your life was destroyed," Yair critiques what I said, "because of our story, or because of what happened after?"

"What happened after wouldn't have happened if not for what you call 'our story'."

Now Maya is holding her hands over her face. I draw near and try to hug her, but she pulls away, cringing.

"Now look," Yair begins, lurching forward and rubbing his beard as though he were trying to solve a Talmudic puzzle. "What Maya's mother means is that we knew each other when we were kids. Her grandparents lived near mine, and we used to play together... You know, the way kids play..."

"We were twins," I correct, my voice choking. "As we grew older, we were in love. He was the focus of all meaning in my life. I lived only to be with him. I loved him more than you can imagine—"

The words strike me as silly and pathetic, but Maya rouses herself, draws close and puts her warm arm around me. "Mom, Mom, why didn't you ever tell me about this?" And I am so happy she is listening to me that I continue to babble, like a little girl tattling on one of her friends to the kindergarten teacher. "We wanted to get married, Mayaleh, we were about to get married. Heaven rejoiced, ask *him* if heaven didn't rejoice—"

But suddenly I am ashamed. Suddenly I remember Iri, remembered Lealeh, remember the young couple...and I am so humiliated at how pitiful, abandoned, and betrayed I am, a forty-year-old woman telling tales like some whiny, spoiled little baby, sobbing like a teenager who's been dumped. And I fall silent, rise from the couch and make a beeline to the door.

"I'm sorry," I mumble as I flee. "I'll be right back." Wandering down the path to the bougainvillea beds and beyond, I am sure Maya will come after me, and then I'll be able to tell her the whole story in a more orderly fashion. But instead of Maya's soft footfalls behind me, I hear other ones, familiar ones. I turn and see Yair hurrying after me, agitated, and I speed my escape. But he catches up with me and silently sticks by my side, directing me toward the perimeter road that circles all the way around Tirza. We walk for a long time without saying a word, and all I can think about is the fact that we are walking a long while without saying a word.

"How embarrassing!" I say after a while, trying to slip back into the mask that I had been wearing for twenty years but which has suddenly fallen off.

"What's embarrassing?" Yair counters, his voice surprisingly soft and warm. "I never knew you felt that way, Shlomtzion. It never occurred to me that it still hurts you this much. I never even imagined you were so badly hurt back then, when it happened—"

"You never imagined I was so badly hurt back then?" In disbelief I slow my pace, nearly coming to a stop.

Yair is searching for words. "I thought...I thought you never really..."

He looks ahead, and I gaze at the profile that has become so alien to me, at the moustache that nearly covers his upper lip, at the beard that conceals the dimple on his right cheek, at the modest belly that has grown out over his belt.

"I never really what?"

"You never really loved me."

We walk on in the dark. To our left are the houses of Tirza, surrounded by trees and greenery like fortress walls; to our right, down the slope, is the Ramallah-Nablus highway, the path where our patriarchs walked when the land was first promised to them. Arab cars drive on it now in both directions, their horns occasionally tooting a gay melody. Scattered along the mountaintops on the far side of the highway are the lights of the Jilazun refugee camp. In the late 1940s hundreds of families were exiled there from their beautiful villages, upon the ruins of which the Jewish state was built. In its squalid houses they now live, raising a fourth generation of refugees who hate Yair and me and all of us and who weave dreams of return to their true homes.

"For me it was really love," the famous rabbi says, his lips quivering between moustache and beard. "But with you it was all sort of cerebral."

A dull weakness begins spreading through me, rising through my chest and working its way toward my fingertips.

"You never really wanted to be mine," he continues, "but

instead to mend the world in the Kingdom of God, or however you said it back then. I felt like I needed a woman who would love me. A wife—not just a partner..."

"And the Rosh Yeshiva?" I ask, enervated, my voice barely audible. "The Rosh Yeshiva's refusal to give us his blessing..."

Yair breathes deeply and with difficulty.

"I thought the Rosh Yeshiva was helping me understand that my concerns were valid ones. I was sure that he opposed our marriage because he saw right away that you were merely dependent on me, that you needed me, but did not really love me."

Could he please cut it out with the "didn't really love me" bit? What could it possibly mean to "really love" someone, if not exactly what I felt for him from the day I could first feel and think?

"Merely dependent on you?"

"Merely dependent on me. Yes. Rabbi Moishe Schor warned me about a marriage of dependence. He said that dependence is not love, dependence is destructive... Today I, too, warn my students against dependent relationships that masquerade as love."

The weakness spreads as I think to myself, *Rabbi Moishe Schor? Was the Rabbanit Hava Schor also part of this?*

"I tried several times to see whether I was mistaken," he continues, "to see if maybe you did feel for me even a tenth of what I felt for you. But every time I tried, you kept saying that you couldn't live without me—in other words, that you were dependent on me. Every time you said that, it strengthened my conviction that I had to listen to the Rosh Yeshiva."

Me? I strengthened his conviction to dump me? Why didn't he just ask me straight out, "Shlomtzion, do you love me?" Why didn't he give me a chance?

And Yair answers, as though reading my thoughts, "There was no point in asking you about your feelings, Shlomtzion. It was obvious that you were absolutely sure you loved me, that in your opinion to love someone was to dominate him, to breathe through his nostrils, to set off with him to lead the Jewish people and to be with him a light unto nations."

Without noticing, our steps have slowed. He hesitates before continuing, apparently afraid of hurting me, but when I purse my lips and glare at him, the words begin pouring out of his mouth again, sharp and clear, as though he has been rehearsing them from the day we broke up. "You were too ethereal for me. You always aimed for the highest mountaintops, for what could never be reached. I worshipped you for this, but when we were about to get married, I got scared."

"Scared of *what*?" I shout, startling a group of girls walking by us.

"Scared—Shlomtzion, I was scared that I wouldn't have the strength to spend my entire life living up to your expectations."

"My expectations!" I hurl at him in a whisper, "When did I ever ask you to meet my expectations?"

"When didn't you?" He stops, raising eyes full of agony and laughs bitterly. "You don't remember the way you drove me crazy during that time when you were so revolted by the things of this world? And then you reversed yourself. Suddenly you wanted the two of us to sanctify the name of God *through* this world like no one had ever sanctified His name before, and you pushed me to go to yeshiva and study Torah like a superhero."

"You yourself wanted that," I protest.

"Because I wanted to satisfy you," his voice is adamant. "That was what you wanted. You insisted that I be perfect and unique, and you kept saying I had to train myself to be a leader…"

"But *you* came up with the idea of Prophets' Town."

"Because you demanded it! You decided that we had to be prophets, you got the idea in your head that the world was waiting for us. The vision of Prophets' Town was yours—I just joined in because I loved you so much."

I want to answer, to argue, but the truth closes in around me like the ancient Samarian mountains that surround us in the dark: *The Rosh Yeshiva saved Yair, he rescued him from me before it was too late.*

"So you went and fell in love with Lealeh." My voice breaks as I formulate the conclusion.

"No, Shlomtzion. The Lord will not forgive me until the day

I die for having betrayed the holy bond between man and wife, the secret, eternal point that is the essence of man, but I never fell in love with Leah. I never was able to love her the way I loved you."

By the side of the path I see a bench under a weeping willow and I drag myself over to it, sitting down, utterly spent. Tirza's newest neighborhood spreads itself out below me, serene and sparkling and bright, with only the far-off lights of Bir Zeit standing between it and heaven.

"You should just know," Yair says in a voice shaking with emotion, getting closer to the bench and lowering his voice so not to be overheard by the packs of teenagers strolling on the road behind us, "just know that when I gave up on you, I also gave up on myself. On the life I had wanted. Everything I had become before the breakup was thanks to you."

I shake my head, trying to dismiss him. "What are you talking about?" I sigh, but he is on a roll.

"You heard me right, Shlomtzion. What was I when we first met? An average kid, imprisoned in a past and a personality that destined me for an unimaginative, uninspired life. Meeting you opened the whole world up before me, opened myself up before me. You made me, for a time, special like yourself. Do you remember what you were like as a girl?"

I do not answer. Yair sits at the end of the bench. I move over to give him room, but he just stays perched on the edge, as though he must leave enough space between us to accommodate another person. His voice is full of affection, almost joyful, as he describes what I was like as a girl.

"You were full of surprises, crazy, like you'd come from another planet. You had me under your spell the moment I met you. You probably don't remember where that was, but that early morning clinging to the bars of the fish store is engraved in my memory. From the outset I ran to help that screaming cat only because I thought you might be there. I had already been keeping tab on you before then, and I knew you always watched out for all those disgusting cats that roamed the neighborhood."

I grin.

"No, really," he assures me, "I can't explain it, but as a child I felt like the Lord had sent you to console me on the loss of my father and to prepare me for life. You were like King Midas, you had a touch of gold, and when you touched me… All those books I read under your influence, the treasures you revealed to me, our philosophical discussions, our adventures—"

Suddenly the joy in his voice diminishes, replaced with a deep sadness. "I wouldn't have gotten anywhere without you, Shlomtzion. When you were in America, and I left high school and entered the yeshiva, it was your inspiration that got me there, and I did it so that I could be more worthy of you than those American friends you loved so much. Later, when I excelled in the army, in my Torah study, it was all for you. Ever since you stopped being a part of my life I've become an ordinary human being, a man of the spirit who lives his whole life off the spiritual reserves he built up in his youth. Of the great maelstroms of the soul, the thirst for the living God, the true aspirations of the spirit—of these I have only memories."

"But all over the country people admire you. Throngs come to attend your lectures. You have your own yeshiva, students, a family…"

Yair lets his head and shoulders drop as though he were a rag doll, as though his life had run out and all that was left of him was colored cloth filled with cotton wool.

"Longing. Longing is what I have. I would be better off never having been created." For some reason he utters these last words with a laugh, or maybe it is a sob.

In the tortured silence that shrouds us my whole world flies up into the air, flips over twice and lands on its side.

"Iri," my voice caresses him at the end of the silence. "Iri."

My heart goes out to this saddened man.

To the teenager.

To the child.

"You just can't imagine," he says hoarsely, his mouth opening and closing and then opening again, "you can't imagine how worked up I got about this weekend… Sure, I had time to prepare for it—after all Maya resembles you so much… But to see you, yourself, here, to talk to you, to sit with you at the table in the house that is mine and Leah's, the house in which I have been trying, day after day, for twenty-one years, to build a life for myself to replace the one I never had with you…"

This confession is difficult to hear. I would have liked to tell him that I too have gotten worked up about it, that I too have longed for him all these years, that I too still love him to this very day—but I no longer know if it is true. *This is Iri,* I remind myself, *Iri, whom your soul loved, Iri for whom you craved with every ounce of your being, Iri who slipped away and was gone, whom you had sought but never found, and now here he is…*

But nothing stirs inside me, for I am an extinguished woman. I extinguished myself many years ago, and I burn no more.

Not looking at him I say, carefully, slowly, "At first I also thought I wouldn't be able to live without you."

"At first?" His voice is full of pain, as though I have slapped him.

"I went on with my life, Iri. I had to survive."

"You stopped loving me."

I am so full of compassion for him, my eyes fill with tears and I bite my lower lip. "I don't know," I say, "I can't tell anymore what it means to love…"

Yair turns his eyes away from me and looks out on the lights of the Arab town of Bir Zeit. From time to time he quickly raises his hand to cover his face, and then allows it to fall back to his knee in despair.

❧

We sit there for a long while. It's already late, and fewer and fewer people are taking walks on the perimeter road.

"It was because of you that I divorced Rosy," I suddenly say, as though this fact could somehow console him for his life without me.

"Because of me?"

"Because I was so sunk in my mourning over you. Because I was sure you and I were meant for each other, and I couldn't live a lie with another man..."

And suddenly I'm overtaken by tears, deep and overwhelming tears of a kind I have not cried since the divorce. I don't know if they are tears of relief at the fact that Yair has always loved me and wanted me, tears of self-pity for the twenty-one years I have been hurting because I did not know how he felt, or tears of unbearable longing for Rosy's glorious body and magnificent soul.

"Oh, Iri, Iri," I sob. All at once I become aware, as though this fact had been burdening my conscience for many years, that I lost Rosy because of the same chronic fanaticism that lost me Yair. I was a creature of black and white, forever refusing to compromise with reality, forever rushing from one extreme to another, forever wanting too much, and forever left with nothing.

Without thinking I allow the weight of my sorrow to knock me over, directly into the narrow frame of the man sitting beside me, and my arms wrap around him as one embraces a brother, or a childhood friend, my face burrowing into his chest. Yair is startled, and I can feel his body stiffen as his heart races wildly beneath my cheek. He looks around to make sure no one sees us and then tightly closes his eyes and touches my hair ever so gently, trembling from head to foot.

❧

The universe is a new and different universe when we finally stand up nearly an hour after midnight and begin treading down the perimeter road, now empty of pedestrians. We are exhausted and hollow as we walk. *Before we were created we were already unworthy, and now that we are created, it is as though we never were created. We are but dust in death—all the more so in life!* In the silence that reigns between us I believe I hear a voice far above, laughing. *He who is in Heaven will laugh, the Lord will mock us.*

"You know," I say, "after you broke up with me I discovered that the lovers in the Song of Songs don't keep missing each other, the way we were always taught. I realized that they avoid each other on purpose, that they deliberately do not allow their love to be fulfilled. The whole Song of Songs is about two lovers who make every effort not to find each other, even by chance."

"Why?"

"Maybe because one shouldn't awaken love before it is desired. Maybe they just understand that the world isn't ready for a love like theirs."

"If she's not trying to meet him," Yair asks disinterestedly, as though he no longer cares, "why does she get up to answer the door?"

"She gets up only when she knows he's no longer waiting on the other side. She opens it only when she's sure that, hearing her stir, he has already run away."

Yair drags his feet, one after another, apathetic.

I rose up to open to my beloved, but my beloved had withdrawn and was gone. I called him, but he gave no answer.

"If you feel nothing for me now," he says flatly, "how can you be so sure you loved me back then?"

"I am not sure of anything anymore."

At the Arbivs' house we find Maya and Ariel sitting on the wooden swing in the front yard. When they see us they get up. Ariel leaves with Yair and Maya follows me into the house. The time has come to tell her how she first came into the world.

Chapter fourteen

It was past four in the morning when we finally fell asleep side by side, the calls of the *muezzins* from the village of Dura and the Jilazun camp interweaving overhead, greeting the dawn. But when I wake at seven thirty, Maya is already up and dressed, standing by the kitchen window and looking out at the rabbit and tortoise cages nestled among the flowerbeds that bubble from beneath the fruit trees in the backyard. All manner of animal and plant life, it seems, give the Arbivs pleasure, and thrive under their care. The windowsill itself is full of glass jars and clay pots, each housing an avocado pit sprouting long, proud fronds, or a sweet potato cascading tiny light-colored leaves upon the wall and window frame. Baby cacti are maturing there as well, and fragrant spices evoke in me a yearning for healthy simplicity.

Maya and I hug each other, exchanging only smiles and murmurs, as though we no longer have a need for words, as though they had all been said the night before.

After my coffee I put a light-colored silk kerchief over my hair, and we walk up to the hexagonal synagogue at the top of the hill. We climb to the women's section and sit in the front row, in the seats Lealeh has saved for us beside her own. She smiles a hesitant, half-smile, as if to ask whether she is still allowed to smile at me.

I smile back compassionately. She's beautiful, she's virtuous, she's wise, and her husband has never fallen in love with her.

Lealeh is not the only one looking at me. Last night I had managed to lay low in the corner of the women's section, but this morning people are stealing inquisitive peeks from all directions at the woman in the light-colored silk kerchief—the Bermans' new *mechutenet* who they say is a secular leftist from Tel-Aviv—trying to see how she is handling the fact that her nice daughter Maya has seen the light and become observant.

❧

In the synagogue they read that week's parashah, *Lekh Lekha,* Genesis 12-17, and I am reminded of how the Rosh Yeshiva used to often speak, in his thick Ashkenazi accent, of the Lord's selection of Abraham. Our patriarch was chosen not because he was righteous, not because he warred against idolatry, but because he was willing to get up and leave the land of his birth and his father's house, and go to an unknown land which the Lord showed him. Again and again the Rosh Yeshiva would repeat this idea in his weekly Torah classes on Saturday nights, and Eden—still Edna—and I would smile at each other forgivingly, patronizingly, as we faced the old speaker through which the old man's voice crackled into the women's section. Yair, however, would later explain to me—he was so cute as his eyes sparkled—that the Rosh Yeshiva deliberately went over the essential points in his classes again and again, drilling the fundamental ideas into us so that we would never forget them.

To my surprise, I find I still remember when to stand during the prayers and when to sit; when and how to bow during the *Amida*; that during *Birkat Kohanim,* the priestly benediction, one has to look down or back but under no circumstances to look directly at the priestly *kohanim* who stand upon the dais in front of the Holy Ark like a gathering of ghosts from a horror film, *tallitot* raised above their heads, covering their faces and upper bodies, arms outstretched toward the congregation, fingers spread to bestow the ancient blessing that flows at that very moment down from heaven through them and upon each and every one of us, *The Lord bless thee and keep thee / The Lord shine His face on thee and grant thee grace / The Lord turn his face to thee and give thee peace.* I even remember the melodies of the prayer service, which have barely changed in twenty-one years, and I don't mind singing with them all—why not?—*Return us to thee, O Lord, and we shall return / Renew our days as of old.*

The community of Tirza is large and close-knit. From the balcony of the women's section I look out over the men and boys swaying beneath the stained-glass windows, mounting the raised platform in the middle of the synagogue and descending from it, lovingly surrounding the Torah scroll, with its velvet cover on which is embroidered, in large purple letters, the name of Yenon, the slain son of my counselor Shlomit. When a bar mitzvah boy goes up to read from the Torah, I throw candies just like all the other women, and watch as dozens of children swarm the platform to collect them like starved birds; I am amused when Maya pulls close to me, her face sour and wincing, and says, "This is the only job they give women in this synagogue—to throw candies. Beyond that we are basically spectators here on this side of the partition."

When I raise my eyebrows, she says, "Look, I'm no feminist, Mom. But Ariel says that after we get married I should start a women's *minyan*, where I can pray without the help of men, and express myself not just as a passive observer. He says there's no problem with halakhah, that rabbis have allowed women to pray on their own for some time now."

❧

After the *shacharit* morning prayers and the reception for the bar mitzvah boy, Yair studies Talmud with his sons while Leah and her daughters enter the kitchen to make salads for lunch. I offer to help and am immediately handed a cutting board and a basket of cherry tomatoes.

Yifat, who is standing next to me peeling boiled potatoes for the salad niçoise, is fuming. "Just look where all this talk about territorial compromise is leading!" she complains loudly. "Now my friends tell me that the dean of their high school has declared that we need to start preparing for the day when we might really have to leave this place."

"Chronic Jewish defeatism," her sisters call from their stations along the kitchen counters.

"Infectious Leftism."

"Conceit."

"Are you one hundred percent sure," I ask carefully while cutting my little tomatoes as precisely as possible, "that it wasn't a mistake to build the settlements? Are you sure it has to be out of the question to withdraw, to evacuate a single settlement, even if it is in exchange for real peace?"

The girls shout, protest, upbraid me for the very way I phrased my question. "You should say 'town' and not 'settlement', 'to give away parts of the Land of Israel' and not 'to withdraw', 'to expel Jews' and not 'to evacuate'. And besides, who, precisely, is offering us 'real peace'?"

I want to explain that we have to at least try, but faced with their righteous rage, I give up.

"The important thing is that most of the country stands with us," Moria sums up.

"The Oslo accords are so unpopular," Maya mocks, "that all the serious musicians are refusing to appear at the Left's rally tonight. They're afraid that if they get associated too closely with Rabin and Oslo, people will stop paying to see them in concert."

"Where will all this hatred lead us?" I whisper to myself, but they all hear me, and their sighs fill the kitchen.

❧

The ceremony of washing hands, the festive meal with baked fish, salads, and casseroles, and at the head of the table a defeated man who does not so much as look at me, then all of us removing to the front lawn for coffee and tea and cake and nuts on white plastic chairs. There we are joined by friends and neighbors who have been invited to raise a toast to the engagement of Ariel and Maya. Among the couples I see men and women whom I recognize from back when Yair studied at the graduate yeshiva, and I am delighted when a gentle woman named Einat approaches me. I still remember how she and her husband had assisted me so many years earlier, at the end of that disquieting Purim party, getting me safely home late at night when Yair was stone drunk.

My daughter and his son politely thank all the well-wishers and go off to talk to their friends. I sit restlessly on my plastic chair, and when Leah goes into the house to bring out more offerings, I follow her inside, as if to help.

"Shlomtzion, we have to talk," she blurts as soon as she sees me. "I came undone last night, you have no idea."

"I wanted to tell you that it's really all in the past," I try to assure her. "I don't know why I freaked out like that last night. It's not that I've been in mourning all my life, or anything like that."

She slices apple-cake and lays the slices out on plates, then pours tea and expertly places the cups on a tray. "Wait for me here," she requests. "I'll serve this and come right back." When she returns, she stands facing me with hands outspread, then brings them together as if to clap. "Before we become in-laws, and grandparents of the same grandchildren," she says, "I want you to know, Shlomtzion, that my life didn't exactly turn out the way I'd hoped, either."

She leads me to a porch off the kitchen, taking two chairs with her. I sit down, and she sits facing me, bringing her chair so close that our knees almost touch.

"I wanted Yair before he broke up with you," she confesses, her voice low as she scans the area carefully to make sure none of her children are in hearing range.

I think of our youth together, of the secrets I'd shared only with her—my feelings for Yair, my dreams of marriage. I think of how Yair and I used to walk her from Geula all the way to her parents' apartment in Kiryat Moshe after the Rosh Yeshiva's night classes. Back then she'd symbolized to me all that was good and pure. Now, looking back, I suddenly see everything in a different light—her sidelong glances at him, her sweet smiles, how she spoke to him in a soft, almost beseeching tone that I had never heard her use with anyone else, how she tried to impress him with her knowledge. At that time I harbored neither suspicion nor fear for I was certain that he loved only me, that I would be his wife—*And then it was morning, and behold, it was Leah.*

"When you ran off to Sinai I knew he was ready for marriage," she continues. "After all, the two of you had been about to get married. I asked my father to make the match, but I didn't tell him that Yair already knew me and that he had nearly married my close friend. My father knew nothing, and to this day Yair has no idea that our whole *shidukh* was at my initiative."

She is quite agitated, her hands compulsively tucking her hair back under her kerchief or adjusting the ends of the ethnic fabric along her high, smooth forehead. "The terrible irony," she says, lowering her voice, perfect lips quirking into an off-kilter rueful smile, "is that I never really loved him. I wanted him—I wanted to please my father by marrying a masterful Torah scholar like him, and I think that most of all I wanted to win him because he was yours. I was always so awfully jealous of you, Shlomtzion—of your vast knowledge of Torah, of your unusual spiritual qualities. I always wished that one day Yair would worship me the way he worshiped you."

I listen to her, unable to breath.

"I didn't love him," she confesses again. "And he didn't—" she looks up with her moist green eyes, "he didn't love me either. I really think he is still in love with you, to this very day."

What can I say to her? What does one say to a woman who has lived her whole life without love?

Leah swallows compulsively, then adjusts her kerchief to rein in her wayward hair. Retarded little Ziv suddenly shuffles out onto the porch, her fat tongue lolling out of her mouth and a look of simple, honest joy gracing her misshapen face. At first she prances over to me but when she notices how sad her mother looks, her smile disappears, and she turns to Leah and hugs her with her short, shapeless arms. "Zivi's a good girl," Leah says, caressing her daughter's head reflexively, looking at me as though inwardly questioning whether she has done right by confessing.

Ziv caresses her mother's face, passing a square hand along her cheek to console her.

"Of course, Yair is very dear to me," his wife clarifies quickly. "We've been together twenty-one years, after all. We've come a long way, and we have wonderful children. He is very dear to me, I don't want you to think otherwise…" And she picks up their special little girl and holds her tight against her chest, as though fearing someone would take the child away if her sin was discovered.

The door between the kitchen and the porch opens again, the face of pure-eyed Hananel popping through the crack. "Mom," he says, "Dad sent me to look for you."

As we go back into the house I wonder why Leah had chosen to reveal her secret. Was the disclosure that she never loved Yair meant to somehow recompense me for the fact that I had never married him? We pass through the kitchen and living room and out the front door back to the front yard, where men and women sit in a circle. Yair shoots an inquisitive look at Leah, and she says quietly, "I'm so sorry, we just had to resolve something in there."

On the white plastic chairs, a harsh political debate is under way. Should the settlers fight for their homes, and absolutely refuse to be evacuated, as the majority of those there argue? Or is democracy to be held over everything else, as a few of those seated assert, and therefore there is nothing left to do but to start packing?

"Maybe if the decisions were made in a legitimate way, I could understand it," a skinny, mustachioed man says in anger. "But when major foreign policy resolutions are made on the strength of the Arab votes in the Knesset, they cannot be considered legitimate, democratic decisions."

His friends nod in vigorous assent.

"The Left," an older woman who sounds like a schoolteacher states, "makes cynical use of the votes of Arab citizens, who have already declared their opposition to a Jewish state and identify publicly with the PLO."

"I heard somewhere," somebody adds, "that they're planning on filling the square with Arabs at tonight's rally."

How distant from you I have become, I think to myself, *and how distant you have become from me.* And at that very moment I notice, to my amazement, that Leah's eyes have rested, with infinite softness, on a stocky, smiling fellow who has joined the circle together with his diminutive, bird-like wife.

"Rabbi Yair will probably tell us that we're never allowed to protest against an elected Israeli government," the object of our hostess' yearning glances smiles, trying to drag our host, who is uncharacteristically silent, into the conversation. "What did the Rosh Yeshiva use to call it, Rabbi Yair? 'Sovereignty', right? 'Israeli sovereignty'."

He pronounces the word 'sovereignty' with a thick Ashkenazi accent, just like the Rosh Yeshiva used to say it, and the Rabbanit Leah smiles with pleasure at his wit.

Maybe Leah's life wasn't really loveless. An unruly thought steals into my head, a thought rooted in a kind of sixth sense I sometimes have. *Leah doesn't love Yair,* the unruly thought says to me, *but she does love this stocky, smiling man, whose eyes are now twinkling affectionately back at her.*

"I don't find the issue of sovereignty to be funny at all, Aviram," the skinny moustache says in frustration. "What, you can't even have protest rallies any more in this 'democratic' country? Trust me—if the Rosh Yeshiva were alive today, he too would think that the Rabin-Darawshe government is not a holy government."

Leah is in love with Aviram, I decide. *She lives with Yair and they raise their children together, but Aviram is the reason she goes on living. Only for Aviram does she get up in the morning, only for Aviram does she go to work, put on makeup, laugh, and live another day. One cannot live without love.*

Without planning to, I hear myself getting involved in the debate.

"Excuse me," my voice sounds, "but there's something I'm curious about. Are you really absolutely sure that you've been right all along, that the Jewish settlements in Judea and Samaria will remain for all eternity?"

The assembly is silenced, and they all look at me, surprised and entertained. It is clear they hadn't even imagined that the secular visitor would have the guts to express her Leftist views in their presence.

"Doesn't it ever cross your minds, once in a while," I elaborate, "that maybe you were wrong? That maybe the entire settlement enterprise was just a mistake, that it never should have happened, and that maybe it will, therefore, come to an end?"

At least five people recover from their initial shock and try to answer all at once. "No," their passions are hot and swelling, "it has not crossed our minds that the entire settlement enterprise was a mistake. What are you talking about? Absolutely not only a defeatist from Tel Aviv could even suggest such a thing. You are *here* and you see all the success around you—don't you?"

With a sweeping hand gesture I am shown the expansive construction, the lush trees, the lawns and flowers and playgrounds with girls in Shabbat dresses and boys with colorful *kippot* climbing jungle gyms, sliding down slides, swinging on swings, their voices like jingle bells. To be honest, it *is* very hard to imagine all this being wiped out, to believe that one could just erase a town so large, so attached to the land, so deeply rooted in it; nor can I imagine emptying it of all the Jews who built it and replacing them with Arab refugees. I am reminded of that day long ago when Yair lay on the earth clinging to the brambles and clutching the raw soil with his fingers, and I am forced to admit, to myself at least, that the settlers' methods of attaching themselves to the land have improved markedly since then.

"At least admit that there's something in what Shlomtzion's saying," Leah interrupts in her calm voice, and now everyone really goes silent. "When we first got here, we thought we would bring the Jewish people back to their historic homeland," she says. "We thought that millions would follow us. But twenty years have passed, and there are only two hundred thousand Jews living in all Judea, Samaria, and Gaza. These lands are alien to the majority of our people."

"So what are you trying to say, Lealeh," Yair wakes from his daze, a hint of reprimand in his tone, "that it was really all a mistake? That we never should have built the settlements?"

"And what's twenty years anyway?" Someone else calls. "Since when do people render historical judgment on the basis of twenty years?"

"I don't think I ever would have admitted it in front of all of you were it not for Shlomtzion's question," Leah says, "but sometimes I think that maybe we, the Jewish communities of the territories, are guilty of the same tragic error of the Israelites who tried to charge up the mountain after the Sin of the Spies."

I listen to her words, and the story comes back to me as though it were only yesterday that I got a ninety-eight on my Bible matriculation exam. The Sin of the Spies, when the chiefs of the twelve tribes of Israel returned from reconnoitering the Promised Land and slandered it, disparaging God's gift; the people's loss of faith in their ability to enter the land and conquer it; and then, a small group of people decides to try to conquer it on their own, to charge up the mountain. By themselves. Without the nation, and against God's will.

"Maybe we, too, are an irrelevant minority," Leah offers. "Maybe we too tried to charge up the mountain, on our own and at the wrong time, and maybe Moses would have told us as well that there is no point in denying reality and struggling against it. That the nation is not ready, and our mission is therefore doomed to failure."

Everyone there, especially the men, shift impatiently in their chairs, not waiting for her to finish before protesting the comparison and rejecting outright the implication that the settlers were to expect an end similarly dreadful to that suffered by those who charged up the mountain in the time of Moses.

Leah steals a glance at her secret love to gauge his reaction, while Aviram, for his part, cracks open a pistachio and steals a glance at me, trying to understand what I have done to cause Leah, so innocent and pure, to suddenly start spouting heresies.

"The poison of the Left seeps into our veins and undermines our self-confidence," someone asserts, giving Leah a reproving look.

"If we had not been sure of our path," a bearded man who had been silent until now says irritably, "we never would have been able to hold out through all the years of the Intifada."

"There cannot be room for self-doubt."

"You really think we had a choice in all this? You really think we could simply have *not* settled Judea and Samaria, leaving our ancient heritage in the hands of strangers?"

"The settlement movement is, if anything, a *restitution* for the Sin of the Spies. We are earning the land of our forefathers through our love for it, our attachment to it, despite all the difficulties."

"And as opposed to those who charged the mountain, we didn't come here on our own accord. Judea and Samaria fell into our hands through a miracle, and only after years did we start settling them."

Everybody yells at everybody else, everybody argues with everybody else, everybody convinces everybody else, and in the end, the guests ask Rabbi Yair to say a few words of Torah in honor of the young couple. Yair, who had slumped listlessly in his chair, now straightens a little and begins to speak in a broken voice about the verse in Psalm 102: *For Thy servants have desired its stones, and for its very dust they have longed.* "We are allowed to raise questions about our connection to the land," he says, "and we're even allowed to doubt. But before all this, and above all this, we must love the land itself with the same natural love that every nation loves its own land. To desire its stones, to long for its very dust."

Maybe I love him after all, I think. *Maybe he loves his wife Leah after all, and he only thinks he could have lived a true life with me. And maybe she really does love him after all, and only convinces herself that Aviram, married and beyond her reach, is her true, great love.*

Meanwhile, the celebrants recite grace and wish us mazal tov and joy. The men rise to attend the *mincha* afternoon prayers in the synagogue, while the women clear the dishes into the kitchen, and praise the lady of the house for her courageous self-criticism and her wondrous apple cake.

Chapter fifteen

Maya and I go back to the Arbiv house for the Shabbat afternoon nap, and I feel relieved, as though I have returned to my natural habitat. I am surprised by the warmth I feel for this simple home, with its abundance of animals, plants, clothes, and toys strewn about its open spaces, bearing witness to the abundance of human beings living there in joy and freedom. *This is the kind of house I wanted,* I think to myself as Maya and I pat the dogs and cats that greet us upon arrival, even the frozen iguana holding a certain charm. Maya feeds and waters the animals, and then immediately falls asleep on the living room couch. I wander from room to room, the little dog jumping at my heels, and I think: *I would have wanted a country kitchen exactly like this one if I'd had a large family, and I would have set up the boys' room just like this if I'd had boys, and I would have made sure to have a broad veranda just like this one, covered with toy cars and tricycles, and a work room with an open gallery where you could see every corner of the house, and a family room just like this one with a television like this, a video player like this, a computer like this, a bookcase like this one filled with board games like these, an ironing board set up for use just like this, and lots of children's drawings just like these, plastered on the walls and doors and cabinets.*

At the end of the tour I reach the master bedroom, which is also, I decide, right for me in every way. There is something warm and reassuring about the two abutting wooden beds, broad and soft, with the wooden headboard separating them from the wall behind, a wall covered with framed family photos. From these I learn that Hana Arbiv is a roundish, cheerful woman with brown curls peeking out from under a decorative straw hat, and Moshe Arbiv is a balding, bespectacled man half a head shorter than she. Both are social workers by profession, Maya has told me. Hana came from America as a young student, met Moshe in college and stayed on in Israel. Their eldest daughter is in the National Service, and there are five additional biological children and three adopted ones.

I am filled with a sense of reverence for these people, reverence which quickly turns to envy. *Here are people with meaning in their lives, people who really know they're alive, that it's not an illusion; they've got hard proof. Theirs is a kind of real-life Nemeczek house: Even when they go to a kibbutz for the weekend for Moshe's nephew's bar mitzvah, they take in a miserable refugee from Tel Aviv who needs a place to stay in Tirza. And once again, they've earned their day's pay, they've punched their card, proving to themselves that they exist and have a purpose in life.*

I sit down on one of the beds just to get a taste of it, like Goldilocks testing the beds at the Three Bears house, imagining myself to be Hana Arbiv, cheery and industrious. Hana Arbiv, for whom it is better off to have been created, after all.

On Hana Arbiv's bedside table there is a reading lamp, an alarm clock, foot cream, the ceramic creation of a small child, and next to all of these there is an English translation of Elsa Morante's *History: A Novel.* This book is on my reading list, too, but the busy Hana Arbiv has somehow made time for it before I have. Her bookmark shows she is more than halfway through. Trying to imagine myself as her, I lie down on the soft bed, take the book in hand, and open it to the page she is on.

I now see that the bookmark is a square yellow Post-it note, the kind people use for reminders. On it is scribbled "Moishik, I stayed up forever waiting for you. If I'm asleep, please wake me up and kiss me no matter the hour."

And in the margins, in a different hand with a different pen: "Hanchiuk, my sleeping beauty. I kissed you in your sleep, didn't want to disturb you so late. See you in the morning."

This personal testament, which I have read without permission, shakes in my hand. My heart is pounding as I reread the exchange, again and again and again, tremors running through me like an electric current. *There is love in this world and I did not know, love that lives and breathes in simplicity, like a dog or cat, like turtles and rabbits, like the iguana that blinks just when it feels like it without even having eyelids.* I hold the yellow note up to my nose as if to draw in the love by smell, then to my lips, which grace the note gently. Then I read again the sweet and incredible words, and suddenly before my eyes, there come together all the estranged couples of my history—Bubbe Malka and her beloved husband who was torn from her because they never had children; her second husband and his first wife, who ran away with the Polish officer and probably never forgave herself; Grandma Rochel with her beloved bridegroom Y.B. just as they looked in the pictures tucked away in *Tzena Urena*; Grandpa Duvid with a woman who loved him, only him, a woman who would not see him as "another husband", but the one and only love. I could even see Aunt Batya in my vision, with someone she loves and who loves her back. And off in the background, transparent and ethereal, little Shayaleh is flying off with his bride, a researcher of cystic fibrosis, and the golden Estherke is letting down her long golden braid from the window of a high tower, and it is falling into the arms of a handsome prince who has finally come to rescue her.

Only when I get to myself I get stuck. I don't know if I should place myself with Yair or with Rosy, don't know which of them I really wanted, which of them I really love more, and what I should do with the other. After a long deliberation I put the precious note back in its place and return *History: A Novel* to the bedside table. The earthly love of Moishik and Hanchiuk stirs my blood and I go to the hallway, take the dog leash off its hook and make my way to the front door. The little dog hears the buckle jingling and runs toward me expectantly, but I say to him, "You've walked enough today—Maya walked you in the morning and the neighbors' kids took you out in the afternoon," and I call out to the big old Dalmatian who has spent the entire day sprawled on the rug. She raises her head and gives me a melancholic look, wags her tail weakly and slowly gets herself up, collecting her tired limbs and stretching them extensively.

We stride out to the perimeter road, walking into the gentle breeze, taking small steps because it's hard for her to move fast and I'm in no hurry either. It is quiet now in Tirza. Everyone naps here on Shabbat afternoons between two and four o'clock, as if it is yet another religious rite that demands full observance. I inhale with a flute-like breath the wind straight from the mountains and sky, drawing it directly into my blood cells and muscle tissue, the words of Hanchiuk and Moishik Arbiv ringing in my ears like a love song, *Forever waiting for you / Wake me and kiss me / My sleeping beauty / Didn't want to disturb you / Kissed you in your sleep / Wake me and kiss me no matter the hour / Forever waiting for you / Didn't want to disturb you / Kissed you in your sleep / Forever waiting for you / My sleeping beauty / See you in the morning.*

Here is the weeping willow and the bench where Yair and I sat the night before and gazed into ourselves. As I approach I see that now, too, someone is sitting beneath the stream of falling leaves, and wonder, *Who other than me would violate the sacred commandment of the Shabbat siesta?* Drawing closer I see that the man who is sitting there is hunched forward, his hands propping his temples, Yair's blue and white knitted *kippa* on his head. He raises a dejected face to me and says "Shlomtzion," then gets up and walks with me and the old dog as though we had worked it out in advance.

❧

"On the last night of his life, my father was unconscious," I tell him. He was connected to every imaginable tube, and my mother and I sat by his bed and waited. The doctor had said the end was near. Suddenly we heard him stir and grunt and try to say something. We quickly got up. His eyes were open, wide open for the first time since the previous night, and he was looking at us beseechingly, desperate, trying to say something and failing, his mouth and tongue not responding to his command. He put out his right hand, reaching up toward the shelf on the wall over his bed.

"'He wants something,' my mother said, terribly upset. 'He wants something on the shelf. Avrum, what is it you want? Avrum!' And my father squirmed on the bed, holding his arm up with the last of his strength, making raspy hissing sounds, like there were dying coals inside him.

"We went completely crazy, Iri. One minute we were sure he was already dead, and the next minute this whole weird thing. We offered him every damned object on the shelf, the glass of water, the Vaseline for his horribly parched lips, the mirror and comb he had still used the previous morning, the oxygen mask hanging there, but he just kept shaking his head, he wouldn't take any of them, and he kept on pleading and hissing that horrible hiss, until I saw there was something else there, and I said, 'Maybe he wants the tefillin?' My mother said, 'But it's nighttime, what does he want them for at night?' And then she suddenly remembered that he had already been unconscious in the morning, and so hadn't put on his phylacteries that day. She turned to him and asked loudly, as though he was already far away, 'You want the tefillin? The tefillin, Avrum?' And as soon as she said 'tefillin', the hissing stopped, and I took the embroidered velvet bag down from the shelf, and my father calmed down, his eyes expressing infinite gratitude. When I opened the bag, he moved his left arm toward me as much as he could, and I understood that he wanted me to wrap the phylactery around it. But of course I had absolutely no idea how to do that. I said to him, 'Hold on, Daddy, I'll be right back,' and flew down the hallway. It was nine-thirty at night and most of the patients in the ward were already asleep, but in the fifth room down I saw someone still awake, a *haredi* man in his mid-thirties whom cancer had turned into a *Muselman.* He was sitting up reading a holy book with a flashlight so as not to wake his neighbors, and breathlessly I made my desperate request, 'Please, could you...quick...my father needs to put on tefillin...'

"I'll never forget the sight of this guy, Iri. He was so emaciated you could see the shape of his skull through his stretched yellowed skin, but he quickly got off that bed, threw a gown over the blue pajamas that were hanging off of what was left of his body, and followed me to my father, who was still lying there with his eyes open and waiting. He took the tefillin out of the velvet bag, rolled up my father's pajama sleeve, and put the arm-phylactery on his white outstretched arm, fastening it on the point aligned with the heart, gently winding the strap seven times. Then he took out the head-phylactery and put it on my father's forehead, securing the knot of the strap on the back of his neck, right at the base of the head, at the brain stem. Then he went back to the arm-strap and tied it around my father's middle finger three times. And you just wouldn't believe it, Iri, but when he started to say the prayer—*And I will betroth thee to Me forever*—an otherworldly glow spread over my father's face, I swear to you, a glow that grew stronger and brighter as the man continued praying—*And I will betroth thee to Me in righteousness and justice and grace and mercy*—and when he got to the end of it, *And I will betroth thee to Me in faithfulness, and you shall know the Lord,* my father was bathed in light. It was unbelievable—a shaft of light washed over his face as though the guy was shining his flashlight at him, and then my father shut his eyes and passed from this world once and for all."

Yair looks at me with the same expression of attention and wonder that I remember from our childhood, and I stop to catch my breath and give the dog an encouraging stroke, since she's having a hard time of it—perhaps it had been a mistake to take her out on so long a walk. People who have wakened from their Shabbat rest are now passing by us and are astonished by the sight of Rabbi Berman going for a stroll with his secular in-law and the retired Arbiv dog. I smile at them apologetically.

"You never really hated him as much as you thought you did," Yair says, pensively.

"Who?"

"Your father. Deep down, you just wanted him to love you, to see, for once, that you were there."

A young couple walks toward us in lockstep, like a two-headed, four-armed, four-legged creature, pushing a baby carriage and ogling their baby with four glowing eyes. The sky is pristine, and from the neglected storehouse of wisdom I had picked up from Yair during the years of our love, I suddenly recall a line of rabbinic lore that offers consolation. "*The azure thread is like the sea / and the sea is like the sky / and the sky resembles the Throne of Glory.*"

"Our Father in Heaven was a convenient replacement for my biological father," I smile between tears, "but then He let me down, too."

At the threshold of the Arbiv house, with the door open and the exhausted dog already inside lapping loudly at her bowl of water in the corner of the kitchen, Yair looks at me intently and asks, voice shaking, "Do you remember the exact words that Rabbi Yitzhak Tzadok said, about the hand of the righteous man?"

Do I remember?! Of course I remember. "He said that 'the hand of a righteous man holds it back.'"

"Well, that's just it," Yair says, moved, and then, from within the deep sadness shadowing his face, a strange, sardonic grin of bittersweet victory appears. "Not 'prevents it', but 'holds it back'."

"What's the difference?"

"You spoke about not awakening love before its time, and I think now I understand. The righteous one's hand did not prevent our marriage, Shlomtzion, only held it back, until its time."

"Until the next generation?"

He's so fragile, I fear I might shatter him.

"Until Maya and Ariel," he nods. "Until Maya and Ariel."

❧

When we gather at the Bermans' house for the third Shabbat meal. Yair looks refreshed and somewhat recovered, though it is still clear he has not slept since my arrival in Tirza the day before, or maybe even for a few nights before that. Yair, Leah, and I make every human effort to act like ordinary parents of an ordinary couple about to get married, and when Maya sees we're managing, her face visibly relaxes and she goes back to being my joyful, self-assured daughter. For the first time she and Ariel tell us about their plans, about the new settlement they are going to build. When Yair asks how they will get government approval for this in the thick of the so-called peace process, they assure him, "It'll all work out. The town is officially a new neighborhood of an existing town, but really we are going to redeem an entirely new area."

"On a clear day you can see to the Dead Sea on one side of it and to the Mediterranean on the other," Ariel beams.

"You can see Tel Aviv," Maya boasts. "I'll be able to stand at my window and wave to you, Mom."

"Nobody there will have televisions," he adds.

"We'll educate the children right there," says she, "with our own methods, not those of the Ministry of Education."

"Everyone there will be vegetarian."

"We'll eat mostly organic products that we'll grow ourselves."

"And dairy products we'll make from milk from our own goats."

"Even our clothing will be a different fashion. We want to return to the styles of architecture and clothing that best fit this part of the world, to stop imitating the Europeans and Americans, and to try to learn from the Arabs who have acquired a lot of experience over the generations."

Yair and I exchange incredulous looks.

"That's Prophets' Town," I laugh across the table at him. "They're going to build Prophets' Town!"

"Build what?" Maya asks, amused, and Yair explains.

"When we were your age, we too wanted to fix the world. We wanted to create an ideal society, and we called it Prophets' Town."

The young couple looks at us with a mixture of confusion and pity. "We don't want to fix the world," Ariel clarifies.

And Maya adds softly, "Only ourselves."

"Prophets' Town!" Leah ridicules good-naturedly, and Yair laughs, spreading his hands as if to say, *What can I do? That's just how silly and naïve we were.*

The sky is darkening beyond the window near the dining room table as the Berman family becomes submerged in the songs of Shabbat's third meal, songs of yearning and wistfulness, "*Beautiful, sweet, Radiance of the World / My soul is sick with love of Thee / Please, O Lord, heal her / And show her the delight of Your radiance.*"

"*This is the hour of divine intent,*" another pearl rises from the treasury of wisdom I had thought lost forever, "*an hour of great desire, in which the soul can reach the level that is highest, truest, closest to the Throne of Glory.*"

My Maya is going to marry Yair's and Leahleh's Ariel, and I had been all by myself in Rosy's and my peeling house when the labor pains had hit. I was deliberately alone then, and deliberately in the house. I had sat in our neglected yard through the long hours of that afternoon, listening to the human creature blossoming inside of me and watching the flock of starlings which daily would come from the south, forming a cloud of little black dots that gradually grew larger and nearer until they would all land on the poplar tree by the fence. It took them awhile, gathered in that tree, to go to sleep, and a storm of chirping came from the branches and leaves, silvered in the twilight, quieting a little as every bird found its place, driving off unwanted neighbors with piercing peeps and inviting friends to come join with a sweet whistle. Then the sky grew dark, and the swarm gradually stilled, and the chirping stopped completely, and the poplar stopped buzzing and no one would have known that dozens of starlings were asleep in its midst.

"*Please reveal Thyself / and spread Thy shelter of peace over me, O my Beloved,*" Yair and his wife and children, and my child, all sing. When I knew it was her time to enter into this world, I left my house. It was two-fifteen in the morning. I could have asked the neighbors to call Rosy ten hours earlier, when the contractions had begun, but I hadn't done it, and Rosy was still on reserve duty. So I put on a coat the buttons of which I couldn't close because my belly was too big, and I took the bag I had prepared in advance, and went on foot to the administrative office of our moshav. I had prepared telephone tokens in advance, but the public phone on the outer wall of the office was out of order, and I was feeling searing pains in my abdomen every six minutes. I kept on walking, not waking any of the neighbors to ask for a ride to the hospital or to call an ambulance, and shortly before three A.M., lights of the moshav behind me, I walked out onto the Tel Aviv highway.

"Light the whole world with Thy glory / We will exult and be joyful in Thee," Maya is now closing her eyes in her focus on her intimate connection with the divine, and she should never, ever know how I stood on the shoulder of the empty highway in the dark, with rain beginning to drizzle on me, my coat open for my abundant abdomen, my bag hanging from my shoulder, or how a powerful contraction that almost tore me in two forced me to lean with both elbows and my forehead against the bus shelter's support column, until a tanker truck pulled over, maybe the same tanker that had pulled over for me nine months earlier at Rosy's seaside haven, and the driver, whom I imagined to be the same driver, jumped from the cab and ran over to me, supporting me and carrying me high up into the passenger seat, and only after ten minutes of driving at high speed, and two overwhelming contractions four minutes apart, did he peer at me and ask reprovingly, "*Where* is your husband?"

❧

The azure thread is like the sea, and the sea is like the sky, and the sky resembles the Throne of Glory. I called my daughter Maya, a name that read backwards in Hebrew yields *hayam*, the sea that her father loves so deeply. When she decided to come into the world in spite of everything, to be created despite how much easier it is not to bother, my life began anew, as though it were not she who came out of my body, but I who came from hers. "Push!" the midwife ordered, "Push, yes—that's it—not right now. Okay go ahead… great! You're wonderful! One more push will do it." And then the miracle happened. The sharpest pain imaginable came to an end, and a starling fluttered out from between my legs and turned into a real-live baby, that I never knew would be mine.

And as I still lay in the delivery room, floating in heaven out of pure happiness, an elderly cleaning lady shuffled in, exhausted and wearing a worn-out green uniform, put down her squeegee and bucket full of soapy water, and looked at me blandly.

"You before or after?"

"After."

"Waddya have?"

"A girl!"

"Ah, don't worry about it," she thought to console me, and bent over with a sigh, extending two wizened hands to dunk the floor rag into the grayish foam in the bucket.

❧

After the havdalah ceremony marking the end of Shabbat, Maya and I walk back to the Arbiv house to clean up and pack our things, and then back to the Bermans' again, to sit with Ariel and his parents and work out the details of the wedding. The young couple wants a reception where they can invite all their many friends, but to serve only light refreshments. It disgusts them to think of serving their guests the usual roasted chicken, and they find it hard to understand why people can't possibly celebrate without shoving dead birds down their gullets. They request that the ceremony be held at sunset on the top of Mount Scopus, with a panoramic view of Jerusalem with the Temple Mount as its centerpiece. Leah brings out a calendar so I can check when the wedding falls out according to the Christian calendar, and I feel my heart slowly expanding—my Maya is getting married and I would be so happy if she would ask me to help her choose a gown.

In the kitchen, the older daughters are washing the Shabbat dishes and listening to radio news coverage of the peace rally being held right then at the Malkhei Yisrael Square in Tel Aviv. Above the clinking of dishes and the din of water running in one sink for meat and another for dairy, I hear Yifat and Moria grousing about the rally's official slogan, "No to Violence, Yes to Peace."

"Like, who are they calling violent?"

"And excuse me, but exactly what peace are they talking about?"

"Peace unto Israel. *Finito la comedia.*"

When the prime minister begins to speak they quiet down, and we also listen from the living room. Rabin sounds lonely and bitter, and I feel sorry for him. "Violence," he shouts at the thousands filling the square, "undermines the foundations of democracy." He promises to continue down the path of peace, and I look at the horrified faces of my daughter and her new family, and realize that they are not hearing in his words the same meaning as I am.

If someone from their side really would try to harm the prime minister of Israel or one of the ministers, I shiver, *it would be the end of the Jewish state. It would be the end of the Zionist dream that has tried to take form and become real in this country over the last hundred years. We would never be able to go on together after a rupture like that, we would never be able to live side by side, us and them.*

Is it good or bad that the Jews built a state for themselves in the Middle East, I ask myself, *and did they have any choice? Is it good or bad that the settlers set up their homes in Judea and Samaria, and did they have any choice? Is it good or bad that I never married Yair, is it good or bad that I was created—and did I have any choice?*

As I say goodbye to my hosts, the kitchen radio is churning out the emotive song being sung at the rally—*Sing / A song of peace / Do not utter a prayer*. Leah presses both my hands on the threshold, and we part, wishing each other joy and hoping that the wedding will take place, at the right place, at the right time.

Yair comes out to escort me, with Ziv holding his hand and waggling her tongue in self-satisfaction, and we pass the bougainvilleas as we walk toward the parking lot. Maya and Ariel decided to accompany me on the ride home, and from the path we can see them waiting by the car, surrounded by a halo of light.

There are my daughter and his son, I say to my heart. *They have awakened love and found it desired and ready.*

But the sky is black and heavy as the bride and groom enter the car, and flocks of clouds hurry westward as I get into the driver's seat, start the engine and pull out of the parking lot, waving goodbye to the graying man standing by the bushes with his little girl.

As we exit the gate of the town of Tirza onto the road to Ramallah, the radio announces that the peace rally in Malkhei Yisrael Square in Tel Aviv had just concluded, and the demonstrators were beginning to disperse. There were unconfirmed reports of shots fired.

Glossary

Agora/agorot (pl.)—smallest unit of value in the Israeli monetary system. There are a hundred *agorot* in a new Israeli shekel.

Amida—lit. 'standing'. The central part of the Jewish prayer service, recited morning, afternoon and night. It is also part of the additional Musaf service, which is recited after the weekly Torah reading every Shabbat, as well as on festivals. The prayer is whispered while standing in place, and hence is also known as the 'Silent Prayer'.

Ashamnu, bagadnu, gazalnu—"We have become guilty, we have betrayed, we have stolen": opening of the confessional prayer.

Ashkenazi—Jews of Eastern European descent, or pertaining to the customs of such people.

Ba'alat teshuva (f.)—loosely, one who "returns" to Jewish religious practice. Someone newly religious.

Bar mitzvah—a coming-of-age ceremony, admitting a boy who reaches the age of thirteen to the Jewish community as an adult member. The female equivalent, which takes place at the age of twelve, is a 'bat mitzvah'.

Baruch Hashem— 'Blessed be the Name'. An expression of thankfulness indicating that all fortune comes from God.

Bimah—the platform in a synagogue from which the Torah is publicly read.

Birkat Hamazon—lit. 'Blessing of the Food'. Grace said after completing a meal which includes bread.

Birkat Kohanim—the Priestly Blessing cited in Numbers 6:23-27. Also known as *Nesiat Kapayim* (raising of the hands), it is a ceremony and prayer recited during certain synagogue services. On Shabbat and festivals, this blessing is said by actual descendants of Aaron, called *Kohanim* (priests), members of Judaism's priestly clan.

Bnei Akiva—a religious, Zionist youth movement, founded in the 1920s, strongly affiliated with the Mizrahi movement.

Chulent—traditional Jewish food. A slow-cooked stew usually eaten for Shabbat lunch.

Daven—(Yiddish). To pray.

Ein Yaakov—a collection of all the aggadic (non-legal) material of the Talmud, compiled by Rabbi Yaakov ibn Chaviv, a fifteenth-century Talmudist.

Finjan—(Arabic), a small coffee pot with a long handle.

Goyim—lit. 'nations'. Non-Jews.

Haftarah—a portion of the book of Prophets read in synagogue on the Shabbat and holidays immediately after the weekly Torah reading. Its theme usually amplifies the themes of the Torah reading.

Hag sameach—Happy holiday.

Hakafah/Hakafot (pl.)—lit. 'circuits'. Part of the services of the holiday of Simhat Torah, in which the synagogue's Torah scrolls are removed from the ark and carried around the bimah. Although each hakafah need only encompass one circuit, the dancing and singing with the Torah often continues much longer, and may overflow from the synagogue onto the streets.

Halakhah—lit. 'the way'. Jewish law as transcribed in the Talmud and subsequent legal codes and rabbinical decisions.

Haredi—'one who trembles [before the Lord]', as per Isaiah 66:2, 5. A term for Ultra-Orthodox Jews.

Havdalah—lit. 'separation, differentiation'. A blessing and ceremony said at the end of Shabbat and holidays.

Hazaka—from the Hebrew root 'to strengthen'. Halakhic term for a pattern that establishes either legal rights or halakhic suppositions.

Heimische—(Yiddish). Homey, intimate, informal.

Hesder—combined program of yeshiva study and military service in the Israeli army.

Intifada—(Arabic). Lit. 'to shake off'. The Palestinian revolt against Israel, begun in 1987.

Kabbalah—Jewish mysticism.

Kashrut—the system of Jewish dietary laws.

Kibbutz—an Israeli community settlement, usually agricultural, organized under collectivist principles.

Kibbutznik—a member of a kibbutz.

Kiddush—lit. 'sanctification'. A liturgical introduction to Shabbat and the holidays usually recited over a cup of wine.

Kippa/kippot (pl.)—a skullcap worn by traditional Jewish Orthodox males.

Knesset—lit. 'assembly'. The Israeli legislative parliament, consisting of 120 members.

Kohen/kohanim (pl.)—'priests', people who have a tradition that they are descendants of Aaron the High Priest. Judaism's priestly clan. Though there is no Temple service today, in present times *kohanim* are still involved in several Jewish ceremonies, including the Priestly Blessing, *Birkat Kohanim,* recited in the synagogue on specific occasions, such as Shabbat and festivals.

Kosher—lit. 'proper, appropriate'. Fit or allowed to be eaten or used according to the dietary or ritual laws of Judaism. Also used loosely to refer to anything proper or legitimate.

Koylel—post-graduate yeshiva, the student body of which is typically comprised of mature, usually married, men, who often receive stipends.

Kugel—(Yiddish). A baked pudding of noodles or potatoes, eggs, and seasonings, traditionally eaten by Jews on Shabbat.

Mechutenet (f.)—mother-in-law of one's son or daughter-in-law.

Mekubal—Kabbalist.

Menorah—the seven-armed candelabrum that was lit in the Temple and is the symbol of the state of Israel.

Mezuzah/mezuzot (pl.)—lit. 'doorpost'. A parchment placed on the doorway of rooms in Jewish homes, upon which the two first paragraphs of the *Shema* are written.

Mikvah—ritual pool used for purification.

Mincha—the afternoon prayer service.

Minyan—lit. 'count, number'. The quorum of ten adult Jewish males required by halakhah to be present for communal prayers. Loosely used for any communal prayer service.

Mizrachistim—members of the Religious Zionist movement, also known as the Mizrachi movement, which is often identified, especially in the United States, with the Modern Orthodox movement, although they are not synonymous. Both are characterized by an approach to halakhah that is less stringent than that of the

Ultra-Orthodox.

Mohel—a person who performs the Jewish rite of circumcision.

Moshav—a cooperative community in Israel made up of small farm units.

Moshavnik—a member of a moshav.

Muselman—term for the "walking skeletons" in Nazi death camps.

Omer—lit. 'bound sheaf'. A barley offering in the Temple on the second day of Passover. Also the name of the period of counting between Passover and Shavuot.

Parashah—a graphically demarcated section in a Torah scroll. Popularly and more loosely used to refer to the weekly Torah portion read in the synagogue on Shabbat.

Pesach—Passover.

Pri Tzaddik—lit. 'the fruit of a tzaddik'. Torah commentary and reflections on the Jewish year by Rabbi Tzadok HaKohen of Lublin (1823-1900), a famous Hasidic leader and Kabbalist.

Rabbanit/rabbaneot (f., pl.)—the wife of a rabbi, or a highly respected woman.

Rebbe—teacher of Torah. Also a Hasidic leader.

Rodef—lit. 'pursuer". Technical halakhic term for one who attempts to kill or willfully endanger another. In halakhah, it is seen as an imperative to kill such a person.

Rosh Hashanah—the Jewish New Year, and Day of Judgment, in which potential for the coming year is allotted.

Rosh Yeshiva—lit. 'the Head of the Yeshiva'. Dean of a rabbinical collage.

Shul—(Yiddish). Synagogue.

Sefat Emet—lit. 'language of truth'. A commentary on the Torah by the great Hasidic leader, Rabbi Yehuda Aryeh Leib Alter of Ger (1847-1905).

Sephardi—lit. 'Spanish'. Name given to Jews of Spanish or

Portuguese origin or ancestry. Also, recently and more loosely, to Jews of North African or Mid-Eastern decent, most of whom originally descend from Jews of Spanish or Portuguese ancestry. Also used to describe the customs of such people.

Shabbat/Shabbatot (pl)—The Jewish Sabbath, which begins at sunset on Friday, and ends after sundown on Saturday. A holy day of rest, in which various activities, particularly those seen as creative, including turning on lights and driving a car, are forbidden.

Shabbat shalom—'A Shabbat of peace'. Traditional Shabbat greeting.

Shacharit—from the Hebrew word for 'dawn'. The morning services.

Shakshuka—a spicy Mid-Eastern egg and tomato dish.

Shavuot—The holiday of Pentecost. Lit. 'weeks', after the seven weeks counted from the second day of Passover in preparation for the holiday.

Shidukh—a marital match, as well as the system of introducing eligible and marriageable singles to each other in Orthodox Jewish communities.

Shiva—a seven-day period of mourning following the death of a close relative.

Shlita—acronym for "May he live long and well, Amen."

Shochet—a ritual slaughterer.

Shofar—a trumpet made of a ram's horn, sounded in the synagogue during the holiday of Rosh Hashanah and at the end of Yom Kippur.

Shteible—(Yiddish). A small, informal, intimate room for prayer and study.

Shtreimel—(Yiddish). A round, fur-rimmed hat worn by Hasidim, especially on Shabbat and festive occasions.

Siddur—the Jewish prayer book.

Simhat Torah—lit. 'the Joy of the Torah'. A holiday immediately following Succot, celebrating the end and beginning of the cycle of weekly Torah readings.

Tallit/tallitot (pl.)—a prayer shawl.

Talmid hacham—lit. 'a student of the wise'. A Torah scholar.

Tefillin—phylacteries. Small black leather cubes containing a piece of parchment inscribed with the verses of *Shema*, worn by Orthodox Jewish men during weekday morning prayers, one strapped to the left arm, the other to the forehead.

Tekiya, shevarim, terua—the three separate tones sounded with the shofar on Rosh Hashanah.

Tikkun—lit. 'repair'. The opportunity for, and the role of humanity in, healing creation. Also the name of night-long prayer and learning services, which facilitate such healing.

Torah—lit. 'the teaching, law'. The Pentateuch, as well as the parchment scroll on which the Pentateuch is written, used in the synagogue. Also an inclusive term for the entire body of Jewish religious literature, law, and tradition.

Treif—lit. 'torn'. Non-kosher.

Tzaddik/tzaddikim (m., pl.)—a person of outstanding virtue; a righteous man.

Tzizit/tzitziot (pl.)—ritually tied fringes on four-cornered garments. Worn by Jewish Orthodox men.

Tzur Olamim—the Eternal Rock, or the Rock of Ages. An epithet for God.

Yeshiva—traditional Jewish school for teenage and young adult males, devoted primarily to the study of the Babylonian Talmud and its commentaries, as well as Jewish philosophy. Also a rabbinical college.

Acknowledgments

I am indebted to Amos Oz, whose generous guidance and assistance made this book possible. I also want to thank Matthew Miller, Deborah Meghnagi, Batnadiv Weinberg, Tzvika Meir, and Shimon Adaff. I am grateful to Yael Mali for her constant encouragement, and to my beloved children, for theirs.

Most of all, thank you, Benny, for your infinite friendship.

About the Author

Emuna Elon

Born in Jerusalem in 1955, Emuna Elon has lived in the settlement of Beit-El since 1982. She is married, and has six children. Elon has published seven children's books, and many short stories, and is currently teaching and writing. *If You Awaken Love* is her first novel.

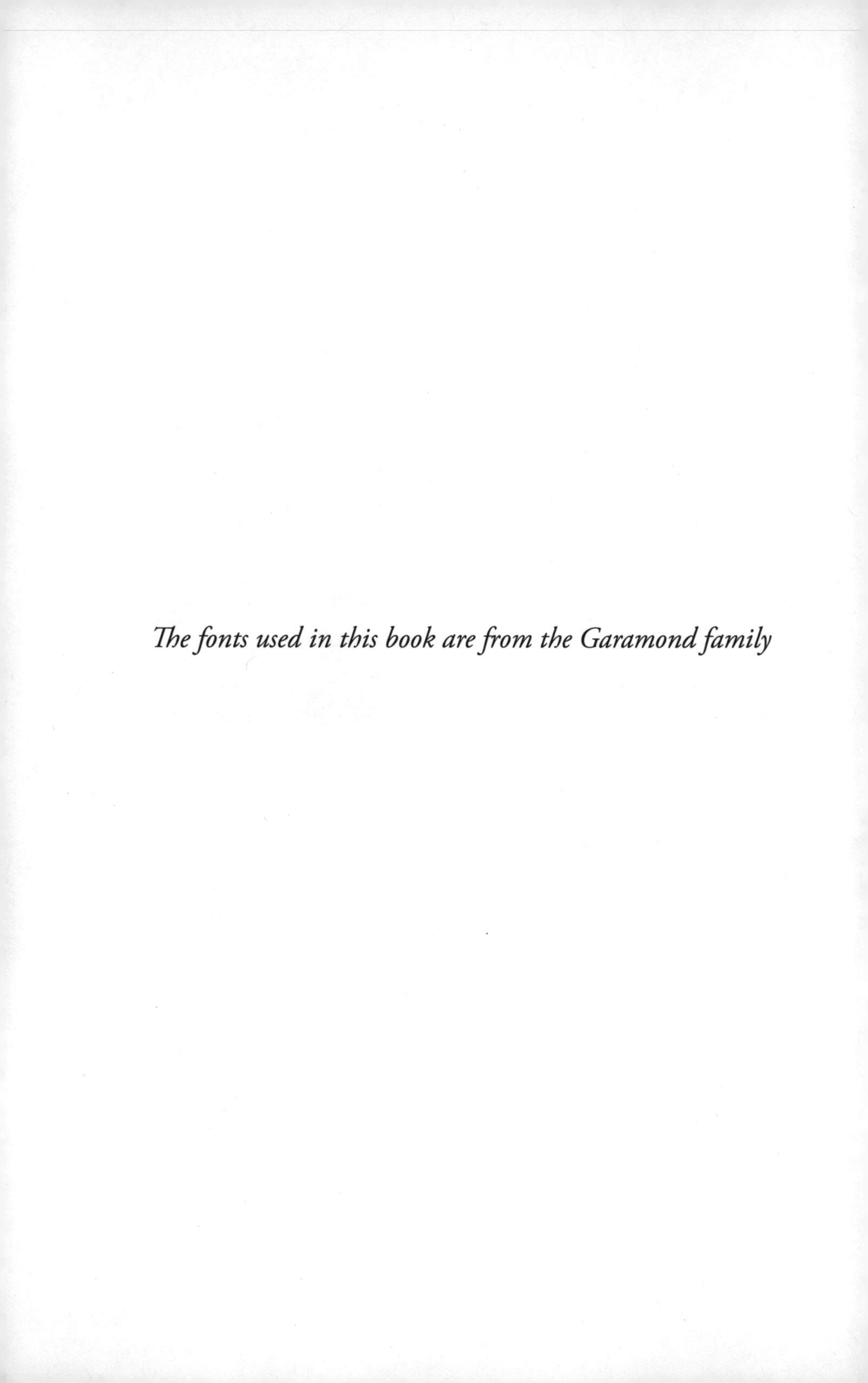

The fonts used in this book are from the Garamond family

The Toby Press publishes fine writing,
available at leading bookstores everywhere. For more
information, please visit www.tobypress.com